THE SHINING YEARS

THE SHINING YEARS

EMILIE LORING

LITTLE, BROWN AND COMPANY
BOSTON · TORONTO

FIRST EDITION

T 09/72

Library of Congress Cataloging in Publication Data

Loring, Emilie (Baker)
  The shining years.

  I. Title.
PZ3.L8938Sk [PS3523.O645]   813'.5'2   72-4473
ISBN 0-316-53285-1

Published simultaneously in Canada
by Little, Brown & Company (Canada) Limited

PRINTED IN THE UNITED STATES OF AMERICA

THE SHINING YEARS

L ESTER Forbes, stiff from an eight-hour drive, parked his car on the Green in the Connecticut village of Waring and got out to stretch his legs before making the final hour's run into New York City. For a few minutes he walked briskly but aimlessly, enjoying the exercise after his long day at the wheel. Then his attention was caught by the glorious color of fall foliage at its breathtaking peak. The maples on the Green were flaming with scarlet and crimson and gold; an ancient oak that had been old when the village was young spread huge gnarled branches, its leaves a russet color like the ground in November when the colors have faded and only a mellow afterglow remains on the landscape. Wineglass elms soared proudly, lifting regal heads over the village to look at the distant gentle curve of blue hills. The white spire of a church pierced the red of maples to reach upward toward the deep serene blue of the sky. Crimson ivy climbed the walls of the library.

Set far apart on spacious grounds, white colonial houses occupied three sides of the Green, their beautifully kept lawns now beginning to be a multicolored carpet as leaves drifted downward.

After the relentless roar of traffic on the highway and

the turmoil, crowding, and smog of a great city, Lester
was struck by the beauty, the peace, and the leisurely pace
of the village. From somewhere there drifted the acrid
smell of burning leaves. Here and there smoke curled
from a chimney into the clear air. Lester paused before a
white picket fence on which late roses climbed.

"It's just a hick town," he told himself impatiently, but
something of its quality caught at his imagination. "More
dead than alive," he assured his questioning mind. "And
yet there is lots of room to live in without crowding and
lots of time and it's — pretty." He felt that the word was
inadequate but he did not try to improve it. Words were
not his business; pictures were. But not, of course, pictures of rural prettiness or the brilliance of autumn colors.
Pictures, to Lester, meant news: street accidents, fires,
criminals being hauled off to jail; people caught in their
moments of grief and terror and tragedy. Pictures, as
Lester always said, must have some life in them, must
shock the hasty newspaper reader into attention. Since
Lester was highly regarded in his profession it is to be
assumed that he knew what people really want.

At the top of the Green he stopped to look unbeliev-
ingly at the great stone house set in a commanding position
far back from the road on a rising bluff, a huge structure built by someone with an unbridled sense of ro-
mance, a medieval castle complete with turrets and narrow
Gothic windows. All it lacked, Lester thought in amusement, was a moat, a drawbridge, and a portcullis.

Automatically he adjusted his camera and took a picture of the house. A man strolling past him stopped to
watch. "Stranger here? It always gets them."

"Who thought that up?" Lester demanded, and the man's friendliness faded.

"That's Holbrook's Folly." His tone was defensive. "Old man Holbrook made a huge fortune in the nineties and built this place. Had it copied from some castle on the Rhine. It's really something, isn't it? And as gorgeous inside as out." There was local pride in his voice. After all, not every American small town could boast of a genuine castle.

Lester laughed. "Suits of armor and a dungeon, I suppose."

"Stanley Holbrook don't keep a museum."

"You mean someone actually lives there?" Lester was incredulous.

"Sure. It's still the Holbrook place. Holbrooks have always lived there. Only Stanley left now. A bachelor. Don't seem like he'll ever marry. Kind of a shame to have the place go out of the family."

Lester shrugged. "No one could keep up a house like that today."

The man laughed. "Oh, he can afford it! That's why people think it's so strange he works. He says he has to have some meaningful job, but it's not what you and me would call work. He reads books. Assistant editor at the Radcliffe Publishing Company in New York." He chuckled again. "Meaningful!"

The daylight was fading and Lester became aware that he was chilly. "Well, I've got to make tracks. A big date coming up in New York tonight. Say, what's the name of this burg, anyhow?"

"This is Waring," the man told him. He added politely,

"You are in Connecticut, in case you hadn't heard of it either."

Lester got back in his car and dropped the camera on the seat beside him, unaware that he had taken a prize-winning picture, which in the long run would profoundly affect the lives of at least six people.

ii

Miss Winifred Holbrook started nervously and then realized that the explosion which had alarmed her was not a shot fired from a gun in the hands of some desperate and dangerous man but the backfire of a truck laboring up the steep San Francisco hill. Nothing in the world to be frightened of or to make her heart pound in that disturbing way. In spite of the doctors' assurances, and Miss Holbrook had consulted a number of doctors, that her heart was sound as a bell — in fact, that she was, as one of them had infuriatingly told her, as strong as a horse — she knew better. She knew she was a sick woman in precarious health. Naturally she worried about it!

Miss Holbrook, indeed, worried about almost everything. She not only devoted a great deal of thought and attention to the proper functioning of her body; she worried about her food. All this pollution! How could she really be sure that the food she ate was pure and wholesome? How, even, could she be sure it would not actually poison her? She frequently encountered such terrible things in the news, and to Miss Holbrook, as to many others, news inevitably meant bad news.

To Miss Holbrook all living was an uncertain if not a

downright dangerous business. With wild young drivers on the road it was hardly safe to cross the street. She felt that she took her life in her hands every time she did so. And planes roaring overhead as though they might crash through the roof. And that door opening so suddenly yesterday, without a knock or anything. The woman had been clear inside the house before Miss Holbrook had heard her. True, she had turned out to be a neighbor who, knowing Miss Holbrook disliked cooking, had brought a casserole for her dinner, but the shock that it had caused! She had had a bolt and chain put on the door this very morning.

The truth was, Miss Holbrook confessed, that she was not fitted to live by herself. It wasn't right for a woman of her age, a woman nearly forty — well, actually, forty-eight, but she didn't look it — to live alone. It wasn't fair. Here she was without a maid again. They rarely stayed more than a few months because they selfishly complained that she called upon them day and night. She couldn't help it, could she, if she had palpitations in the night and the doctors didn't realize that something was wrong with her?

What she needed — what every woman needed — was a man to look after her, take the responsibility, protect her. For some reason, none of the young men who had come to the house when she was a girl had paid much attention to her. They didn't seem to care for frail girls who needed to be sheltered.

Miss Holbrook sighed, put in the oven the casserole her neighbor had brought, and settled down with *The Friday Review*. She subscribed because reading the publication was regarded as a sign of culture, and though she seldom actually read it she kept it prominently displayed on an end table. She flipped the pages casually. This week, she saw with relief, there was no art criticism to baffle her. Only the week before, a critic had bewildered her by talking about "a dialogue between sea and sky." Such stuff! Instead, there was a section devoted to pictures submitted for the annual prize. She got no farther than the first-prize winner: Holbrook's Folly.

For a long time she sat looking at the picture of the medieval castle perched above the Connecticut village. That huge place! It was years since she had visited it but, as she remembered, there were at least twenty bedrooms and in the past few years an adequate number of bathrooms had been added. No one lived there but her nephew Stanley Holbrook and the servants. Plenty of servants, she thought enviously. That poor boy, all alone in the big house. How lonely for him. How sad.

It would be a kind thing, Miss Holbrook reflected, to do her poor bit to brighten Stanley's solitary existence. A great thing for them both. It was a wonder that Stanley had not thought of it himself. After all, since poor Bill's death, she was his only living relative, except for Bill's son who, at six months, did not count as a companion. When she came to think of it she would be doing no more than her duty to go to him.

With unusual energy Miss Holbrook put aside the magazine and went to her desk, where she drew out a piece of blue monogrammed paper.

"My dear Stanley," she began.

iii

Eve Holbrook walked swiftly along the street, eyes straight ahead, ignoring the male glances from the sidewalk tables where a few hardy Parisians braved the chilly air. With her pale gold hair, great violet eyes, beautifully modeled lips, and tall graceful figure, Eve was a girl who inevitably attracted admiring male glances, but she was safe from annoying advances, not only because of the mourning she wore but because of something melancholy in the droop of her mouth and the aloof look in her eyes. Armored in her grief, Eve walked alone without fear of being molested, and unaware, indeed, of the admiration she attracted.

Her steps slowed as she neared the building in which she and Bill had lived for the gloriously happy year of their brief marriage and which she had lived in alone since his death. A year ago today the sun had faded from the sky and her life had seemed to end. Time healed all pain, her friends assured her, but it was not true. She missed Bill as achingly now as she had at the beginning. Only twenty-four years old and her life was already over. No, that was not true; there was Billy, six-month-old Billy whom his father had never seen.

Impatiently she brushed her cheeks with the back of her hand. She wasn't going to face her boy with tears in her eyes. She was all he had and she must be both father and mother and teach him the importance of courage; make life sweet and good and safe for him. But no matter how hard she tried, she could not really take the place of a father.

She smiled at the concierge and glanced indifferently at the meager mail. Her marriage had been so complete that she had not felt the need of friends after she married Bill, and she had no family of her own except for some remote cousins in Florida whom she had never seen. There was nothing but the inevitable appeal for funds from Bill's college and a copy of *The Friday Review*. She tucked them under her arm and climbed swiftly up to the third floor, for as usual the elevator was out of order. Before she could get out her key she heard the sound of Billy's howls and she unlocked the door to find Hortense, her daily maid, running from the dark kitchen, and Billy in his crib, screaming with hunger and rage and a sense of neglect.

"I am sorry, madame. I was preparing the vegetables and I forgot to feed him. But I'm only a little late, just half an hour."

Eve controlled her anger. Half an hour for a hungry child. But she made no criticism. It had been hard enough to find a girl who could cook well and was willing to look after Billy while she was away doing the necessary shopping and taking the daily walk on which her physician insisted.

"Madame has no right to neglect her health," he had said firmly. "You owe it to your son to keep in good condition. One hour a day you must walk. It is understood?"

She picked up the howling child, made him more comfortable, and settled with him on her lap while she fed him, the fat tears still rolling down his cheeks while he gulped hungrily. The feeling of the warm little body in her arms made her smile with contentment. Any woman who had Billy, this enchanting child with the red cheeks and scarlet lips and a glow of health, was rich indeed. She must remember that. She touched the silky fuzz on his head. He was going to have dark hair like his father.

When dinner had been served, Billy tucked in for the night, and Hortense gone home, Eve cleared up the dishes and then sat on in the darkness, looking out over the roofs of Paris, listening to the sounds of an uninhibited quarrel by the couple next door and to the muted noises of the city. This was always the most difficult hour. This was the time when Bill, his work done for the day, had turned to her for talk and laughter and love. This was the empty time.

She made herself get up and switch on all the lights. She was not going to brood in the dark any longer. She picked up the appeal for funds from Bill's college. Perhaps someday Billy would be able to go to his father's old school. She wished she knew more about bringing up a boy. Idly she glanced over *The Friday Review,* flipped pages, saw the prizewinning picture: Holbrook's Folly.

For a long time she stared at it, bemused. Bill had often described his family home, half laughing, half proud. It was absurd, he told her, but he loved it. Someday, when he could find an opening in his profession that suited him, they would return to the United States and then he would take her to Waring. There was no one left in the family now but his older brother Stanley, who still lived at the Folly, and an aunt whom they rarely saw, a tiresome woman who was a hypochondriac. She lived in San Francisco and they wanted no part of her.

"Someday, when we have a child, he may want to live at Holbrook's Folly, darling."

"I thought it was your brother's home."

"No, it belongs to both of us, but my jobs have always taken me out of the country and Stan loves the place just as I do. I doubt if he'll ever marry. I don't know why. He's a good-looking guy and popular with girls, but none of them seem to be up to his standards."

"He sounds hard to please." Eve was uneasy.

"Well, he has a right to be. Stan is quite a guy."

"Oh, Bill, do you think he'll approve of me?"

Bill had laughed and seized her in his arms and said —

From long practice Eve switched her mind away from the past and brought it back to Holbrook's Folly, Bill's boyhood home. Now Bill had a child and perhaps that child had a right to become a part of his own country, to take up his inheritance. Perhaps if Stanley did not marry, he would like to have a nephew, like to have Bill's son in his house, like to take Bill's place as his father.

Carefully Eve weighed the pros and cons. The experiment might prove to be disastrous. Stanley might dislike Eve and find Billy a nuisance. She might hate his kind of life in that preposterous castle. But it need not be forever, she reminded herself. We can visit Billy's uncle, that's natural enough, isn't it? And if it doesn't work out, if we don't like him and he doesn't like us, we'll think of something else. After all, it's such a big house there surely will be plenty of room for us without getting in the way.

It was the first forward-looing thinking she had done since Bill's death. For fear her courage would fail her she went to the telephone and called a travel agency. Then with a lighter heart she went to her desk and pulled out a piece of paper.

"Dear Stanley," she wrote, "I have never thanked you

adequately for your kind offers of help when Bill died or for the wonderful gift you sent when Billy was born. He is six months old now and a beautiful child. I am sure Bill would like to have you know each other. We are planning to leave Paris on Sunday, as that is the first flight I could arrange, and we'd like to visit you for a while at Holbrook's Folly. Bill talked so much about his old home. Your affectionate sister, Eve."

iv

In her bedroom on the top floor of the smart townhouse in the Turtle Bay section of New York City, Ellen rocked back and forth in the chair so thoughtfully provided. "All I need is a bonnet and shawl and some knitting," she told herself grimly, folding idle hands on her lap. Only half-past three and so much of the day and the long empty evening still to get through. What in the world am I going to do with the time?

She had started to rearrange the exquisite crystal she had given her daughter-in-law as a wedding gift on the shelves that had been especially designed and lighted for it, but Thelma had said rather sharply that her maids could do the housework. Poor Thelma, so conscious of what people would think, so afraid of the disapproval of the servants she had imported from England, so arbitrary because she was so insecure! But Ellen had determined at the outset that she would not quarrel with her daughter-in-law, whatever she might do, as long as the girl made her son happy.

She had offered to do some errands for Thelma and

Thelma had been shocked. "Oh, no, Mother, you don't know how difficult it is to drive in New York traffic. You might smash up the car — and yourself as well," she added quickly.

"I have driven a car for thirty-five years without an accident." The words rose to the older woman's lips and were sternly repressed.

It was Thelma's idea, she knew, to relegate her to the top of the house, away from her entertaining, in which, apparently, Ellen was not to be included. Out of the way.

Out of the way. That was what Thelma wanted, of course. Perhaps it was what her only son Bruce wanted too, and that hurt her much more. She had been in the tiny backyard garden, gathering the last of the chrysanthemums the afternoon before when she had overheard him say, "Try to bear with Mother, darling. She's not as young as we are, you know."

"Of course I understand. Perhaps we can find someone her own age for her to meet. She'd hardly enjoy our friends." The unspoken thought was there, "And they will hardly enjoy her."

"I hope she isn't going to be lonely here," her son said uneasily. "She had such a full life at home and so many friends. She was always up to some venture or other. In an unobtrusive way she did a tremendous lot for people, not just in the usual form of charity, but by helping them work out their problems. And she has always been a great traveler, you know, with friends in half a dozen countries. Perhaps I shouldn't have urged her to move here with us."

"Well," his wife said practically, "she could hardly

have let you have so much money for your business and this house if she hadn't sold her own. Anyhow, she's much better off here. That old place of hers and that old furniture — I'd have died with it!"

"It wasn't just old-fashioned," Bruce said with the first sharpness his mother had ever heard him use to his wife. "It was a collection of antiques she had gathered over the years and immensely valuable. Selling it probably provided a large slice of the money she turned over to me so generously. I do hope —"

"Don't worry. She'll be all right."

"You don't understand Mother, Thelma. Somehow I can't imagine her just sitting around idly."

Neither can I, Ellen thought, recalling this conversation. She switched on the radio, listened to the noisy gossip of the world, and switched it off. She was luckier than most people, she knew; she would always be cared for. She had a roof, and a very pleasant roof, over her head. But it was of no avail. She could not contemplate a life spent doing nothing. As things were she was of no use to anyone.

Idly she picked up a copy of *The Friday Review,* saw the prizewinning picture of Holbrook's Folly in Waring, Connecticut. Surely she had heard of the castle and of Waring before. Then she recalled the visit, a few weeks earlier, of friends of her daughter-in-law, people named Mur — Bur — Denton. That was it. The Thomas Dentons. Thelma had told her mother-in-law with considerable pride that Tom Denton had inherited a fortune and a huge shipbuilding business. He and his wife, who was her oldest friend, had bought a quaint old farmhouse near a little village in Connecticut called Waring. It was the smart thing to do these days. Marie Antoinette with a modern touch.

The couple, as Ellen remembered them, had been rather tiresome, but Thelma had been thrilled to entertain them and obviously she was in fear that Ellen would not fit in with such distinguished company. Fortunately Bruce had not observed his wife's attitude because, as Ellen was aware, in spite of his infatuation for his young wife he would not have tolerated any lack of courtesy to his mother. So far he had not discovered the girl's social ambitions and he was blind to her occasional lapses into vulgarity and her tireless efforts to meet prominent people. Sometimes Ellen was afraid of what would happen when Bruce saw his wife clearly.

Ellen's mind still dwelt on that dinner party for the Dentons. She remembered Thelma saying, "I expect you are the most important people in that village of yours."

Doris Denton laughed shrilly. "That's what Tom thought when he bought that old farmhouse, but he's outshone — and how! A castle from the Rhine, no kidding, called Holbrook's Folly. A real castle. This guy Holbrook lives there all alone, a bachelor. How he keeps clear of the girls is beyond me. In his position I'd be hitting the high places of the world but he, believe it or not, has a job as an assistant editor in a publishing house. Says he likes having something meaningful to do. Comes back at night to a real castle. Tom and I went to call one evening when we found out he wasn't going to invite us. — Oh, don't worry, Tom! There's nothing wrong in that and, anyhow, Thelma and I are old friends; we understand each other.

Gorgeous place! I wouldn't mind living like that, I can tell you, but Tom said it was — I don't know — too formal or something."

"All I said was that it wasn't a home. Anyhow I can't afford to live like that, give a wrong impression to people, make them think I want to be better than they are."

At the time Ellen had not been aware of how much of the conversation she had heard. She wondered why she recalled it so clearly now. *It wasn't a home . . . He wanted to have something meaningful to do . . . Out of the way . . . Out of the way . . . Out of the way.*

The chair had stopped rocking. The woman sat still, her face intent, only her hands tightening over the arms of her chair. "I wouldn't dare," she said at length. "They'd never stand for it."

The chair resumed rocking, stopped again. "They couldn't prevent it and I would dare. I do dare."

She went to her desk, reached for her stationery with its monogram, put it aside and found a piece of plain paper. For a long time she stared at it, and then she began to smile.

"Dear Mr. Holbrook," she wrote swiftly, "I have heard of your marvelous house, Holbrook's Folly. Apparently it is everything anyone could wish it to be except for one thing: it is not a home.

"I am not young; I suppose I could be called a rebellious old woman, but I want to do something meaningful. I find it unbearable to be put on the shelf while I am still active. There is one thing I can do well; I am a home-maker. If you are interested you can reach me at this number. Sincerely yours —"

After a thoughtful pause she signed herself "(Mrs.) Ellen Davis."

v

Sherry Winthrop stood before the full-length mirror and inspected herself critically. From the bronze hair with its red lights to the small green satin slippers, there was no fault to find except, perhaps, that she was such a small girl, though nicely rounded, and her chin was rather too firm, a defect belied by the dimple in her cheek. As she brushed her hair vigorously, sparks flew out. That was the effect Sherry had on most people and it was an exhilarating one, except when her quick temper flared.

At the moment, however, Sherry was on top of her world, a world that, at twenty, seemed enormous to her. In a few minutes the doorbell would ring and she would run downstairs — no, on second thought she would be leisurely about it, as though in no hurry at all — to greet Major Douglas Carleton, who had proposed to her a month earlier and had been accepted. She had a huge solitaire on her ring finger to prove it and to disprove the innuendos that he was just amusing himself with her while he was stationed in Minneapolis.

Doug Carleton, tall and handsome and well-to-do, had been the most sought-after man in the city from the time he was stationed there. Almost from their first meeting he had ignored the lures thrown out by other girls and had devoted himself to a determined siege of Sherry. With his dashing sports car, his good looks, his admiration, and the attraction of being older than her other admirers, he had proved to be irresistible. But there had been one flaw in the whirlwind courtship. Doug's army job was one which he could not discuss with her and there were times when he disappeared without warning and reappeared without explanation.

Sherry, studying the lines of her new green dress with approval, smiled to herself and threw out her arms in exultation. At this moment she had everything in life she wanted. In another month she would marry Doug. Even his occasional absences would be bearable because she was, secretly, writing a novel that would, she was sure, make her famous.

A bell rang and Sherry, without waiting for her landlady to open the door, ran down the stairs. The bell rang again, not the doorbell but the telephone jangling insistently. Her heart sank. Surely Doug was not going to break his date, as he had been forced to do several times before, tonight of all nights, when they were going to complete their plans for the wedding and the honeymoon and decide where they were going to live when he would be reassigned.

But it was not Doug's voice on the telephone; it was a woman's voice, impersonal and official. "Is this 354-7111? ... Miss Sherry Winthrop? ... I have a message for you: 'Regret cannot see you tonight. All my love. Doug.' "

Sherry caught her breath. "Where — where was it sent from?"

"Philadelphia."

"*Philadelphia!*" A pause. "Ah — thank you." Sherry put down the telephone and stared blankly at the wall. Philadelphia. Half a continent away. He must have left by plane hours earlier and he hadn't even called her. Twisting the spectacular diamond solitaire that caught the light and reflected it in dazzling multicolored facets, she went slowly up the stairs to her room, mouth drooping with disappointment.

But Sherry was not built for ill humor. Hers was, as a rule, a joyous and confident nature not given to brooding or self-pity, and rarely discouraged. In the long run she always came back to the cheerful conviction that the world was her oyster which she would open by her own efforts. Even her flaming temper went off like a skyrocket and was as quickly spent.

Now she gave herself a disapproving little shake. If her plans for the evening were upset she was not going to sit around being sorry for herself. Instead she settled down at the typewriter she had purchased with the first money she had saved on her job in a day nursery where she looked after the small children of working mothers. She looked at the last sentence of this memorable opus, hesitated for a moment and began to type vigorously. Sherry Winthrop, aged twenty, with no experience beyond high school and her first job, was writing the most exciting story she knew, the story of her own life.

vi

Major Douglas Carleton did not, as Sherry expected, appear to apologize the next day or the next or the next. He did not call. He did not write.

Days grew to weeks and then to a month, two months, three. Hurt feelings turned to growing anxiety and finally to anger. Sherry was aware that Doug was not free to discuss his hush-hush job with her; he had explained that clearly. But she knew that he had given her name as the one to notify in case he should be injured or killed, and there had been no word at all. He had simply dropped out of her life.

For the first time she took into account the warnings of her friends that the glamorous Major Carleton was merely flirting with her and that he had no serious intentions. She had blithely disregarded these as being inspired by jealousy. Now she came to the conclusion that her friends were justified and were more clear-sighted than she had been.

At least there was still the novel. One morning she wrapped it carefully and mailed it to the Radcliffe Publishing Company, as she had long admired the books on their list. Almost before it seemed possible that they could have read it the script came back. With unsteady hands Sherry tore open the letter that accompanied it.

Dear Miss Winthrop:

Your novel, The Shining Years, *has been given a sympathetic reading but we do not feel we can make a place for it on our list. There is an engaging quality of youth in your writing but you would, perhaps, be well advised to live a few more of those shining years before you attempt to write of them. Perhaps you will find that living, rather than writing, is your real forte. Or perhaps you might address yourself to an audience of children. You have an imaginative quality that would appeal to them.*

Sincerely yours,
Stanley Holbrook

Why — why — temper flared. So she was too young to write. The experiences that had seemed wonderful and unique to her merely amused this arrogant man. He didn't even believe she could hold the attention of anyone but little children. She'd show him. She'd —

The anger flickered out. Sherry flung herself face down on her bed. Everything was over. She was a desperate failure both as a woman and as a career girl. Doug had jilted her. Now her hope of a future as a best-selling novelist had faded.

After a night of stormy tears Sherry rose like the phoenix, showered, wiped away the traces of tears and sleeplessness, and squared her shoulders. Her world had not yet come to an end just because she had been jilted. There were other men. If her dreams of becoming a famous writer had vanished there were still a number of exciting things to do and she intended to live her life to the full. But first she would go away and make a fresh start somewhere else. She'd go — why, she would go to the most exciting and stimulating and challenging city in the world — New York. She'd take the city by storm. She'd show people like Douglas Carleton and Stanley Holbrook what they had missed.

As usual, common sense came to the rescue and checked her wild imagination in mid-flight. She examined her checkbook balance and her savings bank deposits. Her father's life insurance had provided her with the backlog of a few thousand dollars. She thought confidently that she would be all right. Of course, she'd have to get a job, and she would try something more glamorous than work in a nursery school. Evidently Mr. Stanley Holbrook didn't think there was anything interesting in the work she had been doing, though it had enchanted her and she had loved working with the children, amusing them, and, particularly, telling them stories. She could hold them enthralled for such long periods of time that the other workers had been amazed.

She performed her usual Sunday chores, washed out stockings, pressed some dresses, and wrote letters. She carried on an enormous correspondence because she was as friendly as a puppy, and wrote gay and amusing letters as spontaneously as she breathed; as a result, people were eager to get them.

She glanced at the Sunday paper and then, weary of conflicts and violence, she picked up a copy of *The Friday Review*, scanning the book reviews with great care to see what attractions other novels had that her own lacked. She read with more than her usual interest the accounts of concerts and new plays. Before many weeks had passed she might be able to enjoy them for herself. She looked at the prizewinning pictures. Holbrook's Folly appealed to her romantic taste. Imagine being able to live in a real castle! She read the brief account of the owner. The castle, it appeared, belonged to Stanley Holbrook of Waring, Connecticut, a wealthy man who preferred to hold a meaningful job rather than live a life of idleness.

She stared at it, puzzled. Then she went to get the infuriating letter from the Radcliffe Publishing Company. It must be the same Stanley Holbrook. As her nimble imagination began to take fire she did not hear the noises from the street, the sound of church bells, or voices on the stairs. There was a challenging tilt to her head, a sparkle of mischief in her hazel eyes that would have alerted anyone who knew Miss Sherry Winthrop.

In a drawer where she kept old letters she turned over envelopes impatiently until she found one with the post-mark, "Waring, Connecticut." It had been written months earlier.

Both my wife and I hope very much that you will be able to visit us when you have your summer vacation, so we can renew our acquaintance with your dear father's daughter whom we have not seen for so many years. Waring is a quiet village but it is only a little over an hour from New York, which I believe you will enjoy.

Your affectionate old friend, Frank Saunders

Sherry rolled paper into her typewriter.

Dear Mrs. Saunders:
I am coming to New York to look for a more stimulating job than the one I have here and I would like very much to accept the kind invitation of you and your husband and spend a few days with you in Waring before going on to New York.

When she had hastily finished the letter she began another:

Dear Mr. Holbrook:
Perhaps you have forgotten me. I hope not because, though our acquaintance was so brief, it has made a lasting impression on me.

(You bet it has, telling me I can't write!)

Of all my memories of you, the ones I cherish most are the times when you talked to me about your delight and pride in encouraging young writers.

(And someday I'll make you sorry you didn't.)

I expect to be in New York before long so we will be meeting again. I wonder if you have forgotten my name.

She did not sign the letter but she addressed and stamped it and ran down to drop it in the corner mailbox.

II

STANLEY Holbrook awakened to see a brilliantly blue sky and the crimson of ivy growing up around his bedroom window. The air was crisp. It was a perfect October day and nowhere in the world, he was convinced, was the autumn season as magnificent as it was in New England.

When he had showered, shaved, and dressed he ran lightly down the great circular stone staircase, which was so striking an architectural feature of Holbrook's Folly, crossed the huge stone lobby with its priceless tapestries, and went into the impressive dining room to his seat at one end of the refectory table that could seat sixty guests. He had once laughingly countered his brother Bill's question as to why he did not marry by saying that the dining room table was so long that if he and his wife sat facing each other at the two ends they would need a telephone to talk to each other.

He smiled a good morning to the maid and ate his breakfast slowly, with the sense of well-being that came from a life neatly planned down to the last detail, excellent health, a sound financial standing, and the awareness of a job ahead which he found stimulating and rewarding, in spite of the gibes of some of his friends that he was

taking bread out of the mouths of people who needed to
work for a living.

He had given up trying to explain why he found it im-
perative to have a job to do, a job that had value and
made sense to him. Books are the last completely free
medium for the exchange of ideas, their contents controlled not by the pressures of advertisers or special interests but only by the canons of need or good taste.
Everyone seemed to be worrying about pollution of one
sort and another but, he argued, the quality of what
people put in their minds was even more important than
that of the air they breathed or the food they ate. It con-
ditioned not only their thoughts but their actions; it
molded their sense of values. When he tried to be completely honest Stanley felt that he sounded self-righteous,
so he had learned to evade all personal questions and to
speak of his work lightly as though of some amusing
idiosyncrasy, which he did not take seriously.

As usual there was a pile of mail beside his plate, almost as much mail, he thought, as would be awaiting him
at his office. Because of his wealth there were always appeals for money. Because of his attractive personality —
and perhaps his wealth and position too — there were always invitations.

Now and then it struck Stanley that his personal mail
was not really very personal. Since the death of his
brother Bill there had been no one who was particularly
close to him, and even Bill, because of the jobs which took
him all over the world, had rarely been at home. Nothing,
however, had ever changed or diminished their relationship, not even Bill's long absences, not even his marriage

to the girl Eve whom Stanley had never seen. But Bill's death a year before had closed that door forever.

Stanley found himself wondering what Bill's son would be like, not what he was like now. A baby only a few months old could not be expected to be interesting. But Stanley thought that later it would be pleasant to get to know the boy, perhaps to be a sort of stand-in for Bill, though Bill's widow would probably marry again. According to Bill, who had adored her, she was fabulously beautiful, and the picture he had sent was certainly charming. Even allowing for the exaggerations of a man in love, Stanley agreed that she was a lovely creature with melting violet eyes and a sensitive mouth. Not his type, however; too much the languorous lily for his taste. He liked girls with more vitality, but he did not like them enough to be tempted to marry, did not like any of them enough to want to bring them home to Holbrook's Folly. His interest in girls was purely ephemeral and he always made his attitude clear at the outset of his acquaintance.

He slit the envelopes open and arranged the mail in neat piles: bills in one place, appeals for money in a second, invitations in a third. This morning there were four unexpected letters. The first, he noticed with a grimace as he recognized the monogram, was from his Aunt Winifred. What new alarums and excursions had she experienced this time? In her last letter she had filled five agitated pages describing what she had thought to be a burglar looking over the neighborhood but had turned out to be a legitimate real estate broker examining some property on the block. The time before that she had been bracing herself for an operation which, apparently, had never taken place.

He read her letter in growing consternation. So she thought he must be lonely in that great barracks of a house, that he would be glad to have company, especially someone of his own family with him. And all those empty rooms! It quite frightened her to think of him rattling around in all that space. As it happened, she had been most unwell and she had lost her maid, an ungrateful, self-centered girl, so she had been quite at a loss until she thought of Holbrook's Folly. "Just as if it had been meant," she wrote, she had seen a picture of the castle and realized that it provided a perfect solution both for her and for her dear nephew Stanley. So, unless he wired her otherwise, she would sublet her house and fly from California on Thursday, joining him some time in the evening, taking a taxi from the airport unless he found it convenient to send a car for her. Otherwise he was not to put himself out. She was quite accustomed, in her lonely life, to having to look out for herself.

Stanley looked up in dismay. "What day is this?" he asked the surprised maid.

"Monday, sir."

"Good God!" He might have known, he thought savagely, that Aunt Winifred would make it impossible for him to refuse her his hospitality. By now she had probably carried out her intention to sublet her house. Then he felt ashamed. After all, she was a lonely woman; understandably so because she thought of nothing but herself and her health, and people had learned to give her a wide berth. Still she was right about the number of unoccupied rooms at Holbrook's Folly. He could take care of her without bother or the total disruption of his daily life.

He turned to the maid who was refilling his coffee cup. "Please tell Wilson that my aunt, Miss Holbrook, will be here Thursday evening for an indefinite stay. Oh, and if I should forget, see that a car picks her up at the airport. Have Roberts check the time. She'll be coming in from San Francisco."

"Yes, sir," the elderly servant said, privately thinking that Wilson would roar like a wounded lion when he heard that Miss Holbrook was coming to stay. She always turned the place upside down with her unreasonable demands, her complaints about the servants, and her determination to set Wilson right about how the house should be run. Last time the enraged butler had gone so far as to threaten to resign, though none of the staff believed him for a minute because Wilson was convinced that without his constant supervision the Folly would crumble away to chaos.

The second private letter was from Paris and addressed in the distinctive hand of Bill's widow Eve. It appeared, Stanley thought grimly as he read it, that Holbrook's Folly would rapidly be filling up. Of course there was always a place for Bill's son and for Bill's wife. In any case, the house had been left jointly to the brothers, and now Bill's son had a right to be there. It was his home too. Anyhow, Stanley owed it to Bill to do what he could for the boy, but between Aunt Winifred and Eve there was apt to be tension, with both women warring for control of the household management. It seemed to Stanley that his peaceful bachelor days were over and henceforth he would be living in a state of siege. His experience of women was that they all had an ungovernable desire to rule him for his own good.

The third letter was signed Ellen Davis and he smiled as he read it. His first impulse was to toss it aside unanswered, but he was struck by the woman's mention of a meaningful job. And she called herself "a rebellious old woman." She also referred to herself as a homemaker. He put the letter down, tapping the paper thoughtfully, letting his coffee cool.

A homemaker. He looked down the bleak length of the refectory table, thought of the echoing emptiness of the great entrance lobby, the splendid rooms that were better fitted for a museum than for human living. Whatever Holbrook's Folly might be, no one could call it cozy.

Ellen Davis, he thought, taking up the letter again, appeared to be an elderly woman with a singular longing for independence and usefulness. Perhaps such a woman might be an answer to his dilemma. With her installed as housekeeper, neither Eve nor his aunt would be able to take over the direction of the house. She might, if she were tactful, be able to arbitrate between the two or possibly even establish some bond of sympathy between them. He glanced at the New York telephone number and tucked the letter in his pocket, deciding to get in touch with her as soon as he reached the office.

He was about to get up when he noticed the square blue envelope, typewritten and mailed from Minneapolis. He read it, his brows pulled together in surprise. Now who on earth — when had he ever talked about encouraging young writers, boasting of it? Could the writer pos-

sibly be making fun of him? Whoever it was — probably
some silly female — sounded enterprising enough, assum-
ing with so much assurance that they would be meeting in
the near future. If they did so, he vowed to himself, it
would have to be arranged without any encouragement
from him. He dropped the letter down with the third-class
nuisance mail to be thrown out.

ii

He drove down the Saw Mill Parkway, the car window
open and the crisp air blowing through his short dark
hair. Dogwood, that generous tree which is as colorful in
fall as in the spring, had changed color again and the
parkway was a glorious tapestry. The beauty of the morning helped to dissipate the annoyance that the mail had
brought. After all, he could keep Aunt Winifred in her
place, and Eve would probably be busy with the child,
and if this Mrs. Davis panned out things might not be so
bad after all.

To his surprise he found himself pondering again about
the writer of the unsigned letter. That it was a girl and
a young girl he felt reasonably sure. About the rest he
was uncertain. If she was going to so much trouble to get
in touch with him she must have liked him a good deal at
one time. Minneapolis? He had never been there and he
could not remember anyone he had ever known from
there, nor did he go around telling people that he prided
himself on encouraging young writers. Somehow that
word stung, and he had an inkling that that was exactly
what it had been designed to do. He shrugged. He had
never yet met the girl he couldn't handle.

He passed the soaring arch of the George Washington Bridge with an endless stream of cars crawling like ants on its two levels; passed the great gleaming body of the Hudson River, blue under a cloudless sky; saw the distant spires of the towers of midtown Manhattan, passed Grant's Tomb and the Soldiers' and Sailors' Monument and, leaving the parkway, crossed town through Central Park and went down past great and characterless steel and glass buildings to his favorite garage and walked the short distance to the building that housed, along with fifty other enterprises, the Radcliffe Publishing Company. He nodded to the receptionist and went quickly to his own office. Before ringing for his secretary he pulled out the letter from the rebellious old woman, Ellen Davis, and asked for an outside wire.

The voice at the other end of the telephone was male and formal. A butler's. Stanley's eyebrows rose and then he realized that the woman was probably employed in the house. There was a brief pause when he asked for Mrs. Davis.

A quiet voice spoke into the telephone. "This is Ellen Davis." A cultivated voice and beautifully pitched, he observed in relief. He disliked strident voices and ugly accents.

"This is Stanley Holbrook. Your letter reached me this morning and I am definitely interested. Would it be possible for you to call to see me sometime today at my office?"

"It would give me great pleasure."

He consulted his calendar. "At eleven-thirty this morning? Is that too short notice? That is, uh, are you free to come at that time?"

He could hear the smile in the woman's voice. "I am quite at leisure, Mr. Holbrook. Where is your office? . . . Eleven-thirty then."

He jotted the time on his calendar and rang for his secretary. After embarrassing experiences with girls who insisted on keeping his desk supplied with flowers, who dressed to please him, and who appeared to take a personal interest in him, he had prudently hired a middle-aged woman with a husband and two children. As a result his work was done more efficiently and without personal complications. He went through the usual morning routine, writing to authors, declining a number of manuscripts, suggesting changes for one, writing encouragement to a beginner. (*Darn that girl, anyhow; her words kept getting under his skin.*) He broke off occasionally to answer telephone calls or to see importunate authors and literary agents, all laden down with masterpieces.

"Well," he said at length, "that seems to dispose of the lot for today, Mrs. Parker."

She got up, gathering the letters and notebook and pencils. "Oh, there's one thing. Mr. Fisk would like to see you in his office as soon as you are free."

"In *his* office?" Stanley raised his brows but the woman avoided his eyes.

When she had gone Stanley picked up a manuscript from one of the company's regular authors, but before he had turned half a dozen pages he leaned back, frowning. Young Art Fisk was a nephew of the president of the Radcliffe Company, one of the few publishers still able to function independently in a period of soaring costs. The uncle had presented him to Stanley the day he entered the company, four weeks earlier, and Stanley had summed him up as brash, encroaching, and ignorant. Fisk had made too much of a fuss over Stanley to be trusted. He seemed inclined to try to get ahead by the way he handled people rather than by the way he handled his job. A warning signal had been hoisted at once.

"I see my uncle has kept to the old lines of the house," Fisk had said, after his uncle had left the two young men to get acquainted, exchanging what he thought was an amused, conspiratorial look with a contemporary. "Kind of out of line with the present world, don't you think? The house needs some new blood and some new ideas. I'm sure you and I can do a nice job of rejuvenation, and weed out some of the dead wood, like old man Wolf, for instance. Historical novels! Who reads historical novels today?"

"About fifty thousand people read Wolf's historical novels in hard cover," Stanley told him dryly, "aside from the book club sales, and they all sell to paperback houses, which bid high for them, as well as abroad. Twelve countries for the last title."

Fisk had been silenced but he was not, Stanley thought, convinced. Uneasily, Stanley shoved back his chair and went down the hall to the cubbyhole that had been assigned to Fisk. Judging by the fact that he had seen fit to send for the assistant editor instead of going to him, it was apparent that Fisk's ambitions were for the head office.

This suspicion was confirmed by the casual way Fisk nodded to Stanley and then waved idly to the one extra chair in the office. "Hi, Holbrook. I expected you earlier."

There was a glint in Stanley's eyes. "Your orders just reached me."

Fisk flushed uncomfortably. "Hell, it wasn't an order, just — well, push those manuscripts off the chair onto the floor and make yourself comfortable. It's all tripe anyhow. The whole place is more dead than alive. I guess my uncle is getting past it. I hadn't figured on going into publishing; I had my eye on a nice spot in an advertising concern but it took a good deal of cash to buy a partnership and my uncle owns most of the stock here; it might be a good thing in the long run, after we've made some changes, of course."

Fisk had a narrow face, made narrower by wide sideburns. He indicated a manuscript on his desk. "This is what I mean. My uncle wants me to arrange some television interviews for this guy — what's his name? Oh, Professor Clovering. Television! Who's going to listen?"

Stanley held on to his temper with some difficulty. "Quite a lot of people, I think. He is one of the most distinguished economists in this country if not in the world and, though his sales are not high, his prestige value is immense."

"Oh." After a moment Fisk said less certainly, "Well, I'll see what I can set up."

"Once the broadcasting companies know he is available they will jump at him. You won't have to do anything but arrange the details."

"I'll leave the details to my secretary."

Stanley sounded a warning note, though he knew it was more than the cocksure Fisk deserved. "There is nothing writers appreciate more than personal interest and attention. Publishing is a personal business, just as writing is. Sympathetic relations are important."

Fisk laughed. "You sound like my uncle."

"That's natural enough. All I know about publishing I learned from him."

"Well, I'm going to bring in some new ideas and the first thing is to get some life into our list. As a matter of fact, I've been kind of cultivating some promising writers in my free time the past few months while Uncle Jim was being talked into giving me a job."

It was Stanley's conviction that the only place where Fisk met anyone was in a bar or night spot. "Who are they?" he asked with foreboding.

"Ever read *Man's World?*"

"I've seen it around now and then. It's not on the newsstands, is it?"

Fisk laughed. "Strictly under the counter. But, man, does it sell!"

"I can't imagine what place there could possibly be on the Radcliffe list for books made up of centerfold cheesecake."

"It's not just the illustrations; those boys can write too." Fisk snickered.

"You aren't seriously considering —"

"Look, Holbrook." Fisk's eyes narrowed and so did his lips. "I've come into this company. It's my uncle's company. Someday it will be mine. I intend to see that it makes some real money. So I want you to run along and read these two manuscripts. They're hot stuff and that's what people want. You're not with it, man!"

Stanley fought down an almost overpowering temptation to knock the smug Fisk off his chair. Then he wheeled without a word and went striding down the corridor to Radcliffe's big corner office. As usual the door stood open. Radcliffe believed in being accessible not only to his staff but to his stable of writers at all times.

He was going over advertising appropriations and he looked up with a frown at the interruption, which turned to a welcoming smile when he saw Stanley. "Sit down, Holbrook. Be with you in a minute. My God, if prices soar any higher —"

At length he pushed away the papers. He was a tall, silver-haired man with a scholarly face. "What's on your mind this morning? Any more trouble about that plagiarism suit?"

"Oh, no, it was a trumped-up charge by an unsuccessful writer making a fool of himself in an attempt to get some attention he couldn't earn legitimately."

Radcliffe nodded. "Thought that might be it. We get about one of those a year." He leaned back, watching Stanley, appearing to have all the time in the world, though he was notoriously overworked and almost always took home a well-filled briefcase at night.

"I've come to hand in my resignation."

Radcliffe did not attempt to conceal his dismay. "I'm sorrier than I can say. I don't scruple to tell you that you are the most promising editor I've ever had. Frankly, when you first came to me I thought you weren't serious, that a job was just a new experience for you; but you have a nose for good writing and you know how to get the best out of your writers. I like the kind of books you have added to our list, books I am proud to publish. I had begun to hope —" he broke off to fill and light his pipe. "I had begun to hope," he repeated when it was going well, "that you-would become editor-in-chief when Brooks retires next year and eventually, I even imagined," and there was a wry twist to his mouth, "that you might be interested in buying out my stock in the business and running it on your own."

When Stanley made no comment the older man laughed at himself. "Oh, well, I should have known better ever since I saw that picture of your place in *The Friday Review*. I suspected then you wouldn't be satisfied to go on working indefinitely at a modestly priced job."

"A question of salary isn't involved."

"What is it to be: politics or sports or travel?"

"None of them. I'll look around for another job I like."

Radcliffe's eyes searched the younger man's face. Not a regularly handsome face, he thought, but an attractive one with glinting humor in the eyes to lighten the thoughtful brow, and an engaging smile that softened the firm mouth. Not a face that gave anything away. Holbrook had too much reserve; he was friendly with everyone from the president to the office boy but, paradoxically, he had no close friends.

"I see." He puffed on his pipe. "I see. It's my nephew, isn't it? I was afraid that he might make a nuisance of himself. One of those kids who want to start at the top." He puffed in silence, ruminating. "He's the only child of my sister and the poor girl has had a difficult life. Married a no-good drifter who died young, mercifully; married a second time, Art's father, a man who wanted to live on her money. And did. Got all she had and sank it in bad investments. So she has nothing left now but Art. Between them I've been persuaded against my better judgment to give the boy a chance. I couldn't refuse, Holbrook. I owed the poor girl that." Again Radcliffe searched Stanley's unrevealing face. "But if he has any idea that he is going to supplant you, he is mistaken. I hoped you could give him some idea of how the house is run." He broke off as he saw Stanley's expression. "What is it?"

"He is giving *me* ideas of how the house ought to be run. Get rid of old-fashioned historical novels like Wolf's. Drop Dr. Clovering. Add some juicy numbers from writers for *Man's World*."

There was a long silence while Radcliffe forgot to smoke, sunk in troubled thought. Then he went through the leisurely ritual of relighting his pipe. "I don't like asking favors but I'm asking one now." As he saw Stanley's lips press firmly together he added quickly, "Just give it one more month. Will you do that? I'll talk to Art. If he has any idea of taking over the editorial policy I'll nip it in the bud right now. What he needs —"

Stanley smiled briefly. "What he needs is a good left to the jaw."

Radcliffe shook his head. "All that bluster is an attempt to cover up his sense of inadequacy. So far he's failed at everything — If you could —"

"Accept his authors?"

"Don't be a fool! He will never be permitted to choose titles for our list; I'm planning to use him only in the publicity department."

"I am genuinely sorry. The job suited me to a T, but I

can't work in an atmosphere of hostility, of conflicting values and interests. Fisk is determined to rule the roost and I'm getting out. It will take me the rest of the week to clear up all the loose ends."

Radcliffe held out his hand. "Good luck to you, Holbrook, and remember if you ever change your mind there will be a place and a welcome for you here."

"Thank you. I'll remember that." But both men knew that Stanley would not return as long as Fisk remained.

It was eleven-thirty when Stanley got back to his own office, feeling curiously lost now that he had broken with his job. Othello's occupation's gone, he thought. Now what?

His secretary, who had been on the lookout, came in to say, "There's a Mrs. Davis waiting to see you. She says you are expecting her."

Davis? Preoccupied with the problems raised by Art Fisk, Stanley had forgotten about her. "Oh, yes. Bring her in, please."

In a few minutes his secretary returned, escorting a white-haired woman of sixty, wearing a well-cut gray suit with a smart black hat. She was not a handsome woman but he liked her at once. Deep-set dark blue eyes were unfaded and observant and there were lines of humor and compassion at the corners of her mouth.

Stanley stood up. "Mrs. Davis?"

"Yes, I am Ellen Davis, Mr. Holbrook."

He had been right about her pleasant voice. This was no typical housekeeper, this was a woman of poise and cultivation. His curiosity was aroused. What had led such a woman to write the letter he had received? *A rebellious old woman*. Rebellious, perhaps, but not actually old. She had good health, vitality, and alert eyes. He found himself wishing he could have known her when she was a girl.

When she was seated beside his desk, hands resting quietly on her lap without fidgeting, eyes fixed on his face, a faint question in them, he abandoned any idea he might have had of conducting the usual interview with a prospective employee.

"You know," he found himself saying frankly, "your letter came like the answer to a prayer. I found myself in a real quandary and I didn't have the slightest idea of how to cope with it." He told her about the impending visit from his aunt. "My aunt is a hypochondriac and she always upsets the whole house when she comes for a visit. My butler Wilson has been with the family since before I was born, and he's been running things pretty much to suit himself ever since my mother died. I suspect he's a bit of a domestic tyrant but I'm lucky to have him. I can't imagine the Folly without him. He handles everything, so you can guess what it's like when my aunt tries to take over and change his routine and complains about the servants."

Mrs. Davis smiled without speaking. She was, Stanley thought, a restful woman.

"On top of that my brother's widow is flying over from Paris with her baby. Of course the house belongs to the boy as much as it does to me but," he flung out a hand, "there are bound to be a number of changes. Well, the thing is I need someone to —"

"To assume the reins of the household without putting Wilson's back up and at the same time make Miss Holbrook feel that her complaints are being heeded, while persuading Mrs. Holbrook that she is actually the hostess."

"Put that way," Stanley said gloomily, "it sounds impossible."

Mrs. Davis had a quiet laugh. "Oh, I think with a little tact it could be done."

"You mean you are ready to take on the labors of Hercules?"

There was genuine mirth in her laughter. "I can't think of anything I'd enjoy more than a challenge like that," she surprised him by saying. "For six months I've been little more than a — a spare tire, sitting around with idle hands. A useless old woman on the shelf."

"I don't think of you as old."

"Anyone is old who is told constantly that he or she is old; anyone is old who is of value to no one; anyone is old who is regarded as incompetent to carry out a useful, meaningful job." There was passion in the woman's voice and her eyes glowed with the intensity of her feeling. Then she mocked at her own impassioned utterance. "I warned you that I am a rebellious old woman."

"Then thank heaven for it! Shall we call it settled? Will you come up to the Folly and get established before my guests arrive?"

"Of course I will."

"Today?" he asked, naming a healthy salary.

"Today," she agreed promptly, accepting his salary offer.

"If we are going to make this work, we'll have to think of some reason for you being in my house."

"But I'm to be housekeeper!"

He shook his head. "There would be conflicts with

Wilson. Anyhow, that isn't what I need. Look, I have an idea! Why can't you be the aunt of an old friend of mine, a childhood friend. My mother died when I was quite young and you've practically been a substitute mother. How's that?"

She laughed at the pride with which he produced this bit of fiction. "I'm sorry to break up this dream but your aunt and sister-in-law would know it couldn't possibly be true."

"I've never met my sister-in-law," he told her, "and she doesn't know any of my friends. As for Aunt Winifred, she has visited the Folly only half a dozen times over the years, and I was usually away at school when she came, or off on a visit to escape her."

There was a twinkle in the woman's eyes. "Then we'd better find a name for my nephew, hadn't we?"

"Archibald," he suggested.

She was revolted. "Certainly not. Wilbur?"

"I will not," he declared, "have a friend named Wilbur."

"What about Henry?"

"Not my favorite name but acceptable. By the way, what's happened to Henry?"

"We don't want the wretched creature around here. Let's say he's a mining engineer in South America."

"Married?"

"No, we'd be bound to get confused about the details. He's just a rover by nature. And why am I so at home in your house?"

"Don't you remember? You're a substitute mother. You've been staying there, for months at a time, over the years."

"What about your servants and neighbors?"

"I'll take care of the servants and I don't really have neighbors, in the sense of close friends — oh, there are two or three, of course, but mostly it's just a question of people who entertain me and who come to dinner a few times a year."

The shrewd eyes gave him a fleeting glance. He had revealed more than he had intended. This attractive and wealthy young man was, on the whole, a singularly solitary person.

"Well, if you think it will work out without involving you in too many difficulties, we can at least try it."

"Fine!" Stanley smiled. "I think I had better call you Aunt Ellen. Will that be all right?"

"Of course, Mr. Holbrook."

"As you've known me all my life you had better call me Stanley." He groped for some tactful way of framing his next comment. "You'll be dining with me, of course, and I do not want you to go to any extra expense —"

She guessed at the cause of his embarrassment and reassured him. "I have an adequate wardrobe."

"Good. Then I guess we've settled everything. I'll call for you, wherever you say, at five o'clock."

There was a moment's hesitation. "Perhaps it would be better if I met you here in the lobby."

He started to protest, wondering uneasily whether this woman's desire for independence was leading her to run away from her own people. He didn't want any problems with outraged or indignant relations. However, something in her manner prevented him from asking personal questions. "As you like. At five o'clock downstairs then, Mrs. Davis."

When she had gone he called the Folly. "Wilson, I am bringing home a Mrs. Davis tonight. I'll need her when the other ladies arrive. You might give her that suite of rooms in the tower. I think she would enjoy it. And, Wilson, you are to remember and inform the staff that Mrs. Davis is an old friend of mine and that she has spent so much time at the Folly that it is practically a second home to her. Got it?"

"Mrs. Davis," Wilson said woodenly, "is an old friend and the staff all know her well." His voice was stiff with disapprobation.

Stanley sighed. If Wilson was going to be hostile, Mrs. Davis would have her work cut out. How peaceful it would be to live in a world without women!

III

W HEN Stanley stepped out of the elevator that afternoon Mrs. Davis was waiting in the lobby of the office
building. There were two suitcases on the floor beside
her, a weekend bag in her hand, a lined cape over her
arm. The lobby was thronged with people crowding
toward the revolving doors, pushing their way out into the
street.

Stanley saw her before she saw him and he was aware
that her expression had changed since their interview that
morning, during which her eyes had so often twinkled
with amusement. Now they wore a strained expression as
though, during the intervening hours, she had had a
change of heart or had begun to have qualms about the
step she was taking. Perhaps, when it came to the pinch,
she was not quite as rebellious as she had believed.

He thought ruefully that perhaps they had both been
precipitate, she with a desire to break with her former
life and he to break with his job. On sober second thought
he was not at all sure he had made the right decision in
severing his connection with the Radcliffe firm. He was a
man who hated change and he had fitted comfortably into
a pleasant groove: the publishing house by day and his

well-stocked library at night. And now, in a moment of impulse, he had shattered his routine. He tried to comfort himself with a statement he had once heard that there is no such thing as a snap decision. The decision we make at any given time represents the sum total of the person we are at that moment.

News of his resignation had filtered through the office grapevine before the end of the day. Art Fisk, much of his cockiness gone, had come awkwardly to apologize and to say that his uncle had made clear that he was to keep his hands off the editorial policy.

"I guess," he said, his expression resentful, "I built too much on his promise of a real future here. The old man seems to think I'll be satisfied to be nothing but a glorified clerk and I don't believe he intends to leave his share of the business to me when he quits. Oh, well, I'll get him to lend me enough to buy into a good live outfit; so you can carry on in your old way here, Holbrook."

"That's good of you," Stanley said evenly, "but I'm clearing out at the end of the week."

"You needn't go on my account, you know; I'll find a place for my writers somewhere else. There must be a house that wants to make a mark for itself. I wouldn't like to see you jobless."

Stanley grinned at that. "Don't let it keep you awake." In some amusement he watched the young man leave his office, but he was not amused to find his secretary in tears over his impending departure. "You aren't losing your job," he assured her.

"It's not that but where will I find anyone like you to work for?"

"Well —" he had begun in embarrassment and he was relieved to have the interview interrupted by other members of the staff, resentful or angry to hear that he was leaving and that his departure had been caused by Art Fisk. Knowing that their enmity would make Fisk's position all but intolerable, he assured them that he was going on to a job that offered more scope. This seemed unfair to Radcliffe but it was better than leaving his nephew on the firing line. However, it made no difference because none of them believed him. Radcliffe's secretary had overheard the interview and it had lost nothing in the retelling.

Having triumphantly carried his point Stanley was humanly regretful that he had been impulsive and that he had burned his bridges behind him, so he was in an uncharacteristically sober mood when he went to greet Mrs. Davis, take her cape, and pick up the two suitcases.

Madison Avenue was thronged with office workers hurrying for subways and buses. The roar of traffic, the racing of motors, the sounding of impatient horns, the piercing whistle of a traffic policeman made conversation difficult unless it was conducted in loud voices. Neither of them spoke until after Stanley had retrieved his car at the garage, stowed the suitcases in the trunk, and helped Mrs. Davis into the passenger seat.

For a few minutes his attention was fully occupied by easing his car into traffic and holding it in its lane, with taxis and trucks jockeying for position. Only when he had gone up the long ramp onto the Henry Hudson Parkway could he relax and take a quick look at his passenger. She seemed unaware of the heavy traffic or the gleaming windows of the apartments on Riverside Drive reflecting the afternoon sun. Her gloved hands were tightly clasped.

"Any regrets?" he asked. "You aren't committed to anything, you know. If you'd be happier going home I'll take you there."

There was a pause and then she said, "Thank you. No, I don't want to go back." Unexpectedly she smiled. "What would my nephew Henry think of such poor-spirited behavior?"

He grinned. "I wonder sometimes if you don't have too high an opinion of Henry."

"Henry is a paragon."

"Then he is no friend of mine."

"Well, perhaps, he has a few human weaknesses," she conceded. "Has it been an exceptionally difficult day, Stanley, or are you still worrying about the invasion of your house by your uninvited guests?" As he looked at her in surprise she explained, "I have a son about your age and I recognize the symptoms."

Stanley had never been addicted to talking about himself, much less to discussing his personal problems, but he found himself telling her about the outrageous Art Fisk and how, in a moment of anger, he had resigned from the job he enjoyed. Urged on by a few intelligent questions and Mrs. Davis's genuine interest, he told her how he felt about publishing and the necessity of having a real job to do.

"You don't have to tell me that," she assured him. "I understand how you feel. But, after all, at your age you aren't condemned to a vacuum in the sense that I was. You have only to stretch out your hand to find a job that needs doing."

"I am not," he admitted honestly, "quite as philanthropic as that. I'm looking for a job I want to do for my own satisfaction."

How it came about he did not know but he was soon talking to her as though he had known her all his life. He described the Folly, laughing at the absurdity of its presence in a New England village, but betraying his love for it. "You were right, of course, when you wrote that it was everything but a home. It needs — I don't know what. Warmth, perhaps. What they call 'a woman's touch,' though I've never known just what that means."

"Perhaps you need a wife, Mr. Holbrook."

"Stanley," he corrected her. "You're my Aunt Ellen. Remember?"

"How stupid of me to forget," she said equably, aware that he had warned her off his personal preserve, that he had posted a sign: PRIVATE — KEEP OUT.

ii

Three days later, Stanley came down to breakfast to find the long refectory table unoccupied and to hear voices in the narrow ell at the end of the room. A round table had been set beside a window. Mrs. Davis was so deep in conference with Wilson that she was not aware of his approach.

"Just what I always say myself, ma'am," Wilson was agreeing.

"I imagine so from the way this house is managed," she said warmly. "Everyone knows his job and just what he is expected to do. I've seen houses where the staff is confused and the servants don't know what to do next or what responsibilities they have. But the worst is when the routine is changed every day."

"Badly trained." Wilson shook his head in disapproval.

"Well, more than that, I think. A house needs one good managing head. I've always been so grateful that Mr. Holbrook has you."

Mrs. Davis's magic was such, Stanley realized in amusement, that she had hypnotized Wilson into believing that she was indeed an old friend as well as a frequent guest at the Folly. She had also won his complete allegiance, a victory for which Stanley gave her full marks.

"Good morning, Aunt Ellen. The table seems to have shrunk."

She gave him her warm smile. "I hope you don't mind. Wilson thought this would be pleasanter for breakfast, especially as this window gets the morning sun."

"It's a great improvement," he agreed as he shook out his napkin, and Wilson beamed, apparently convinced that this had been his own idea. Aunt Ellen, Stanley was beginning to think, was a very clever woman.

"What's on the agenda for today?"

"Miss Holbrook is arriving this afternoon and Wilson has already instructed Roberts to pick her up; I agree with him that she will be comfortable in the small yellow suite at the back of the second floor. You will probably want Mrs. Holbrook to have her husband's old rooms, which your aunt usually occupies. We are sending out for flowers later as there is nothing left in the garden since the frost. Oh, and you are entertaining a Mr. and Mrs. Saunders for dinner tonight." Her eyes warned him. "Old friends of yours, apparently, though I don't recall meeting them myself."

"I wonder how that could have happened?"

"Probably it was one of those times when Henry was ill," she improvised. "You know how susceptible to childhood illnesses he always was!"

"What do you hear from Henry?" he asked wickedly.

Momentarily at a loss she made a quick recovery. "You know what a wretched correspondent he is! Oh," she rushed on to a safer subject, "Mrs. Saunders called to ask whether they would upset your table if they bring along a house guest. She said she knows you well enough to be sure you'll be frank with her. It's some girl whose father was an old friend of Mr. Saunders and she has come rather unexpectedly to pay a visit before going to New York to look for a job."

"Oh, sure. Sure. Tell them to bring her along. But as for being an old friend," and he laughed, "Frank Saunders is the friendliest man I ever knew, and the chances are he won't even remember this girl's father. She is probably just another —"

"Another what?" she prompted when he hesitated.

"Another self-seeking woman expecting to exploit her father's friendship with Saunders and to take advantage of anyone she can."

Aunt Ellen buttered a piece of toast, wondering as she had half a dozen times before what had caused Stanley's bitter disillusionment with women.

iii

Miss Holbrook looked around the small suite of rooms, a sitting room with a fireplace and an easy chair drawn up before it and a television set which, it had occurred to Ellen, might keep her in her rooms at least a part of the time. There were spicy carnations both in the sitting room and in the bedroom, which had a canopied four-poster bed and yellow draperies to counterfeit sunshine. Beyond was a gleaming bath, its shelves stocked with bath powders and salts, with eau de cologne and tooth-brushes in their cellophane covers, with scented soap and soft thick bath towels. The whole effect was not only comfortable but charming. It would have been hard for anyone else to find fault. Not so with Miss Holbrook.

"I don't know that I've ever seen these rooms before. How small they are! I usually have that big suite on the east corner of the third floor. I believe I'll speak to Wilson about it. Perhaps Stanley did not remember that those have always been my rooms."

"He is putting Eve there," Ellen said in her quiet voice. "Eve is bringing her son with her, of course, and it seemed important for her to have as much space as possible and plenty of sunlight for the baby. By using the two rooms next to it there will be a nursery and a room for the baby's nurse."

"Eve? Oh, Bill's wife. I had no idea she was coming." Miss Holbrook was displeased. "I must say, if I had been informed — my nerves won't stand having a baby crying and upsetting everything. I think it is most inconsiderate of Stanley to let her come here while I am in the house."

"Well, of course," and Ellen's voice was deceptively mild, "he did not have much warning of your arrival and he has no idea how long you plan to stay." As Miss Holbrook was silent she went on, "And then, as you know, it's the boy's house as well as Stanley's."

Miss Holbrook took off her coat and dropped discontentedly into the big chair in front of the fireplace, in which logs had already been laid in preparation for lighting. She was a restless woman whose hands were never still. Now she ran the beads of a long necklace through her fingers. "Surely the girl isn't going to make her home here permanently! I thought she was settled in Paris. A country village is no place for a French girl."

"I believe Eve is an American, born in Ohio."

"Well, I didn't mean it literally, of course, but it's safe to assume she'll be the fast, restless type."

Ellen surprised her by laughing. "Sorry," she apologized, "but I was remembering a comment I read about France when I was a little girl. It said, 'The French are a frivolous people, fond of dancing and light wines!' " Seeing that Miss Holbrook was not amused, she glanced around her. "Well, if you have everything you want —"

Miss Holbrook's manner was aloof. "Mrs. — ah — Davis, I haven't quite grasped what your position is here. Are you the housekeeper?"

It would be difficult to explain what it was in Ellen's manner that made Miss Holbrook uncomfortable. "Oh, no. Indeed, no! It wouldn't occur to me to interfere with the management of a house as well run as the Folly. I am merely an old friend of Stanley's, a kind of substitute mother, a relationship that has grown over a number of years. It all began with a close friendship between Stanley and my nephew Henry and, little by little, I came to spend a great part of the year here at the Folly." Ellen was amused to hear the glibness of her reply. "If you aren't careful," she warned herself, "you'll begin to believe in Henry yourself."

"Oh, I see. How odd of Stanley never to have mentioned you."

"Well, no, you know how reticent he is and how disinclined to discuss personal matters with anyone, even a relative like you, though, of course, he has seen you so rarely."

Miss Holbrook looked around her, determined to assert herself and unsure as to how to do it. "I am quite worn out from my trip. Kindly tell Wilson to have a tray sent up to me. I won't come down to dinner."

"Very wise of you; especially as Stanley is giving a small dinner party tonight; it wouldn't suit you at all."

"Dinner party!" Miss Holbrook quickly reversed herself. She smiled in a martyred way at Ellen. "Then of course I must make an effort. I suppose I am actually the hostess here. The very least I can do for dear Stanley is to make an appearance and receive his guests. And will you kindly see that someone brings me some tea?" She dismissed Ellen with a gracious nod.

Ellen smiled at her and hastened away to relay this order to a smoldering Wilson and to placate him. "Mr. Holbrook and I are relying on you, Wilson, to keep the peace. You will know just how to manage Miss Holbrook so she will keep in a good humor and Mr. Holbrook won't be disturbed."

"It will be all right," Wilson assured her, determined that the Holbrook female was not going to make life miserable for this kindly lady who understood and sympathized with his problems. Not a mite of trouble, bless her; always a pleasant word and already the maids were thankful for the day she had come inside the castle. She was the one who had seen that Jane had a toothache and had taken her to a dentist. She had persuaded the outdoor man, who resented orders from anyone but Mr. Holbrook, to have the gravel on the driveway raked where it had been cut up by an oil truck, and had him liking it too. If Miss Holbrook thought she was going to give orders to her as though she were a servant and not Mr. Holbrook's old and valued friend, he'd make her know how matters stood.

When Stanley came down for dinner, his aunt was already waiting, wearing a dress that was rather low-cut for her meager frame and several jingling bracelets on a thin arm. She had, he remembered, a misguided passion for this form of adornment and she went around like an animated Christmas bell, jingling in and out of season.

He came forward to give her a light hug and kiss her cheek. "It's fine to see you, Aunt Winifred. You look flourishing."

"It's nice to be here, dear Stanley. I felt — you will laugh, but I really felt as though I were coming home."

Stanley felt no inclination to laugh. "I hope we can make you comfortable."

"Well, of course, the rooms you have given me are comfortable enough, though — shall I say — a trifle small. Of course, I am accustomed to my rooms at home which are really spacious, so I feel a bit crowded. But I know

I'll get used to it in no time. As I informed Mrs. — ah — not a housekeeper, I believe —"

"Mrs. Davis."

"Yes, I told her I was looking forward to peace and quiet. I'm not very strong, you know. So when I learned from Mrs. Davis that Bill's widow is actually coming with her baby, I was upset, I can tell you. What possessed her to come here of all places?" She was as plaintive as though it were her own home that had been invaded.

"This was Bill's home and it belongs to his son as much as it does to me. Naturally Eve has every right to stay here as long as she likes."

"Well, I — I'm really thinking of you and of the upset it will make in a bachelor's household to have a crying baby around."

"He won't cry all the time," Ellen said in an amused voice as she came into the room. She wore a long, simply cut dress of some soft gray material and she had an unstressed dignity that Miss Holbrook resented without being able to emulate.

"I was just telling Mrs. Davis," Miss Holbrook said with her toothy smile, "that I was surprised to find her so at home here when I had never heard of her."

"So far as I am concerned, it *is* her home," Stanley said rashly. "She's the only person I ever knew who can manage Wilson and not have him fly into a rage. If you want anything done I suggest you relay your wishes through Aunt Ellen."

Whatever indignant protest Miss Holbrook might have made was checked by the announcement of their guests, and Stanley went to greet them. Frank Saunders, sixty, overweight, bald, all the lines of his face curving upward from his ready laughter, was one of the few people whom Stanley liked immensely. His wife was a pleasant, good-humored woman of fifty, who found village life exactly to her taste because she enjoyed knowing her neighbors and their problems and being involved in them. She was kindly and helpful without being officious or carrying tales from one to the other, although they all confided in her.

But it was their house guest who attracted and held Stanley's attention. She was a small girl with a vivid face and bronze hair with red lights, sparkling eyes, and a determined chin, with a most enchanting dimple beside her mouth.

"This is Sherry Winthrop, the daughter of an old friend of ours, who has come to visit us," Mrs. Saunders said.

"I'm afraid I've really crashed your party, Mr. Holbrook," Sherry said.

"Not at all. Delighted to have you." He introduced his guests to his two "aunts," Miss Holbrook and Mrs. Davis, and saw that Miss Holbrook, who had already met Mrs. Saunders, had responded to a casual, "How have you been?" by launching into a lengthy account of her ailments. Ellen, he noticed in approval, had suggested that Saunders try the biggest chair and was already engaging him in talk which he apparently enjoyed as Stanley heard his hearty laugh. He was free to turn to the girl, who was frankly examining her surroundings with wide-eyed curiosity and wonder. He sat beside her, saying, "I understand you have come east to take New York by storm."

As she had expected, he sounded exactly like his letter, making fun of her ambitions. "Other people have done it," she said defiantly, a spark in her eyes.

"They have indeed. And what do you plan to do?"

"I had hoped — that is, I thought maybe Mr. Saunders would know of an interesting New York job but he says he rarely goes there anymore and he doesn't even have any friends there, that is people who really work in the city, except —" She broke off tardily.

"If he was counting on me, I'm afraid I'm going to prove a disappointment. As of tomorrow, I am joining the unemployed."

His words fell into a momentary pool of silence and then Wilson announced dinner. Stanley took in Mrs. Saunders, and Miss Holbrook hastily laid a hand on Saunders's arm, leaving Ellen to follow with Sherry. What, Ellen wondered, could Stanley have said in so short a time to take the sparkle out of the girl's eyes?

It wasn't until crabmeat cocktails and a clear soup had been removed that Saunders took advantage of the small party — for again the round table in the ell had been used — to say, "What's that I heard you telling Sherry, Stanley? Are you leaving Radcliffe? I thought you'd found just the right niche."

"So did I. But a situation came up, not worth repeating but tiresome, and I realized that in the future there would be a totally different and uncongenial atmosphere."

"The only time I met Radcliffe I liked him and he was certainly sold on you. Matter of fact, I got the idea that he had you in mind as his successor."

"It wouldn't have worked." Stanley tried to change the subject.

Saunders, however, was not to be balked. "I must say that personally I am glad to hear it." As Stanley's brows arched in surprise, he explained, "I'm giving up the *Courier*. My wife and I have been confining ourselves more and more to Waring, rarely even going as far as New Haven to see a play. We're not getting any younger and we've decided to carry out a lifelong ambition and go around the world while we are still able to get around on our own two feet. I've known too many people who postpone seeing and doing interesting things until they are too old to enjoy them, or handicapped in some way so they can't maneuver easily. Only trouble is that I've built the *Courier* from a little four-sheet weekly to a sixteen-page paper. That may not strike you as much of an accomplishment but I have subscribers all over the state because they like the editorial policy. It may be only a country newspaper but it is quoted quite frequently in big-city dailies and it carries more weight than you might believe."

"It's a good paper. You have every right to be proud of it. But what will happen to it now?"

"That's just it." Saunders leaned forward earnestly. "Do you know Thomas Denton, the guy who is remodeling the old Cathright place?"

"Shipbuilding firm? I met them both. Denton and his wife came to call on the Folly."

Miss Holbrook laughed. "I think you mean call *at* the Folly, Stanley dear."

"It struck me that their sole interest was in the house. They did everything but demand a guided tour. I wouldn't have put it past them to offer me a tip."

"That sounds like the same people. Well, the thing is

that he got wind of my plans, heavens knows how, and he called from New York to make me an offer."

"I hope it was a good one," Stanley said idly, his attention on the girl who sat beside Ellen, thinking he had never seen anyone so alive in his life. And her hair — he felt that if he put his hands on it they would be warmed. An idiotic idea.

"Oh, it was a good offer. He told me to name my own figure."

Stanley's eyes came back incredulously to the older man's face, and the editor nodded. "Yeah, exactly. Denton really wants it, but no one could convince me that he wants a country sheet like the *Courier*, so —"

"So he wants to use it for his own purposes, take advantage of its reputation, turn it into a propaganda sheet."

Saunders nodded. "That's what I make of it. I said no, of course. He didn't like that; used to getting his own way. He seems to think he can have anything he wants if he just pays enough for it."

"He probably can."

"Last time he was in Waring he came to see me himself instead of sending one of his deputies. Very hearty. Very friendly. Very persuasive. I still said no. Fact is, I only put an end to it by saying I had already made the sale."

Stanley laughed. "What will he do when he finds you don't mean it? Did you put a name to the buyer?"

"Oh, yes, I said it was you."

"You —" Stanley put his fork down on his plate, staring at Saunders in mingled amusement and consternation. "But, hang it, Saunders, that's not my field. I like dealing with ideas not with news; it's too ephemeral."

"But, Stanley," Ellen pointed out in her quiet voice, "news is the most — the most human thing there is, reflecting the changing picture of our daily lives and the world around us. Fleeting, of course, but essential. A free press is the most vital and important element in a democracy. Why, you can always tell when democracy is threatened because attempts are made to stifle free expression and keep people from knowing what is going on and forming their own judgments." She added thoughtfully, "It is terrible to see news distorted and falsified for private ends or personal gain or to engender hatred or serve totalitarian purposes as has happened abroad and is happening here every day."

Saunders took immediate advantage of the suggestion she had dropped. "That is just what would happen if Denton got his greedy paws on the *Courier*. And you are at a loose end now, Stanley."

"But," Stanley protested, feeling that events were moving too fast for him, "I don't know the first thing about running a newspaper."

"You wouldn't have to do it by yourself. I have a small staff but it is experienced. Spend a couple of weeks with me. I could show you the setup, enough to start on, and the momentum will carry it along while you are feeling your way. You will find it is a lot more exciting to dig up the news and discuss what is happening in the world every day than reading about far-off things, I can promise you that."

"But —"

Sherry smiled sympathetically. "I don't blame you for hesitating, Mr. Holbrook. Men are so much more conventional and less adventurous than women and they are afraid — that is, they hate to make changes. I can remember that if we even moved the furniture my father would be upset for a week and pretend he couldn't find his way around the house."

Stanley was annoyed. He wasn't so cut and dried that he could not make changes, and he did not care for girls who stated their opinions so bluntly. She spoke as though she represented the spirit of youth and he was an old fogy, set in his ways.

"We'll discuss it later," he told Saunders, ignoring the girl.

"Good!" For some reason Saunders seemed to feel that he had won his point. "Now that brings up another question. Since you aren't going to be working in New York any longer —"

"I haven't said that." Stanley felt that he was fighting a last-ditch battle. "I don't know where I'll be working."

"Well, the thing is I've been worrying about Sherry. She is looking for a job. If you should take on the *Courier,* you'll need a woman to do what my wife's been doing, cover the social events and the personal items, births and deaths and all that. Sherry is a live wire and you might put her through her paces. Anyhow, if we go on our trip around the world, it would be nice to know that the daughter of our old friend has someone to keep an eye on her."

Sherry smoldered. "I don't need an eye kept on me!"

"At your age?" Stanley mocked her, "with your uncurbed love of experience and change and adventure?"

"I am quite capable of taking care of myself and of finding my own job. I don't need yours."

"I haven't offered it to you. That will have to wait until I've had time to make up my mind." Stanley's eyes laughed at her and, in spite of her indignation, Sherry wanted to laugh back. She restrained the impulse.

"I like cautious men," she told him. "You remind me so much of my grandfather. I don't believe he ever made a hasty decision in his life."

"Or a foolish one?" Stanley asked.

"Oh," she said earnestly, "he was never foolish, just dull."

Ellen's lips twitched.

Stanley shot a keen look at the girl with the sparkling eyes and the vivid mouth. She was deliberately baiting him, a new experience for a wealthy and personable young bachelor who was accustomed to flattering attentions from the girls he met. It would be amusing to cure her of her mockery, but he noticed the diamond flashing on her left hand. He might have known that a girl like this would not be left long unclaimed by someone. Keeping Sherry in order would be a full-time job, he reflected, as he followed his guests out of the dining room. On the whole, he did not envy the guy his job.

"My handkerchief, Stanley," Miss Holbrook said with a touch of impatience. "I've asked you twice."

"Sorry." He bent to retrieve it, aware that he had been watching the red lights in bronze hair as Sherry walked ahead of him. She was, he told himself, an infuriating girl and the less he had to do with her the better.

One of the changes inaugurated by Ellen was to have fires lit in all the fireplaces. In one of the smaller rooms there were flowers, and a few upholstered chairs had been brought from other rooms to replace the stiff-backed carved ones which, whatever their virtues, had not been designed with an eye to human comfort.

Mrs. Saunders sank back into her chair with a sigh of relief. "I've always loved this room. In fact I love the whole preposterous castle, but I must say I never liked those hard chairs. You're making the place much more livable, Stanley."

"The credit belongs to Aunt Ellen, not to me."

Miss Holbrook sighed. "I suppose I'm too much of a traditionalist; I hate to see changes come in these wonderful rooms."

"How much you resemble your nephew!" Sherry beamed at her. "I can see you will both always resist change."

"When things are right as they are I always say we should leave them alone." Miss Holbrook turned to Stanley. "I do hope Eve will not turn the place upside down when she comes."

"Eve?" Mrs. Saunders asked.

"Bill's widow. She is actually planning to settle down here with her son," Miss Holbrook told her in indignation.

"He is Bill's son too." There was a note of warning in Stanley's voice, which his aunt did not heed.

"I can tell you right now, Stanley dear, if this outsider tries to take over the management of your house I'll have a few words to say. It has always been the home of Holbrooks, and it would be insufferable to have its character changed by an outsider."

"Oh, she won't do that." Stanley's manner was relaxed. "The management of this house is in Aunt Ellen's hands and no one would be foolish enough to interfere. As you say, Aunt Winifred, when things are right as they are we should leave them alone."

There was speculation in the glance Sherry gave him but she made no comment. Easygoing as he appeared, Stanley Holbrook had a way of drawing a clear line beyond which he would brook no interference. Probably, she thought, mindful of his amusement when he had asked her about taking New York by storm, he was as disagreeable as he was tyrannical. People had to do things his way — or else.

It was much later, while she was driving back to the Saunderses' sprawling and comfortable house on the outskirts of the village, that she said casually, "What kind of person is this Eve who is coming to the Folly?"

"She's the widow of Stanley's brother," Mrs. Saunders replied. "Stanley and Bill were always unusually close and there was only a few years' difference in their ages. They complemented each other: Bill was always one for trying new things and Stanley provided a balance wheel. He has become a bit set in his ways as a bachelor and he probably isn't looking forward to having Eve and the baby there, but Winifred Holbrook, if she has the sense she was born with, won't be disagreeable to Eve. Stanley won't stand for that on Bill's account. However, Bill always had good taste. I can't believe that any girl he married would be anything but charming. Those men, with their attractive looks and their nice manners and their money, could have had any girls they wanted. They could pick and choose. I've always thought it a pity Stanley never married. I suspect he was disillusioned by girls who threw themselves at his head for his money or for a chance to live in the castle. With all his pleasant ways he's a lonely man. Do you think, Frank, that he will buy the *Courier?* I can't help but think it would be a relief to have the whole thing settled before we leave. Perkins is sound enough but I don't believe he could carry on the paper without someone to assume responsibility. The poor man is so afraid of it and, heaven knows, responsibility is practically Stanley's middle name."

Her husband chuckled. "Not a doubt of it. From the moment when Mrs. Davis pointed out what could happen if it fell into Denton's hands he was hooked."

"But you would never have sold to Denton!"

"Stanley can't be sure of that."

"Well, I hope you haven't made a mistake. If Stanley takes over the newspaper, he'll settle down in Waring the way we have, and just let life pass him by."

When they entered the house she looked at the unusually silent Sherry. "You go straight up to bed, my dear; you must be very tired after your flight and a dinner engagement on top of it, and at the Folly, of all places. The castle may be as absurd as some people say, but I've always loved it and I always find it an exciting place to visit. It has never lost its romantic appeal for me. You run along and I'll send up some hot milk as soon as you are in bed."

"You are being incredibly kind to me when I'm almost a stranger," Sherry told her.

"Nonsense, my dear. It's a delight to have a young person in the house. Like sunshine. Frank and I always wanted children. All that worries me is what you will do when we leave, and as we've made all the arrangements, you know, we could hardly, at this late date —"

"Of course you aren't to change your plans on my account."

"Well, when we heard that you were coming we wanted to see that you were established in a pleasant job in New York and had a suitable place to stay where you would be safe and have a chance to make nice friends, but —"

"Do you think," Sherry turned back from the stairs, "that Mr. Holbrook would really give me a job on the paper?"

"He hasn't bought the paper yet and, I must say, Frank, I don't think you should have urged him as you did."

"Stanley would be a natural for the job. As soon as he grows reconciled to the idea he'll love it."

"Reconciled! Well, if he does take it, do you think he'll let Sherry handle the social news?"

Saunders gave his hearty laugh. "That depends on Sherry. My personal opinion is that she bowled him over."

"Why he didn't even like me," Sherry said in astonishment. "Didn't you hear the way he talked to me?"

"I did and the way you talked to him, young lady." He chuckled. "But I also saw the way his eyes followed you."

"They — did?"

"Frank," his wife said sharply, "you shouldn't give the child ideas. Stanley is a hardened bachelor, my dear. Anyhow, if he did give you a job where would you live? There are only two rooming houses in Waring and they wouldn't be at all suitable for a girl like you. The only alternative would be an apartment in that new development that just went up but you'd have to buy furniture, which is a big expense."

"There are lots of rooms at the Folly," Saunders said, "and plenty of chaperons."

As Sherry closed the door of her bedroom behind her she heard Mrs. Saunders say indignantly, "Pandarus!" and heard Saunders laugh. What she did not hear was Saunders's comment, "Actually the girl is in no danger, if that engagement ring means anything, and she'll be good for Stanley. Girls always hurl themselves at his head and she acted as if he was pure poison."

"Sometimes," his wife said gloomily, "I think I've been living in a fool's paradise all these years, believing you were a brilliant man. When it comes to women you are blind as a bat."

"Blind! I told you in the beginning the girl is a beauty."

"I don't mean that. For my money that engagement ring doesn't mean a thing. She hasn't the look of a girl in love."

"I suppose you'd know," her husband jeered affectionately.

"Of course I know."

When Sherry had changed to white nylon pajamas and brushed her hair until it sparked, she slid into the comfortable bed and switched off the light. But even after sipping the warm milk her kindhearted hostess had brought her she lay wide awake.

The trip east, which she had undertaken so impulsively, had in the past few hours been so eventful that she was still endeavoring to absorb all her impressions. She had landed at the exciting La Guardia Airport, and driven in to New York, dazzled and breathless at the impact of the thrilling skyline, and the crowds and the towering buildings, and the shattering noise. She had taken a bus to Waring and then the local taxi had delivered her to the Saunders house, her volatile spirits sinking at the thought that, after all, in spite of the warm letter from the Saunderses, she might not be welcome.

The first sight of her hostess, simple and kind and beaming with goodwill, had set her heart at rest. She had soon found herself pouring out her problems and her ambitions. She wanted to find an exciting job in New York and she had no training except in a nursery school. She longed for adventure.

Mrs. Saunders studied her in amusement and consternation. The girl was distractingly pretty, wildly romantic, and much too innocent to be left to her own resources in New York.

"My husband and I have a dinner engagement for to-night and Stanley says we are to bring you along. Stanley Holbrook is an old and dear friend of ours. You'll love his house. It's a copy of a real castle on the Rhine and simply fascinating, and as Stanley is with a publishing house in New York it is just possible that he might be able to help you get a job."

When Sherry had planned to visit the Saunderses it was in the hope that she would meet Stanley Holbrook but it had not occurred to her that her wish would be fulfilled on her first evening. She dressed with more than her usual care for the dinner party, wondering anxiously whether a dress that had seemed smart in Minneapolis would do for a castle. It was almost dark when they reached the Folly but she could see dimly the towers etched against the sky and she caught her breath. The vast entrance hall with its stone floor, fabulous tapestries, and circular staircase made her feel that she had strayed by chance into Carcassonne, the walled city which had snared her fancy when she had seen pictures of it as a little girl. Even now in dreams she walked through its fabled streets or looked out of its narrow turret windows.

And then she met Stanley Holbrook, the owner of this incredible castle. She had hoped to find the man who had written her that mocking letter diminished by his surroundings, somewhat absurd in all this grandeur. Instead he seemed to belong here, a tall man who moved with loose-limbed grace, who had a lurking smile in his eyes when he looked at her, and who dared — actually dared — to let her see that she amused him. She thought she was furious with him but she could not put him out of her mind. She had dreamed of an exciting job in New York. Now she wondered if Stanley Holbrook would buy the *Courier* and if so whether he would give her a chance, as Mr. Saunders put it, to go through her paces. She would show him! She would be a girl Friday to end girl Fridays. As she fell asleep she was imagining that she had made a great scoop; the presses had stopped for huge headlines. Even the moonlight catching sparks from her diamond did not disturb her. Tonight the thought of Major Douglas Carleton was dim, almost unreal.

IV

ON Saturday, Stanley lunched at the country club after a golf game. Ellen suspected that he was avoiding his aunt, but Miss Holbrook had decided to have her lunch on a tray in the library. Ellen devoutly hoped that she would not be impelled to complain again about the food. After her third complaint the cook threatened to resign. He had, he said, received a flattering offer from a major New York restaurant.

When this threat was relayed by Wilson to Ellen she went in search of Miss Holbrook, who was, little by little, appropriating to herself Stanley's favorite chair in his favorite room, the book-lined library with its hanging ladders for the high shelves of the two-story room, and its balcony at the second-floor level. She had finished her lunch and she was working a jigsaw puzzle on a small inlaid table. She looked up in annoyance when Ellen came in. When she moved, the bracelets on her arm jingled.

Ellen's agile mind was at work. Somehow she had to keep the peace with the temperamental cook and yet make Miss Holbrook feel that she was getting her own way.

"I was just trying to compose myself before Eve and

the child get here," Miss Holbrook explained. "I suppose this is our last day of peace. I had Wilson bring in this table. From the fuss he made you would think it would disrupt the whole house to get me a table for my jigsaw puzzle."

"I'm afraid it will disrupt Stanley's peace. This is his favorite room, you know; a place where he can get away from us all. Perhaps you can have the table taken to your own sitting room, which will be a kind of refuge for you if the baby is too troublesome." Ellen let this thought sink in before she went on. "But what is really disrupting is the cook's threat to resign if there are any more complaints. Stanley would be greatly annoyed if that happened. Excellent cooks are hard to find and they must be treated with a great deal of tact."

"Well, I must say that all I've done is to point out that I must pay strict attention to my diet and usually I have to refuse at least half the dishes he serves."

"How tiresome for you," Ellen said with ready sympathy, "especially with a *cordon bleu* chef in the house. I wonder if perhaps you are not overdoing your diet, so very underweight as you are, and you know, my dear, when we are over fifty we cannot afford to let our strength diminish."

"Over fifty!" Miss Holbrook was outraged.

"Oh, aren't you? No, I suppose not. That's the trouble with being underweight, it does age one so. Here's the menu for tonight. I suppose you won't care for any of the pheasant, though the way Pierre cooks it is simply delicious."

"Pheasant! Well, perhaps just a taste." Miss Holbrook

looked over the menu. "And a cup of the lobster bisque. I really must force myself to eat and gain some weight. Over fifty! No dessert, of course. Oh, it's a chocolate soufflé. That's so light it will be quite safe." She handed back the menu. "I wish you would talk to Wilson about the waitress. She spilled the water last night and spotted my dress. I had to speak to her pretty sharply. Hands shaking! Probably the woman is a secret drinker."

"Oh, I wouldn't dream of interfering with the way Wilson runs the house," Ellen said. "We'd upset all the peace and have the place in a turmoil, so unfair to poor Stanley. And as far as the waitress is concerned, it probably won't happen again. She was greatly upset, you know. She had just had word of her father's death, and she was trying to carry on. Most courageous of her, of course. If she had let us know — but she is one of those brave souls who don't complain of their personal problems."

Miss Holbrook gave her a penetrating glance but she could read nothing in Ellen's bland face. But Ellen did not tell her that the elderly waitress, driven to tears by Miss Holbrook's recriminations, had poured out the story of her father's death. "And she can take the price of her dress out of my wages," she had said.

Ellen had reassured her as deftly as she had placated the irate cook. Wilson brought her all his complaints and she was reasonably sure that she could keep him in good order. When she could hit on something that would interest Miss Holbrook enough to take her mind off her imaginary ailments, the house would run smoothly enough, always providing the unknown sister-in-law did not prove to be a disturbing element.

"I do hope at least I won't disturb dear Stanley by taking some books from his library."

"Of course not. Have you found anything to interest you?" and Ellen's eyes traveled over the shelves, which held over fifteen thousand volumes.

Miss Holbrook's eyes brightened. "Travel books! Except for my trips from San Francisco to the Folly I haven't been anywhere. I'm an armchair traveler. Accounts of far-off lands have a fascination for me."

Ellen tucked this bit of information away in her mind and helped Miss Holbrook select a book on Sweden and one on southern France and watched her retreat to her room in good order.

Feeling reasonably satisfied with the results of this sparring engagement with Miss Holbrook and, indeed, rather invigorated by it, Ellen went up to her room to rest until it was time for Eve to arrive. But though she lay quietly on her bed she was sleepless. Already she had ceased to feel like a stranger in the castle. She had become involved in the household as she could not in her son's house. The memory of her daughter-in-law's anger when she had learned of Ellen's plan had begun to fade.

"No better than a common servant! You are deliberately trying to humiliate me and shame your own son. I suppose you want people to think Bruce took all your money and you've been thrown out in the cold to starve!"

Well, Ellen answered silently, he did take all my money but it seemed to be the best thing for him, and I'm not being thrown out. I'm running away.

"Like King Lear," Thelma said. "You see yourself like King Lear. An outcast! When Bruce knows what you have done to him he'll be sick. Just sick! And my friends!

How am I going to account for you? People like the Dentons! It's so embarrassing."

Ellen had felt a pang of sympathy for her insecure daughter-in-law who was so anxiously asserting herself and so eager for approval.

"Tell them what you like, Thelma. But what people think of us isn't as important as all that. We have to learn to live with our own approval first."

Thelma had looked at her with puzzled eyes. She could live only according to a pattern imposed from outside. She had no private criterion.

Ellen hoped that Thelma would be wise enough not to report that painful interview to Bruce. She had packed her suitcases and left a brief note for her son, saying only that she had become bored with having nothing to do and feeling useless. She would be all right and she would be in touch with him. She signed it, "Your loving mother."

Ellen lay remembering that and thinking about the change that had come to her life since she had moved to the castle. She was helping to turn the Folly into a home, warm and bright and welcoming, without sacrificing its special qualities. The thing she would most have liked to do and so far had failed to do was to bring Stanley out of his shell. She was aware that the invasion of his house and the inevitable changes in routine involved were only minor annoyances. Even Miss Holbrook's maddening ways were only an irritation. What had upset him was finding himself at loose ends, without the job he had enjoyed. She was aware that Mr. Saunders was continuing to urge him to take over the *Courier* and that Stanley was reluctant to do so. Privately she felt that the job of running a newspaper would be the best possible thing for him, driving him out of himself, forcing him to deal with people.

Things will work out, she told herself, but I hope he will make the right decision. The choice of a life work is as important as the choice of a life partner. It influences all your future comfort. She thought of her daughter-in-law and sighed. But, after all, Bruce loved her. That was what mattered.

When she went downstairs she was relieved to learn from Wilson that Miss Holbrook had had the little table taken from the library to her own sitting room. At least Stanley would have one sanctuary to which he could retire when his guests became too much for him. She noticed Wilson's gloomy expression. "We'll soon have Mrs. Bill and the baby here," he said. "I suppose it will make a lot of extra work."

Something in his expression made Ellen say quietly, "Do you remember her husband?"

"I was here when he was born, and a nicer boy you wouldn't want to know. Always in some scrape and always laughing, and a fine man he turned out to be; like Mr. Stanley, only more outgoing."

"Then I know what it must mean to you to welcome his wife and baby to their home."

"Yes, ma'am." The butler went toward the door. "A taxi with a load of suitcases. That will be Mrs. Bill." He was beaming when he went out to collect the luggage.

A tall slender girl dressed in black, her fair hair curling shoulder length, her face an exquisite oval, was staring transfixed at the imposing entrance to the castle, and tilting back her head to look up at the turrets. In her arms she held a baby.

Ellen went down the steps. "Welcome home, Mrs. Holbrook. Do come in and let me take the baby. I am Ellen Davis, an old friend of your brother." She looked down at the sleeping child, saw the red of his cheeks, the crimson of his mouth, the deep-set eye sockets so like Stanley's. "Oh, what a beautiful child!"

Eve's sad face lighted with pleasure. "He's a happy child and he doesn't cry much. He won't be any trouble and I'll take all the care of him. I do hope Stanley will like him." There was so much anxiety in the girl's voice that Ellen was about to reassure her when she was forestalled by Stanley himself who had just driven up from the golf club and had left his car behind the taxi.

"Not like Bill's son? Of course I will! I am so glad to have you here, Eve." He took her cold hand in a warm clasp and bent to kiss her cheek. She was as lovely as Bill had claimed, with great violet eyes that were scanning his face uncertainly. How lost she seemed; how uncertain of herself and her welcome. For all her beauty she had no self-confidence. "This is your home, you know, Eve. Yours and Billy's." He lifted the baby out of Ellen's arms, smiling down at him. As he did so the baby opened wide blue eyes, blinked, yawned, and then gave a wide toothless smile while a tiny hand closed firmly around one of Stanley's fingers.

For a long time he looked down, a curious expression on his face, while both women watched him. "You wouldn't think," he said at last in a hushed voice, "that anything so small could be so strong. I'll bet he's going to be football material like Bill."

By the time Miss Holbrook had jingled her way down to dinner, Stanley had taken Eve on a tour of the castle, so delighting her that the melancholy left her face and her eyes shone with pleasure.

"Bill talked about it so much but I never really grasped what it was like."

Stanley laughed. "It has to be seen to be believed."

"You mustn't make fun of it. It's wonderful."

Miss Holbrook looked critically at Bill's widow. A beautiful girl if you cared for that kind of blonde; rather insipid really, she thought, though she had a sweet enough expression. No drive in her. It was unlikely she would try to take over the management of the house. She shook hands, asked about the flight from Paris without listening to Eve's reply, and said, "I've always wanted to travel but the details of tickets and foreign exchange and what to tip bewilder me. Anyhow, I don't know any foreign language and it would be awful not to be able to make yourself understood. Imagine being ill and not being able to explain. I suppose you enjoy being on the go."

"I'm not at all adventurous," Eve replied in her soft voice.

"Well, living in Paris, after all —"

"That's where Bill's job was. Wherever he went was home."

"Are your rooms comfortable?" Stanley asked.

"Just perfect."

"They were Bill's rooms, you know. We thought you would like to have them."

Miss Holbrook said, "You'll find them very comfortable. Until you came I always had them."

Eve flushed. "I'm sorry if I have upset anything."

"Upset anything! You forget," Stanley said, an edge

on his voice, "that you aren't a guest here. This is your home."

Something in his tone silenced Miss Holbrook for the time being, but not for long. She resumed the attack. "Are you prepared for the rigors of a New England winter?"

Eve was at a loss. She had hoped to find a home in Bill's old home, to find a father substitute for Billy in his brother. But it was apparent that Miss Holbrook regarded her as an intruder. "Well, I — haven't any plans really."

"I'm afraid Waring will seem dull after the gaiety of Paris."

"Gaiety!" The violet eyes regarded her blindly. "Since Bill's death I've gone out only to shop and to take walks."

"Leaving your child alone?"

"Of course not. I had a most reliable maid."

"That reminds me," Stanley said, "we must get a nurse for Billy."

"I don't need anyone," Eve said.

"That won't do." Stanley was firm. There was something helpless about his lovely sister-in-law that brought out all his protective instinct. "You aren't to be tied down. You have your own life to live."

Eve shook her head. "All that is over."

"That," Stanley told her bracingly, "is what you think. Bill would have wanted you to be happy."

"Yes, he always did. All he had to do was come in a room to make it brighter and gayer. He always made me laugh. We'd sit around just giggling like children from sheer — oh, I don't know, a kind of champagne gaiety bubbling up. I can't believe all that is just—silenced."

"For his sake, if not for your own, you've got to try to build a new life, Eve. Bring back the laughter."

"I don't believe that can be done," she said, her lips quivering.

"Yes, it can," Ellen told her. "I know because I have done it. Twice."

"You must be a very brave woman."

"You are certainly to be envied, Mrs. Davis," Miss Holbrook said, her bracelets jingling as she helped herself lavishly to chocolate soufflé. "No nerves. Such a blessing. I am a martyr to nerves."

She was still happily discussing the state of her nerves when they returned to the smaller drawing room but she broke off in indignation when, at a gesture from Ellen, Wilson set the coffee tray before Eve. "Well, really!"

The latter flushed. "I wish you'd carry on just as you did before I came. You are all incredibly kind but, after all, I am a stranger here. Who has been the hostess for you, Stanley?"

"Aunt Ellen," he said firmly, and Wilson moved the tray.

It was some half hour later when the butler came in to say, "Mr. and Mrs. Thomas Denton are here."

"Say I'm out — oh, well, I'll get rid of them as quickly as I can."

But Stanley had reckoned without the brashness and the hard self-possession of the couple who were determined to storm the castle. They stood in the doorway behind Wilson. Though they must have overheard Stanley's impatient words they were both smiling broadly.

"Good evening, Holbrook. I hope you don't mind our

barging in like this. Neighbors, you know. We never stand on ceremony. I wanted a chat with you and I thought we could talk more comfortably at home." Denton took Stanley's hand in a crushing grip, looked around, and gave a laugh. "Well, well, all these lovelies! Three ladies all to yourself. I don't believe I know them." He waited for Stanley to perform introductions.

"My sister-in-law, Mrs. Holbrook; my aunt, Miss Holbrook; Mrs. Davis."

Denton was a big man, taller even than Stanley, with heavy shoulders, a deep chest, a short thick neck and hair growing low on his forehead. His wife in an evening dress that made the women gasp and enough diamonds to stock a jeweler's window laughed shrilly. "I just couldn't keep away when Tom said he was coming to the castle. How do you do, Mrs. Holbrook. Miss Holbrook. Mrs. — Davis, did you say? I am bad at names but I never forget a face. Haven't we met before?"

Only Stanley was aware of Ellen's moment of discomfiture but she recovered herself almost instantly, saying, "Will you have some coffee?" He stepped forward to bring a chair nearer the fire for Mrs. Denton and to indicate one for Denton.

The latter shook his head, laughing. "No, no. I prefer to sit by a beautiful woman when I have the chance," and he settled himself on the seat beside Eve. "And how does it happen I've never seen you before?" Bold eyes summed her up.

"I just flew in from Paris today. I'm a stranger here."

"We must change all that," Denton declared in his booming voice.

Miss Holbrook had observed Ellen's willingness to remain in the background and Eve's shrinking from Denton's loudly expressed admiration. She smiled graciously at Mrs. Denton to indicate that she was the hostess at the castle. "I believe I've heard of you quite recently, Mrs. Denton; we have a mutual friend."

"Who's that?" To Eve's relief Denton stopped staring at her.

"Frank Saunders, the owner of the *Courier*."

"Owner!" Denton turned sharply to Stanley. "I understood from Saunders that you had bought the paper. Matter of fact, that's why Doris and I dropped in this evening. As I get it you took pity on the old guy who wants to stop working and most generously bought the paper. Of course you wouldn't want to be bothered with it so I'll be glad to take it off your hands."

"Why?"

Stanley did not attempt to elaborate his question and Denton hesitated before replying. "It's about time someone did something to stop all this subversive activity in the press."

"Subversive?"

"Ever read the *Courier* editorials? You'd think Saunders had a personal grudge against me or believes me to be Public Enemy Number One. Writes about my tax deductions, hints I'm putting a lot of money in numbered Swiss bank accounts. He does it so cleverly I can't get him on libel, according to my legal staff."

"You want to buy the *Courier* so you can stifle it. That the way you see things?"

"I'm willing to pay for it. You'll find me reasonable. After all, it isn't as though you wanted the thing for yourself. A small-time sheet like that."

"The thing is," Mrs. Denton said, "and I don't see why Tom pussyfoots about it like that, he wants to run for governor. That's why he bought property up here in Connecticut and established residence. He's got all the money he needs and he wants to branch out. Maybe he could move on to the Senate or even the White House. It has happened. But a local paper like the *Courier* can do him a lot of harm, it maybe could even queer his chances. People take it seriously."

"So do I," Stanley said. "I won't have a part in silencing a single independent voice. In the long run, in spite of all the pressure groups, it is still the individual who counts most in this country."

"You mean you are actually going to publish the *Courier* yourself?" Denton was incredulous.

"That's just what I mean."

"Look here, Holbrook, it's all right to be quixotic but we have to be realistic. The *Courier* can't do anything for you."

"Not a thing. I have no ax to grind."

"Okay. So I have. Doris is right. I have big ideas and, frankly, I don't care about obstacles. I can do things for this country, get rid of the radicals and the loudmouths and the longhairs. Take away relief and let people starve if they won't work —"

"Or if they can't find work?"

"Well, you can't make an omelet —"

"I'd hate like the devil to be a broken egg."

"So you're a wise guy, Holbrook. Let's put the cards on the table. Like I said, I have big ideas. No pint-size newspaper is going to get in my way. You're well heeled, according to what I can find out, but it won't last forever. And running the *Courier* could become an expensive proposition. Might cost you a whole lot more than you want to pay and in ways you never thought of."

Denton glanced at his wife and got up. "Well, that seems to be the end of the dialogue. Luck to you with your project. I hope you won't have too much trouble getting advertising." If there was a threat behind the words his tone was affable enough. "If you should ever change your mind you'll find I am in the market, only maybe," and he gave a wide smile, "my price won't be so generous. Coming, Doris? Nice to have met you ladies. See you around." He turned abruptly to the door.

"I hope you'll dine with us some night." Doris addressed herself to Miss Holbrook in whom she had instinctively recognized an ally. "Tom has bought the dearest old place, two hundred and fifty years old, so you can imagine how quaint. Of course we've made a lot of changes. All right, Tom, you can see I'm coming. Good night, all." She went out, giving Stanley, who had accompanied her to the door, a cool nod.

"Well, I must say," Miss Holbrook broke out as soon as the door had closed on the Dentons, "I can't understand you, Stanley dear. Saddling yourself with a country newspaper and alienating a really important man who may someday be president."

"God forbid," Stanley said fervently.

"Don't be so sure. A man like that always gets what he wants."

"Not always. He didn't get the *Courier*."

V

S HERRY was not a girl to sit still and wait for things to happen. It was more interesting to try to make them happen or at least go where they were happening. So while Mrs. Saunders bustled around, drawing up lists, planning the things necessary to be done in closing the house for a number of months, the clothes to be packed and those to be stored, and, most important, those to be shopped for in New York, Sherry was free to explore Waring by herself.

Already the trees were nearly stripped of their leaves. One heavy wind or rainstorm and the branches would be bare until spring. In her dreams of the glittering lights of Manhattan it had never occurred to her that she could love a little New England village, but she had a curious sense of belonging. She walked along the streets and peered into windows and looked at people, her head tilted a little on one side like an inquisitive robin on a lawn, her eyes bright with interest.

At the end of three days she had already begun to make acquaintances, but not those Miss Holbrook would have approved of. She had had several interesting talks with the crossing guard who conducted children safely across the street. A clerk in the store where she bought stockings had exclaimed over her ring and told her about her own engagement. She and the shoe-repair man had a long and serious discussion about arthritis. "Been a victim of it for years," he told her. "Tried everything. A regular guinea pig for new remedies." And Sherry had described the similar dilemma of one of her friends.

She saw a man run out of his house with a large portfolio, which he handed to the driver of the New York bus, and then run back. This was too much for Sherry's curiosity and as the bus was loading she fell into conversation with the driver, who was standing beside it while he waited for the passengers to file in. She asked about the portfolio and the driver explained. "Fellow is a commercial artist who used to ride the bus regularly to New York. But now and then he gets rush orders and I take the stuff in and leave it with a guy at the terminal who delivers it for him."

"How nice of you!"

The driver expanded at the approval in the vivid face under the bright bronze hair. "I always say," he said sententiously, "we ought to help each other."

"How right you are!" Mischief glowed in her eyes. "Do you think — that is, if I give you a letter now and then could you have the New York man mail it?"

"Well," he looked again at the pretty girl with the friendly ways, "well — why sure." He climbed into the bus and Sherry waved as he drove off.

It was inevitable that she saw a great deal of the castle in her daily rambles because of its commanding position on the bluff above the Green. Even by daylight it lost nothing of its romantic appeal, and Sherry's step inevitably slowed when she went past it, recalling the great arched lobby and the formal drawing room with its chairs upholstered in rose brocade, and the smaller, more intimate drawing room in which they had sat after dinner on the most memorable evening of her life.

She had not liked Stanley Holbrook's aunt with her tart comments about her niece-in-law whose coming she so much resented and her attempts to assert herself as the hostess. Mrs. Davis, with her unstressed breeding, her basic kindness, and the smile in her eyes, she had liked much better. As for Stanley Holbrook she had to confess to herself that he was the most attractive man she had ever met. He was not as flamboyantly good-looking as Douglas Carleton, nor was he as lively. What he needed was someone to break down his reticence and make him more human.

It was on one of her walks that she encountered the lovely girl in black, with gold hair and a sad face. They had passed each other several times, Sherry looking at everything, the older girl with vague eyes that saw nothing outside her thoughts. On the second occasion Sherry smiled and, after a pause, the girl returned the smile. On the third meeting Sherry impulsively spoke to her.

"Isn't it good to be out on a day like this! I feel so sorry for people who are stuck indoors."

The tall girl in mourning smiled down at the vivid, friendly little face. "Why — I don't know. I walk because my doctor said I must get out for at least an hour every day."

"But don't you enjoy the exercise and the fresh air

and seeing things? There's always so much to see."

"I'm not much used to doing things alone."

"I'm sorry," Sherry told her with ready sympathy. "I am Sherry Winthrop."

"I am Eve Holbrook."

"Oh, you are *his* sister-in-law."

Something in the unconscious betrayal made Eve's face light up in amusement. "Yes, my husband was Stanley's brother."

"You're very beautiful, aren't you?"

"Well —" Eve, unaccustomed to such frankness, was at a loss.

The two girls walked on together, Sherry slowing her pace to fit the more languorous step of her companion, Eve's look of depression fading as she listened to Sherry's chatter. By the end of a half hour she knew that Sherry was an orphan, that she was engaged but her fiancé was in the army and she had not seen him for a long time, that she had come east to go to New York and look for a job and fill in time while she waited, and that she was now visiting old friends of her father, and, like Eve, was a stranger in Waring who knew no one.

"But you've already met my brother-in-law."

"Well, the Saunderses know him well and they sort of rang me in when they were invited to dinner."

Eve smiled. "I suspect Stanley didn't mind. He needs some young people around."

"I should think he could have all he likes."

"Perhaps he could but he's a lonely person, not at all like his brother. Bill always had a lot of friends . . ." Eve stopped abruptly.

When they finally parted at the foot of the driveway leading up to the Folly, they had agreed to take their walk together the next day.

Sherry returned to the house to find Mrs. Saunders busy with lists as usual. She looked up to smile and say, "I have good news for you, my dear. Stanley Holbrook has decided to buy the *Courier* and he is with Frank now, working out the details and getting all the legal and financial part settled. We'll be leaving in ten days and Stanley is going to work with Frank right up to the last minute, getting briefed and meeting Perkins and the other people on the staff. Oh, and he'll give you a trial at doing the social news. I think you'll enjoy it. It is really fun if you like people, and you seem to get along with them. Actually a lot of people supply their own social news. I asked Frank to bring home some papers so you can see how I handled it, and I'll tell you what I know about the job, what people you must be careful about, and how to reach other people."

She looked up into the glowing face of the girl standing beside her chair. Heavens, she thought, how young she is! Like a small child seeing a lighted Christmas tree with presents stacked under it for the first time in her life. So young, so vulnerable. I do hope she's going to be all right.

"Oh," she exclaimed, "I nearly forgot. Frank says that Stanley wants you to stay at the Folly, at least until you can find a place that suits you."

Stay at the Folly! This was like a dream come true. Live in a castle and, even more important, under the roof of Stanley Holbrook. See him every day. Sherry managed to say lightly, "I'll bet it was Mr. Saunders's idea."

"Well, perhaps he just mentioned it but there are so many empty rooms up there it would be absurd to leave them unoccupied, and heaven knows it would be proper enough, even to suit Mrs. Fosdick, with three chaperons in the place."

"Mrs. Fosdick?"

"She's one of the people I want to warn you about, Sherry. A good woman in her way and well meaning, but if there is any possibility, however remote, of reading impropriety into any situation she will inevitably do it. She lives across the river from the *Courier* building and Frank swears she gets the news before the *Courier* does. Be careful not to give her any occasion for gossip."

"I'll be careful. Are you sure Mr. Holbrook won't mind my staying at the Folly?"

"Mind? Of course not. Why should he?"

ii

Stanley's casual announcement that Sherry Winthrop was going to stay at the Folly while the Saunderses were abroad, or at least until she could find a place that suited her, met with a mixed reception.

"A very sensible idea," Ellen said, "and I think she would love having a room in the tower. It would appeal to the child's romantic ideas."

"I suppose there is plenty of room," Miss Holbrook said discontentedly, "but I must say it is apt to cause talk, having a young girl staying here, especially when she is working for you, and I must say, Stanley dear, I think it is a mistake to give that girl a job when she doesn't know the first thing about reporting, and such a bold little thing too. People are apt to think she is pushing."

"Oh, surely not," Eve protested. "I've met her and we've been walking together. She is just friendly."

Miss Holbrook flashed a toothy smile. "I think I'd be safe in saying she was the one who made a point of getting acquainted."

"Well —"

"Eve, you must bear in mind that when a young woman has a wealthy and unmarried brother-in-law there will be a lot of enterprising girls who will try anything to strike up an acquaintance with him."

Eve was silenced and Stanley looked thoughtful. Once more Ellen yearned to throttle Miss Holbrook. She had planted a seed of suspicion in a mind already distrustful of women.

So when Stanley greeted his new society editor on a Friday morning his manner was guarded and carefully impersonal. Whatever happened he was not going to be entangled with her.

"Too bad you'll be starting on a Friday, which is press day," Saunders had said, "but most of the local stuff has been set up already. It won't be too difficult."

The building which housed the *Courier* was a shabby, two-story affair, on the outskirts of the village and across the river. The first floor held the printing plant and up one flight of stairs there were desks, typewriters, telephones, gooseneck lamps, masses of files and two long tables, one cluttered with out-of-town papers and the other used for making up the paper.

During the crash briefing sessions, Stanley had met his staff: Jones, the printer, and an errand boy Dick Flint; Perkins, a thin worried-looking man who had been Saunders's second-in-command; Worth, an elderly accountant who doubled as a kind of information clerk and had a memory like a card index; Wally Evans, a retired clerk, who handled the advertising; Neil Gordon, the photographer-reporter, a college graduate learning the ropes before moving on to bigger and better things in the city. He was undecided as to whether he would prefer to report foreign news or to be a famous columnist, but for the time being he took pictures of people whose houses had been robbed and of the man who had just been made head of the local hospital, and wrote extravagant and melodramatic accounts which a disapproving Perkins cut down to size.

It was not, Stanley admitted, an inspiring crew. A small cubbyhole had been enclosed for his private office and he settled himself in the swivel chair in front of an old rolltop desk with a covered typewriter of ancient vintage beside it. He recalled that Saunders had typed his editorials on this machine and wondered how he was going to manage. He'd have to hire a stenographer.

Meanwhile he began in longhand to write his first editorial, in which he would indicate that he planned to continue unchanged the policies established by the *Courier* and to maintain the standards of the former owner, Frank Saunders, whose courageous stand had led to the widespread influence of the small local paper.

"It is our conviction," he wrote, "that the voice of the individual remains the most potent force in a democratic society."

He broke off in irritation as he heard heels tapping on the stairs and Sherry's voice rising above the clatter of Perkins's typewriter and the ringing of the telephone.

"Is Mr. Holbrook here? I'm the new society editor, Sherry Winthrop."

"He's in the office," Perkins said. "Oh, sure. Go on in." He added gloomily, "Everyone does."

The door opened and Sherry looked in cautiously. This morning she wore a plain jumper dress of dark blue with a sweater in a lighter shade; her bronze hair was burnished and her eyes shining, though they surveyed her new employer doubtfully. He noticed that she was carrying two heavy suitcases and went to relieve her of them and stand them against the wall out of the way.

"Sorry, Miss Winthrop. I forgot that you'd have luggage. Did the Saunderses drive you here?"

"No, they had to leave very early but it was all right because I hitched a ride to the *Courier*."

"That's a foolish thing to do." He spoke more sharply than he had intended. "Just asking for trouble."

"Well, it wasn't. It was a very nice man and, what's more, he knows you, Jake Ives who runs the hardware store, and he gave me a story to start with. His wife is holding the parent-teachers' meeting tonight and I'm to call her for the details." She looked so triumphant that Stanley found it difficult not to laugh.

"You'd better ask Mr. Perkins to arrange for you to have a desk and typewriter. Can you type?" He was dubious about her qualifications.

"Yes, and I know shorthand too. I learned in high school. But I'd have to brush up on the shorthand."

"How about typing this editorial?" he asked.

She nodded and carried it into the big office where he heard her clear voice. Then his telephone rang and he was plunged into the work of the day.

What with deciding on lead stories — local news first, Saunders had instructed him — and determining the makeup of the paper, Stanley heard the rumble of the presses almost before it seemed possible. The day had been exhilarating and confusing. There were so many snap decisions to make, so many new impressions, so much to learn, that he was unsure whether he was more confused or exhilarated. Poor Perkins, with his terror of responsibility, brought almost every item to him for his decision. Where was this news story to go, how much space should be given to that, how should another one be handled? But when the office boy clattered up the stairs to bring the first copies of the paper, the ink still wet on them, Stanley felt a thrill of pride as he leaned back to read.

His mood of euphoria dissipated when he found a number of typographical errors, misspellings of names, and learned in some astonishment that Mrs. Yates had given birth to a *sun*.

With a glance at his watch he got up and stretched. He was, he discovered, ravenously hungry, and remembered that he had eaten nothing but a sandwich Sherry had brought in from the drugstore along with a container of coffee, holding it carefully and setting it safely on his desk with a little sigh of relief.

"Thank you but that's not part of your duties, you know."

"Well, you haven't had a chance to get anything to eat, what with half the village either coming in to look at the new editor or calling you up." She was bursting with excitement and a longing to talk, but Stanley, recalling his aunt's words and certain disillusioning experiences of his own, nodded curtly.

"Are you getting your own job done?"

Her smile faded and Stanley looked after her remorsefully, while he unwrapped the sandwich and drank the coffee.

At the end of his first day, with the telephones stilled at last and no sound but the rumble of the presses, Stanley prepared to call it a day when he was brought up short by the sight of Sherry sitting in the empty office, reading the *Courier* with absorbed attention, the tip of her tongue between her lips, a streak of ink across one cheek.

"Good lord," he exclaimed in consternation, "I forgot all about you." He went to collect her suitcases. When he returned her smile had faded and she was looking at him uncertainly. "Let's get along," he said, and she preceded him down the stairs, pausing to wave to the teen-aged office boy. "I hope she's all right," she called.

"Thanks, Sherry."

"What was that all about?" Stanley asked as he stowed her suitcases in the car.

"Dick's mother has been sick for a long time and she just went back to work today. He's worried for fear it will be too much for her because she hasn't got her strength back."

"How did you find that out?" He was amused.

"Oh, we got to talking when I was asking him how to get to different places."

"Did you find any social news?"

She nodded. "Mr. Perkins told me about getting the vital statistics, births and marriages and deaths, you know, and I went to see Mrs. Ives. It seemed more friendly than calling up. So she told me about the parent-teachers' meeting — with names — and she suggested some other people to call. Mrs. Jones's family has come to visit her and Mr. Howe has gone to Chicago on business and the Gateses are having people in for bridge and the Greens' daughter is engaged to be married."

"What a riot of activities! You've had a busy day."

"I loved it, meeting all those people and everyone was so nice and interesting."

Stanley found himself smiling down at the bright head beside him and then his eyes were caught by the glitter of the ring on the left hand. "Watch it, Holbrook," he warned himself.

As he drew up before the castle Sherry asked, "Mr. Holbrook, is it really all right? My staying here for a while, I mean. I'm not so dumb I don't realize that Mr. Saunders practically forced you into having me."

"Nobody forces me to do anything and Saunders wouldn't try. There's plenty of room. You won't be in the way, and I understand you've already met my sister-in-law."

"Oh, yes. She's very beautiful, isn't she?" Sherry said wistfully.

"Very." He led her into the lobby.

She looked around, her heart thumping. It was wonderful to be in this house but Stanley's careless, "You won't be in the way," his startled comment in the office that he had forgotten her, were somewhat blighting.

Fortunately Ellen was walking down the stairs while Sherry stood hesitating, looking lost and a little frightened, and she came forward with outstretched hand. "It's so nice to have you here, Miss Winthrop. We've put you in one of the tower rooms and I think you'll love it; like living in Carcassonne, you know."

The sparkle returned to Sherry's eyes. "Oh, that's what I thought when I first saw the Folly, and all my life I've dreamed of seeing Carcassonne." Then her cheeks flamed.

"I'll take you up to your room and you can unpack after dinner. We keep country hours here, you know. Dinner at a quarter of seven."

In the round room in the tower Sherry looked around her in delight. "Oh, it's lovely."

"I do hope you'll be comfortable. If we've forgotten anything don't hesitate to ask."

"I really haven't any right to be here," Sherry said soberly.

Ellen twinkled at her. "Nonsense. You are going to be good for us all, especially Eve, poor darling. She needs someone like you to give her back an interest in life, and, believe me, that's the most important thing you could do. We'd all be grateful to you, Miss Winthrop."

"I wish you'd call me Sherry, Mrs. Davis."

"When you're ready you'll find us in the small drawing room. Do you know your way? On your left past the brocade drawing room and the library."

Sherry went down the great winding staircase to the

impressive lobby, feeling as though she were living in a dream. As she passed the great formal drawing room with its exquisite upholstery and the two-story library with its brightly bound books lining the shelves, she pinched herself to make sure all this was real.

She found everyone in the small drawing room waiting for her. Ellen, knitting beside the fire, looked up to smile and Eve came eagerly to meet her. "Oh, this is so nice! I was delighted when Stanley said you were coming to live here with us."

Miss Holbrook, who was glancing through the *Courier* with a sharp eye for its shortcomings, bowed her head graciously. "Good evening, Miss Winthrop." She turned to Stanley who was standing moodily at the window looking out on the bleak ground that a month before had been a garden. "I believe Wilson is waiting to announce dinner, Stanley dear. You know we are somewhat delayed tonight, and that is so hard on the staff."

Color flamed in Sherry's cheeks, and Eve, who seemed to be defenseless when Miss Holbrook's barbed comments were addressed to her, said quickly, "You must be awfully tired after the first day on a new job. I do admire a girl who can do things on her own."

"Your circumstances aren't quite the same as Miss Winthrop's," Miss Holbrook pointed out. "It isn't necessary for you to earn your living."

The red in Sherry's hair was not there for nothing. "I don't think of it just as a way of earning my living but of justifying my existence," she flamed.

Stanley stifled a desire to say, "Bravo!"

It was apparent from the outset that Miss Holbrook

had declared war. She addressed all her conversation either to Stanley or to Eve, whom hitherto she had disregarded much as she did Ellen. Working girls, she was making clear, had no place in her company, certainly not at Holbrook's Folly. Now and then she would drop a gentle comment about the new apartments that had been built on the highway leading into the village. Some small apartments for working people, she believed, and there were rooming houses that were very pleasant for girls living alone.

Eve, seeing the brightness die out of Sherry's face and the eagerness fade from her eyes, was roused from her apathy and absorption in her own grief to try to talk to her, to draw her out, to ask questions about the day she had just spent.

Sherry was not made for ill humor or depression, and Eve's efforts were rewarded when she began to talk about the people she had met that day, and the things she had learned about them, and how friendly they had all been, helping her to find stories and social notes.

Miss Holbrook laughed at that. "I should think so. People of a certain sort will do anything to get their names in the paper."

Ellen said quietly, "I read your editorial, Stanley, and I liked it very much. You have set just the right tone, I think, and the subscribers who have been wondering what will happen to the *Courier* will be greatly relieved."

Stanley, who had been thinking gloomily that his worst fears had come true, and that the peace and comfort of the Folly had vanished with the arrival of

Sherry Winthrop and his aunt's evident hostility, brightened.

"I'm glad you approve."

"Was it a difficult day?"

He grinned at her. "Confusing. There's so much I don't know and have to learn as fast as I can."

"I do hope," Miss Holbrook said in a tone of foreboding, "you won't find that you have made a mistake."

"I'll probably make a lot of mistakes before I'm through," he said cheerfully, "but I hope I won't make any of them twice." He had accompanied the women back to the small drawing room. "I'll leave you. There's some work I want to do. Good night." And he went into the library and closed the door, but not to work. He stretched out in his favorite chair facing the fire, filled his pipe, and sat staring at the flames, going over the experiences of the day. He'd made a few blunders; he had been curt to several well-wishers because he was in a hurry; he had cut off Perkins when he had asked for orders for the fifth time; and he had driven the smile out of Sherry's eyes. It was one thing to steer clear of her and another to be unkind. He'd have to set a course and stick to it or Sherry, with her impulsive friendliness, was going to go straight through the barriers he had erected, unaware that they existed.

At least she seemed to have landed on her feet in her new job. She had not only hitched her way to work but, instead of running into trouble — as she deserved, he told himself — she had got a story and a lead to other stories and, probably, made a new friend.

iii

Ellen sat beside the fire, her knitting needles flashing in the light; Miss Holbrook was reading a novel, Eve was laying out a game of solitaire, and Sherry sat turning Doug's engagement ring, watching the reflections of the light, remembering his arms around her, remembering his kisses. The curious thing was that she could not remember his face very clearly; it seemed to fade day by day. Already she had almost stopped wondering where he was and why he had disappeared without a word. Probably there had been another girl, a girl he had fallen in love with as rapidly as he had fallen in love with her, and he had hated to tell her the truth. It all seemed far away.

She had worried a great deal about the ring. She knew that it was a valuable one and she felt that she had no right to it, but she had no possible way of returning it; and, anyhow, it was safer on her finger than put away in a drawer. So she continued to wear it. Perhaps it gave a false impression but Sherry, honest as she was by nature, found it impossible to confess to anyone that she had been jilted. That was too great a humiliation. What she had told Eve about her engagement was, after all, the truth, just not the whole truth.

Eve finished her game and put away the cards. "I'm going up to look at Billy. Stanley hired a nurse with fine recommendations, but I'd be happier if I check on her closely for a while; anyhow I haven't seen the baby for hours." She laughed at herself and turned to Sherry. "Would you care to see my son?"

"I'd love it." Sherry followed the older girl out of the room after saying good night. In Eve's suite they tiptoed into the baby's room. Through the open door of the next room they saw the nurse engaged in mending. She looked up, smiling.

Eve bent over the crib and looked at the sleeping baby, her heart in her eyes, touching one soft cheek gently with the tip of a finger.

"Oh, he's beautiful!" Sherry whispered. "The most beautiful baby I ever saw. You must be terribly proud of him."

"I am."

After a whispered conference with the nurse, a healthy-looking girl with an expression of sturdy common sense, Eve led the way back to her sitting room, kicked off her shoes and settled in a deep chair, waving Sherry to another. Looking around her, Sherry thought that she had the prettier room of the two. Eve's seemed incongruous as a setting for the exquisite girl, with tweed and leather upholstery on sturdy furniture and none of the daintiness one would have expected.

"These were my husband's rooms when he was a boy," Eve said, interpreting correctly Sherry's expression, "just the way he left them, except for his personal belongings, of course. They are still in my flat in Paris. I didn't know what to do with them and I couldn't bear to give them away. Now maybe I can have them sent here for Billy when he grows up. But Aunt Ellen thinks I should have these rooms redecorated to suit me."

"I think she's right."

"Yes, but — anything that was Bill's is important to me just as it is."

"You were Bill's," Sherry said daringly. "Tell me about him, Eve."

"I can't talk about him."

"Oh," Sherry said impulsively, "don't do that."

"Do what?"

"Leave him in silence. He'll be so much more alive if you can talk about him."

So Eve began, fumblingly, unsteadily, telling about her first meeting with Bill, about falling in love almost at once. "Stanley looks so much like Bill that I was startled when I first saw him, but Bill was gayer, more of an extrovert, and always full of the wildest ideas. We were married in six weeks and no one ever had such a happy marriage. Then he died in a stupid traffic accident and — that is all."

"But there is Billy," Sherry pointed out.

"Yes, there is Billy." Eve's face softened, her lips curved in a smile, which faded. "But he needs a father. He'll need one more and more as time goes on."

"He has an uncle."

"But Stanley will marry. He's bound to marry, a man as attractive and eligible as he is, and he'll have children of his own."

"You mean he's engaged?" Sherry's tone was carefully casual.

"Oh no, he doesn't seem to be much interested in girls. Tell me more about the man who gave you that stunning ring."

After all, fair was fair and Sherry had urged Eve to talk about Bill, so she said obediently, "His name is Carleton. Major Douglas Carleton, and he has a hush-hush job in the army which is why I don't get any letters from him. So I came east to get a job and keep myself busy while I wait."

"What is he like?"

"Big and handsome and full of life and — exciting. He has a funny way of looking at you with one eyebrow cocked up, a kind of way of laughing." Afraid of being led into some indiscretion, Sherry yawned. "Well, I'm a working girl and I've got to get some sleep. Last night I was too excited to sleep."

"I envy you. There's nothing for me to do here."

"Let's plan to redecorate these rooms and get some new clothes with color in them." As Eve started to protest Sherry said quickly, "You don't want Billy to think of his mother as a woman in black."

"No, I don't. Good night, Sherry. I'm so glad you are here."

VI

ELLEN looked from one to the other of her two
silent breakfast companions. On Saturdays they did not
go to the *Courier* and, as a rule, Sherry at least slept late.
But Ellen had been watching with sympathetic interest
the growth of the attraction between them. They belonged together, she thought; Sherry had the ability
to force Stanley out of his tendency to withdraw from
people, and he could curb her wild imagination and her
quick temper. Only two factors disturbed Ellen; one was
Miss Holbrook's constant hints to Stanley that Sherry
was doing everything in her power to attract him and
make a permanent place for herself at the Folly as his
wife. The other was the magnificent diamond on Sherry's
left hand. Like Mrs. Saunders, Ellen was shrewd enough
to know that Sherry was not in love with her major; on the
other hand, she was not a girl to jilt a man who was serving
his country.

Usually breakfast was a cheerful meal since only
Stanley and Sherry appeared. Miss Holbrook had a tray
in her room, and Eve, who preferred to bathe Billy herself, had breakfast at a later time. As a rule, Stanley
was lighthearted, reminding Ellen of the outrageous ex-

ploits of her mythical nephew and keeping Sherry helpless with laughter. Everything would be gay until he
looked at the ring that sparkled on her finger or remembered Miss Holbrook's comments· Then he would become guarded and Sherry would be subdued.

Sherry had performed miracles with Eve who, at her
insistence, had gone to New York and bought herself
a complete new wardrobe, and was now blossoming out in
bright colors. If the shadow of her sorrow was still deep
in her face, at least she had taken a step in the right
direction. Now, with Sherry's enthusiastic assistance,
Eve was redecorating her rooms, replacing the tweed and
leather with satin and delicate fabrics, and the heavy,
sturdy furniture with lighter pieces. All this met with
Ellen's warm approval, but Miss Holbrook took the
stand that nothing in the Folly must be changed.

This, Ellen reflected, would be such a happy house
without Miss Holbrook's disturbing influence. If only
she would go away! Something might result from her
passion for travel. Whenever they fell into conversation
Ellen had learned to switch from Miss Holbrook's complaints to world travel. If the food served the day before
had not agreed with her delicate digestion, Ellen described the lavish use of olive oil and resinated wine in
Greece. If she complained of the hazards of traffic, though
these could not be considered excessive in Waring, Ellen
related her experiences on a camel in Egypt. If only the
poor woman were not so afraid of trying things on her
own, something might be done, after all.

Ellen glanced at Stanley who was going through his
mail, flipping through the envelopes beside his plate and

reaching, as he had done for weeks, for a square blue envelope. He read it, his mouth quirked in a smile. Several times he chuckled and Sherry looked up quickly.

He laughed. "This is the darnedest thing! Every morning I get one of these cockeyed letters."

"Anonymous?" Ellen was startled.

"Not signed."

"Threatening?"

"Heavens, no. Gay and mocking and amusing."

"But who on earth is writing them?"

"I haven't the ghost of an idea. I've wracked my brains."

"Why," Sherry suggested, "don't you advertise: 'Blue Envelope, who are you?'"

He chuckled. "Good Lord, no! She might have a face like a pudding or be the last leaf left on the tree. But why does she do it? Talk about mysteries! I never, to the best of my knowledge, knew anyone like her. Sometimes she is gay; sometimes she deliberately needles me."

"At least she interests you," Sherry said.

"Sherry," Ellen exclaimed in distress, "you are awfully hoarse. I thought last night you looked a bit feverish. I'm afraid you've caught cold. You need a warmer coat than you are wearing, particularly when you are out of doors so much of the time, trotting around to see people."

"I don't need a new coat," Sherry said quickly. "Mine is plenty warm enough and I don't think I've caught cold. I feel fine, really I do."

"You are trying to do too much," Stanley told her.

"Oh, I love the job!"

"I wasn't thinking of that. You run your feet off all day and then most evenings you go gadding around with Neil Gordon. I should think you'd have enough of War-ing's Jack London during the day."

He sounded so irritable that Sherry looked at him in astonishment and Ellen bit her quivering lips.

"He's very nice and he is ambitious and planning to be a foreign correspondent, maybe for the *New York Times* or the Chicago *Tribune*."

"Hasn't he decided yet which of them to honor with his services?"

Sherry's quick temper flared as she rushed to the de-fense of the young reporter. "He's not stuffy. He is young and ambitious and he needs someone to encourage him instead of being a wet blanket. You probably have for-gotten what it's like to be young."

As Stanley had reached the ripe age of thirty this was too much. "Gordon needs encouragement the way I need another head."

"Well —" Sherry surveyed Stanley's head critically.

He burst out laughing. "You really are a brat."

"I'm not a brat and you are prejudiced against the young."

Ellen lifted her napkin to her lips.

When Sherry had excused herself and left the room Stanley said, "I suppose I shouldn't have said anything about Gordon. It's none of my business what she does with her free time."

"The child is upset because she has a cold, although she won't admit it. She should have stayed in bed today. Instead she has offered to look after the younger children during the town meeting this afternoon so people can attend without hiring baby sitters."

"Why does it have to be Sherry?" he said crossly.

Ellen was amused. "It doesn't, of course. She volunteered. She is really involved in this community. I went shopping with her the other day and I was astonished to find out how many people she knows."

Stanley frowned at the table. "You think she caught cold because she hasn't a warm enough coat? Couldn't you get her one — I'd pay for it, of course — but make it appear to be a present from you?"

"No, Stanley, I couldn't. Not possibly." Ellen's tone was firm. "The child has a lot of pride and it is important not to hurt that, especially as your aunt makes her feel unwelcome here. She is young and inexperienced and, though she has lots of courage, she hasn't yet acquired a lot of self-confidence."

"I'll speak to Aunt Winifred."

"You'll be tactful, Stanley? Good heavens, what right have I to advise you? Sometimes I'm afraid I've come to believe the fiction of our relationship and my being a substitute mother."

"It's not a fiction any longer, is it, Aunt Ellen?" He smiled at her. "When I think of the change that has come to the Folly since I answered the letter from a rebellious old woman, I tell you it makes my blood run cold to think I might not have answered it." He was only half joking. "I can't remember my own mother but it seems to me that you have taken her place."

As Ellen looked at him, speechlessly, he said, "You know there is one guy I envy and that is your son."

To his consternation and embarrassment her eyes filled with tears. Then she said hastily, "About Sherry —"

"If she won't take a gift, how about giving her a raise?"

"She would guess what you are up to."

"Well, what can she do to rate some extra money?"

Ellen pondered. "Have you ever thought of having a column giving a different menu for every day in the week to solve that 'What shall we have for dinner tonight?' problem? I could help her with it."

"That's an idea. Aunt Ellen, you are a darling and a pearl among women and this house couldn't survive without you for a day."

She was laughing when he followed her out of the breakfast room but she was wondering unhappily if her own son ever thought of her or worried about her. Once a week she sent him a brief note to assure him that she was well and happy, but he had never replied to any of her letters. Perhaps Thelma had persuaded him that his mother was a troublemaker. Sometimes Ellen believed that the pangs of childbirth were not the worst pain a mother suffered for her children.

"Has Aunt Winifred said anything about returning to San Francisco?" he asked hopefully.

"Far from it. With Christmas less than a month away she is suggesting that we get busy and plan something for the holidays."

Stanley groaned and went to look out of the window and down at the Green. He saw a small girl with bronze hair and a blue tweed coat run down the driveway to the bus stop at the top of the Green, her hair blowing in the wind. The bus pulled up at the curb and the driver got out while the passengers, always a number of them on Saturdays and more during the Christmas shopping season, filed out. Sherry ran up to the bus. Stanley caught sight of a familiar square blue envelope which she handed to the driver, saw him wave cheerfully, while Sherry came back to the house.

"Well, I'll be —" Stanley began to whistle to himself.

ii

It was midafternoon when Stanley came down from his daily visit to his nephew.

"You must stop bringing him presents, Stanley," Eve protested. "He has a whole bin full of toys now and he's much too young for trains. You'll spoil him. He'll get so he expects to be given something every day."

Stanley laughed unrepentantly, while he looked at his sister-in-law. She was beautiful and sweet and grateful for everything that was done for her, unaware of her just claims, unconscious of her beauty. What, he wondered, had Bill seen in her? A quarter of an hour in her society and the pall of boredom fell over him. He had no interest in girls who agreed with everything he said and who waited passively for life to do something for them.

"I am going to the town meeting," he announced. "Anyone care to go along?"

"It's the flu season," Miss Holbrook said. "I prefer to stay out of crowds. I always say there is no point in asking for trouble."

"Eve?"

"I don't know anything about village affairs."

"Aunt Ellen?"

"What are they going to talk about?"

"Raising money for an extension on the school for a kindergarten, but usually the discussion ranges over all the village problems."

"I believe you are beginning to feel like a villager," Miss Holbrook commented.

"Well, I am one. Now, of course, it is part of my job to attend the town meetings but I've always gone when I could. If I am going to live in Waring I want a voice in the way it is run."

But the dominant voice at the town meeting was not Stanley's, it was the shrill voice of Mrs. Thomas Denton who was determined to be heard. She had stood up as soon as the meeting had been called to order, waiting to be recognized and oblivious of the business on hand. She wore a smart mink coat and a mink hat, and diamonds glittered in her ears and in a brooch fastened at the neck of her dress.

She introduced herself. She and her husband, she said, smiling brightly around her, were newcomers but they felt that Waring was going to play an important part in their lives and they wanted to contribute their little mite to the community. If Mr. Denton could be here he would be talking to them himself but, as of course they all knew, he was a man of wide responsibilities and involved in many enterprises, so she had come to do her poor best to take his place.

What Mrs. Denton had to say was that her husband wanted to contribute a Christmas tree for the Green and provide a Santa Claus who, on Christmas Eve, would distribute free gifts to every child in Waring under fifteen years of age. What Mrs. Denton meant, of course, was that her husband was making his first bid for the governorship and was trying to buy the votes and the goodwill of the people of Waring. He must be amused at the quandary in which he was placing his declared enemy, Stanley Holbrook, who was in honor bound to give this generous offer a fair play in the *Courier*.

Watching the faces of the audience held captive by Mrs. Denton's shrill and determined voice going on and on about the spirit of Christmas and her husband's magnificent generosity and noble virtues, Stanley was unable to gauge the effect she was having. He was bitterly aware, as he had been for the past week, of the disastrous inroads Denton was having on his advertisers. During these weeks the paper should be carrying its heaviest advertising of the year, but Stanley's advertising man came back day after day to say that no one was buying space this year. One store manager said the *Courier*'s circulation was too small to justify the expense; another said that the people of Waring had to shop at his store anyhow for their daily needs so there was no necessity for advertising; a third said bluntly he did not like the editorial policy of the *Courier* and he would not support it.

Stanley smiled grimly to himself. He was continuing his editorials, hammering home that clean government concerned every citizen, condemning special privilege, and demanding that political ethics be as scrupulous as personal ethics. He had not encountered Denton since the night he had failed to purchase the *Courier* but he knew that the shipbuilder was behind the attempts to sabotage the paper, that he was determined to destroy it. If he should succeed in drastically curtailing the advertising, Stanley would be forced to give up the paper sooner or later because he could not afford to carry it indefinitely at his own expense. But how far was Denton prepared to go? How strong was his determination to have a political career and gain power? Before now men had bought high office by an unlimited expenditure of money and ruthless methods. At least Stanley would fight it out as long as he could.

When the meeting came to an end (some angry people had not been able to discuss urgent village problems), Stanley was surprised and pleased to have a number of them gather around him. Apparently the *Courier* played an important part in their lives and the voice of its publisher carried weight in the community.

For the first time Stanley was fully aware of the value of the job he was doing and of the respect in which it was held. He looked around at the town meeting, aware that this was the essence, the backbone of America. He liked the questions he was asked and the diversified opinions that were so openly stated. Across the hall, Mrs. Denton was holding court, not as a member of a town meeting but more as though she were the wife of a presidential candidate, distributing smiles and handshakes to everyone in reach.

"A whole afternoon wasted and no chance to talk about a kindergarten," a woman said angrily. "It's all right to give Chrismas presents but it is more important to give the kids an education. What do you think, Mr. Holbrook?"

"*Timeo Danaos.*"

"And what does that mean?"

"I fear the Greeks even when bringing gifts."

"Oh." A thoughtful pause. "I understand Mr. Denton has political ambitions."

"I gave up my weekly visit to my grandchildren," said an irate man, "to see what could be done about a school bus, and what do we talk about? Santa Claus!"

"You know," Ellen remarked when they went out to get in the car, "people are really awfully sensible on the whole. Give them all the facts and they are to be trusted."

"All the facts, yes, but if they don't get them, or get them watered down or distorted, what then?" He started to help her into the car.

"Oh, wait, Stanley. We can't go yet. Sherry is here, entertaining the youngsters in the basement while their parents are at the meeting. She said she knew she could handle them because she was accustomed to working with nursery school children. We ought to take her home, especially as she has a bad cold."

"Of course. Wait for me in the car, will you?"

Stanley ran down the basement stairs. Accustomed to nursery school children. What did that remind him of? The life story of a girl who, so far, hadn't had any life, but had got tremendous excitement out of working with children in a nursery school. The — the — *The Shining Years.* Stanley began to laugh to himself. So that was the secret of the letters! Sherry was determined to prove that he was wrong and that she could write something that would hold his interest.

Then his amusement faded. There had been a love

story in the novel. A tall, handsome, dashing soldier, with irresistible ways, and a final clinch fading into the sunset in the best tradition of the movies of some years ago. But the part about the children had been true. The love story might be true too.

He found Sherry in the center of a circle of children, their faces intent. She was weaving a romantic tale about the walled city of Carcassonne, with a knight in armor fighting to the death for an imprisoned lady who watched from the narrow window in the tower. When she had concluded triumphantly, "And so they lived happily ever after," she got up. "The meeting is over, children."

"No, Sherry. Don't go. Just one more story. Just one!"

"Well, I'll tell you about the white crane who learned to tap-dance."

"It sounds like a fine idea," Stanley intervened, "but Aunt Ellen is waiting for us, Sherry."

"Come back, Sherry," the children called. "Come back soon."

"I will," she called, and began to cough.

Stanley's hand tightened on her arm and he led her out to the car. Aunt Ellen was in the back seat. Sherry was about to join her when Stanley pushed her firmly in front.

"That was quite a story you were telling the children, Sherry. They were literally hanging on your words."

"I enjoyed doing it. I love telling stories to children."

"I've been thinking," he said mendaciously, "that the *Courier* hasn't been paying much attention to children. I've had in mind a column of stories addressed to the younger ones, something to take the place of cartoons, something any fourth grader can read for himself and perhaps get the habit of reading and eventually turn to books instead of television."

"That," Ellen said from the back seat, "is a splendid idea, Stanley. If you could only find someone —"

"How about it, Sherry?" His tone was carefully casual, while his eyes rested fleetingly on the worn cloth coat. "Think you could manage it? We could give it a try, if it isn't imposing on you too much; you could work on your stories in the evenings unless you are committed to spend all your free time with Neil Gordon."

This was so manifestly unfair that Sherry was about to retort when a startling idea struck her. Could Stanley possibly be jealous? She considered it and then, regretfully, discarded the idea. Stanley could have any girl; he'd never think of her seriously; he just joked with her. And a man of his quality could not possibly be jealous of a boy like Neil.

"I'd like to try."

"Naturally you aren't supposed to do that as a part of your regular duties. I had in mind an extra thirty dollars a week for a children's column."

Sherry heaved a sigh of sheer delight which set her coughing again. Then she asked, "How did the meeting go? I didn't expect it to be over so soon."

The account of the meeting dominated by Mrs. Denton holding out the bribe of Christmas gifts in exchange for the goodwill of the people of Waring lost nothing in the telling.

"She is a dreadful woman and quite unscrupulous," Ellen concluded, "and I can tell you one thing, Stanley; she and her husband are determined to become the guid-

ing spirits of Waring. I thought the first time I met her
they were vulgar, pushing people."

"You'd met them before?" Stanley's tone was casual.
Somehow one did not probe into Aunt Ellen's life, though
he was deeply curious about the situation which had
turned her into a rebellious woman and driven her away
from her home, which he was fairly sure was the case.

"I met them just briefly but quite casually, and I mean
it, Stanley. That offer of hers was just the opening wedge
for Thomas Denton."

"You are wrong there, Aunt Ellen. Not the opening
wedge. They've been trying to undermine me ever since I
refused to let Denton have the *Courier*." Stanley went on
to describe the raid that had been made on the advertisers who were the chief support of the paper. "Wally
Evans, my advertising man, hasn't sold any space in
nearly two weeks except to the grocery stores for their
regular specials."

"Wally Evans," Sherry said vigorously, "couldn't sell
anything if his life depended on it." She turned her head
to look at Ellen. "He's kind of a floppy man."

"Floppy?"

"Well, you know, his hands sort of flap from loose
wrists when he walks. I don't suppose he knows how to
make a sales talk. I can just see him go in and wait patiently for someone to ask to buy space. He hasn't any
push. You should do it yourself, Stanley. Make these
people see what Denton is trying to do and what would
happen to Waring if his became the dominant voice, and
ask whether they really want a man like that as governor
of their state."

"Maybe you've got something. The trouble is that there is less than a month before Christmas; there's no time to plan a campaign or a sales talk to give them. Unless I am to go fatally in the red, I need to have ads in Friday's paper and that is only six days off and it's too late to get them now. Even if I tried to work something out on Monday, you know how it is, people coming and going all the time, and the telephone ringing and a dozen interruptions an hour."

"It's not too late. There's tonight and tomorrow," Sherry said. "Let's work out something. You can do the planning and I can type it for you."

"But —"

"Oh, please, let's try! There's still time to do it and I'd like to help spike Mr. Denton's guns."

"You can help spike them tomorrow," Ellen intervened, "and nothing would give me greater pleasure than to see you succeed, but you are going to bed as soon as we get home and you are going to stay there until morning. A light supper with some soup and a lot of orange juice and a hot toddy before you go to sleep. Then, by tomorrow, if you've shaken off that cold, you can go into battle with my blessing."

VII

STANLEY spent most of the night in the library, drinking countless cups of coffee and drawing up plans of campaign to convince the local shopkeepers that they should support the *Courier* and not be guided by Thomas Denton. The attacks on Denton, as he had written them, sounded more malicious than plausible; and the appeals to support the *Courier* appeared, he thought in annoyance, as though he were asking for a handout.

By four o'clock in the morning, when he gave up, he had a wastepaper basket full of crumpled paper, a bad headache, and nothing to show for the night's work but a sense of frustration. He felt that he was letting down the *Courier*.

After a few hours of restless sleep he got up, heavy-eyed and dull, to find that during the night snow had piled up outside the Folly. The Green lay under a mantle of white. In the early morning there were lights in a few houses and smoke curling up from chimneys, and the stained-glass windows in a church gleamed in soft rose and blue and gold.

This is my village, Stanley thought, looking out at the gentle peace and beauty of the scene. It is not going to be spoiled by one selfish and unscrupulous man. Somehow I'll find a way.

He was not surprised to find Ellen at the breakfast table, looking as alert and rested as ever, her white hair beautifully dressed, but he was surprised to see Sherry.

"Look here," he said in concern, "you shouldn't be up."

"But I'm going to help you work out a plan of campaign to save our advertising," she reminded him.

"Have you looked out of the window? You'd get pneumonia if you went out on a day like this."

"Oh, please," she said eagerly, "I want to so much. I've been thinking and thinking; I'm sure some of my ideas are good. Honestly I am."

Seeing the determination in her face, Ellen wisely refrained from trying to dissuade her.

With heavy boots on her feet and a wool scarf twisted around her head and two sweaters under her coat, Sherry slipped and slid her way, with Stanley's help, to the waiting car, and closed the heavy door with difficulty because of the force of the wind. As Stanley turned the key in the ignition there was a shout and Wilson staggered out to the car carrying a basket which he deposited on the floor in back.

"Mrs. Davis thought it might be difficult to come home for lunch and this is a bit of food."

"Thank her for us, will you, Wilson?"

As they reached the open Green, the full force of the wind struck the car; snow blew crazily in all directions so that the windshield wipers could not provide clear visibility.

The newspaper office, for the first time in Stanley's experience, was dark. Worse, it was cold.

"Good Lord, I hadn't thought that the heat is turned off on Friday night after we go to press. You keep your coat on, Sherry, until I turn on the oil burner and get the place warmed up."

While Stanley busied himself in the basement she seated herself at the typewriter, the gooseneck lamp making a thin pool of light on the paper, and began to type out the ideas she had had during the night.

When Stanley came back she pushed toward him several pages of notes a little shyly. When he did not speak she explained, "You see, I got to thinking that a man like Mr. Denton is devious, but your strength lies in the fact that you are completely straightforward. Tell them what the *Courier* stands for and explain why they need it and that they can't be free men if they sell out their rights to anyone. Do that and then go to see them in person and take a copy of your story to each one. They'll believe you, Stanley. Anyone would believe you."

He looked at the wide, earnest eyes and for a moment he lost track of what she was saying. He found her returning his look, her own eyes startled, with a questioning, arrested expression. He forced himself to look away, to be businesslike. "This may be a long job, you know. I want to get this thing right."

"Don't hurry it."

"You'll be all right?" He was aware of the absurdity of the question.

She laughed. "Of course I will."

For a while she watched the fury of the storm, looked at the river, now ice-covered, stared at the old Queen Anne house across the narrow river, which belonged to Mrs. Fosdick. On this dark day the lights were burning and, as usual, Mrs. Fosdick was seated at her favorite observation post, a chair near a living room window which provided an excellent view of the highway and the *Courier*. The wind blew snow into miniature cyclones and sleet rattled against the windowpane. The sky was so dark that it might have been night instead of midday.

Then, remembering that she had come here to work, she rubbed her cold hands, which felt stiff, and rolled paper into the typewriter. She stared at it for some time and then she began to make notes for stories.

Little by little, she became absorbed and she no longer heard the savage scream of the wind or was aware of the way the building shook under the onslaught of the storm, almost as heavily as it did when the presses were running. She was not aware of the darkness outside the pool of light on her typewriter. What did arouse her was the realization that she was hungry. She looked at her watch. Unbelievably it was nearly two o'clock.

She cleared her desk, opened the basket which Ellen had, with typical thoughtfulness, provided, and set out the food. There were thermoses of coffee and soup, and sandwiches of roast beef, chicken, and cheese. When she had poured soup and coffee into the cups she called Stanley.

He looked more rested than he had in the morning and there was a new alertness and confidence in his manner. "I believe I've got it. Read this, will you, Sherry, and tell me what you think?"

"Of course, but first you had better have some of this nice lunch Aunt Ellen sent us."

"A real picnic. I haven't been on a picnic since I was a kid." He bit hungrily into a sandwich.

"How like Aunt Ellen that was! Is Henry as nice as she is?"

"Henry?" Stanley was at a loss, his mind on Sherry. He had never known a girl like her with the warm and genuine friendliness which was making her so successful as society editor, her quick flashes of temper, her eager helpfulness, her gaiety. And she was lovely too, not with the stunning beauty of Eve but with something deeper, warmer, more alive.

It was curious that she never spoke of the man to whom she was engaged. Eve had told him that the major had a hush-hush job and Sherry could not hear from him. Tough on a guy to have to leave a girl like that for months at a time without a word.

"Yes, Henry," Sherry said, and brought him back to the question. "You know, Aunt Ellen's nephew, the one you are always telling the crazy stories about."

"Oh, Henry."

She looked at him, her head tilted a little on one side. "Are you feeling all right, Stanley?"

He laughed. "Well, the thing is — there isn't any Henry."

This really alarmed Sherry. "Isn't — what is wrong with you, Stanley?"

"We made him up."

"Made who up?"

"Henry."

"Oops! Here we go again."

"Henry," Stanley explained with a straight face, "was the reason I met Aunt Ellen."

"The Henry you made up?"

"Sure. Isn't that perfectly clear?"

"I'm beginning to hear noises in my head," she wailed.

He relented. "You see one morning I got a letter from Aunt Winifred saying she was going to descend on me for a long visit because I'm such a lonely guy. That same day I heard from Eve announcing that she was coming to see Bill's old home and that she would bring her baby. Well, I didn't know Eve then but I did know Aunt Winifred, and I could imagine a battle to the death between the two of them for control of the house, and that same morning there was a letter from Aunt Ellen."

He told her about the letter from the rebellious old woman.

"And so — is there any more soup? Oh, well, how about another sandwich? No, I'd rather have roast beef — so she came to see me and we cooked up the story about my old friendship with her nephew Henry to account for her being practically the official hostess for the Folly, and she was installed that very day. How she has managed to keep Aunt Winifred in order and handle Wilson the way she does is beyond me — and beyond praise."

"But why is she, Stanley?"

"Why is she what?"

"A rebellious old woman."

"I don't know. I've told you all I know about her. I've never asked. But knowing her is one of the best things that ever happened to me. There's not a day when I don't have some reason to be grateful to her."

"Me too," Sherry admitted. "Heavens, it's getting awfully dark. What time is it?"

"Just three o'clock." Stanley went to look out the window. The sky was blotted out by low-hanging clouds, thick and dark, telephone wires were heavily encased in ice, only one car was in sight, headlamps dimmed by heavy snow, crawling and sliding along the road with the click of chains on frozen snow.

Sherry came to stand beside him. "It doesn't seem natural for it to be so dark in the daytime." Her voice was hushed. Her arm brushed against him and, as though the touch had ignited a spark, he turned suddenly, reaching for her. "Sherry!"

She drew back, saying breathlessly, "I'd better start typing your report for the advertisers. You'll want an original copy for each one, using his own name. That's important, I think."

He had himself under control. "You'll need more light." His voice was cool and he went to bring a second lamp and plug it in near her desk.

That was a stupid thing to do, Holbrook, he told himself. She's another man's girl. Just remember that. And she was entrusted to your care by an old friend. You'd better watch your step, boy.

Sherry, her color heightened, was reading the report. She looked up, her momentary embarrassment forgotten, her face glowing. "Oh, this is good! It's really good! You've said just the right things in the right way."

While she typed Stanley paced restlessly from his cubbyhole office to the big room where he stared sightlessly out of the window. The fury of the storm was such that the building was jolted as though shaken by a giant hand.

The wind had risen to a shriek and the windows rattled. Sherry gave a nervous start and then resumed her typing, the tip of her tongue showing between her lips while she concentrated on the reports she was writing, pulling each one from the machine to read it carefully before she added it to the pile beside her.

The lights dimmed, flared, dimmed, flared again, and then went out. Sherry gave a little exclamation of dismay though not of fright.

"It's all right," he assured her. "Nothing to worry about but we'll have to call it a day. Probably wires down somewhere from the weight of the ice."

"But I'm not half done," she wailed, "and there won't be a chance in the morning. Anyhow, that's the only time when you'll be able to go around and see the men yourself."

"Well, you can't work in the dark."

"No, but there's a whole box of candles downstairs and there is a kerosene lantern, too. I can find them. They've been there for years. Dick showed them to me one day."

"You aren't going anywhere in the dark. Probably break your neck," he growled because he was afraid to take a softer tone. "Tell me where they are."

When she had done so, he groped his way down the stairs, holding his lighter above his head, found the box she had told him of and noticed, in concern, that with the power failure the oil burner had gone off.

When he had adjusted the candles for her he said, "You'd better put on that coat."

"I can't work in it."

It was a long time later when she said in relief, "There, that is the lot. Can you see to sign them?"

He pulled up a chair beside her and signed the reports, which she folded and put in the envelopes she had already addressed. As she leaned forward her hair touched a candle. Stanley leaped to blow it out and to crush out the singed hair.

"Sherry! You might have been hurt. Sherry!" She was in his arms and he was holding her crushed to him. "Oh, darling! darling!" He bent his head and covered her mouth with his. And then her arms crept up around his neck.

At last she pushed him away, lifting her head.

"Sherry!" he protested.

She laughed. "Let me breathe."

"I'm in love with you," he said in a tone of wonder. "I never meant — I had no right — and you're too loyal to let your Major down. Forgive me if you can."

"There's nothing to forgive," she said. Doesn't he know, she wondered, how I feel about him? How can he help it?

"We've got to leave now," he said abruptly and lighted the kerosene lantern and then blew out the candles and pocketed the reports while she pulled on her heavy boots.

He looked down at her, at the flushed cheeks, the mouth whose lips seemed warmer and fuller from the pressure of his kisses, took a step toward her and turned away. "Let's go," he told her, his tone peremptory.

Outside they braced themselves against the onslaught of the savage wind, the bite of ice crystals on their faces. Stanley, holding the lantern in one hand, shielded her as best he could from the fury of the storm, supporting her across the treacherous ice on the sidewalk to his car. While she held the lantern he unlocked the door and then took the lantern from her, the light falling on her face. Across the river he could see the Fosdick house lighted up and in the window on the ground floor a shadowy figure. Mrs. Fosdick was at her favorite lookout point.

Of all the rotten luck, he thought. Apparently the *Courier* was the only place to experience a power failure. He could imagine what Mrs. Fosdick would make of that darkened building. Well, he wouldn't worry Sherry about it; he could deal with it when the time came.

He was too intent on the job of keeping the car on the road to speak. Beside him Sherry was content to be quiet. He loved her. He had told her so, his voice and his eyes and his lips had told her so. I didn't know, she thought, that it was possible to be as happy as this. It is almost frightening. And then the bright spark of joy in her was dimmed. He felt that he was being unfair to Doug, and she would have to tell him the humiliating truth, that Doug had jilted her. How would that affect him? Would he scorn marrying a girl whom another man had turned down? But I'll have to do it, she told herself. I'll have to. Only how can I say it so it won't sound so awful? Her thoughts went around, whirling like the snow outside the car. I can't think of what to say, she admitted in despair.

As it happened, she did not have to say anything.

There were lights outside the entrance to the Folly and when Stanley had flung open the door there was warmth. From the brocade drawing room Sherry heard Eve cry, "There they are! Oh, thank heaven! I was so afraid of an accident."

Before Stanley and Sherry reached the big drawing room, a tall man appeared in the doorway and then he crossed the lobby with long strides, not deterred by a limp. He took Sherry in his arms, crying, "Sherry! At last."

VIII

DOUG! Doug here at the Folly. Doug still in love with her. It was many weeks since Sherry had believed she would ever see him again. She had been convinced that he had simply disappeared of his own accord. And all the time he had been unchanged in his love for her.

Sherry was too dazed to think. There were cries of concern about Stanley and Sherry, who were sent to their rooms for warm, dry clothing.

Eve accompanied Sherry, for once bubbling with excitement. "We've been so worried about you with the storm getting worse."

"I'm all right." Sherry belied her words by sneezing. "It's just that the power went off in the building and it got awfully cold. I never realized how chilled I was until we got back here and the Folly seemed so heavenly warm."

"You can imagine how excited we were," Eve said, "when Major Carleton came. I'd have known him at once by your description and the way he cocks his right eyebrow when he looks at you. Anyhow," she rattled on with unaccustomed loquacity, "Aunt Ellen said he was to wait for you. He said he had gone nearly crazy when he got back and telephoned Minneapolis and you weren't there.

Finally he ran down the head of some nursery school and she put him on the right track."

While Sherry changed to a white wool dress and fastened a narrow black belt, her hands shaking with nervousness, Eve, curled up on the edge of the bed, went on. "He's really charming, Sherry, so good looking and so terribly in love with you. He said he didn't think he could have stuck it out much longer without having any word from you but now his hush-hush job is over and he has decided to leave the service. He's been doing all sorts of exciting things and apparently he has been in danger and was wounded in the leg. But he said the lameness won't last long. And he said nothing mattered because he had you to come home to."

"Oh!" It was a whimper of pain. If only Doug had come one day earlier, before Stanley had told her he loved her and taken her in his arms, where she had felt that she belonged.

"Your Major is so much like Bill, not in looks because Bill resembled Stanley, but his manner, his quality. If you're ready let's go down now. Major Carleton is staying for dinner and the night. Aunt Ellen insisted, and anyhow, where could he go in this storm?"

That night Stanley played the courteous host but he was white and he did not look at Sherry. Eve, having recovered from her unaccustomed spate of words, was her usual reticent self. The Major was radiant with happiness. There was no cloud in his sky. He could not take his eyes or his attention off Sherry. He said little about the work he had been doing, and nothing at all about where he had been. He had been sent on a mission, he said, and he had been refused permission to get in touch with

Sherry beyond the telegram he had sent from Philadelphia.

"If she had been anyone else," he said with a laugh, "I might not have felt as easy as I did about it, but knowing her and her loyalty I knew she'd wait, no matter how long it was."

Color flamed in Sherry's face and faded again. She sat twisting her engagement ring and not eating. Doug had changed in the months since she had seen him. He was thinner and there were lines in his face that had not been there before; the months had obviously been difficult ones for him, and dangerous. And he trusted her, trusted her loyalty, knowing he had her to come back to. She looked up to meet the confident, adoring eyes that watched her and she put away her dream forever and smiled back at him.

After dinner they were discreetly left alone. Doug sat on the love seat, one arm around her, her hand in his. "I wouldn't have believed it possible that you could be any prettier, but when you came in with Holbrook with a glow in your eyes that made you so lovely — oh, Sherry, I don't know how I've stood it all these months!"

He told her how he had tried to call her from New York as soon as his mission was completed and he had arranged for his discharge, and learned from her landlady that she had left Minneapolis. Then he had started telephoning frantically until he had run down the woman for whom she had worked at the nursery school and got word that Sherry had gone to Waring, Connecticut, to visit old friends and then went to stay at the home of people called Holbrook while she worked on a newspaper.

"I didn't get the setup quite clear," he admitted, "until I came here this afternoon. I thought I was seeing things when I found you were living in a castle. Craziest thing I ever saw. And the lady of the house, Mrs. Holbrook, is the most beautiful woman I ever encountered. That husband of hers seems to be quite a distinguished guy, too. How on earth did you meet them? So far as I could make out from Miss Holbrook, you are employed by her nephew and I didn't care much for her tone. As though she were in a position to patronize you! Well, that's all over now. There's nothing to prevent us from getting married at once. I'll be out of uniform soon, and I'm not planning ahead for another job until after our honeymoon."

"But, Doug," Sherry protested, "I can't walk out on my job without warning, and this is the busiest season with all the extra work on the paper and more people entertaining and all that, and I was going to start a column after the first of the year and get a raise of thirty dollars a week. Thirty dollars!"

"Sherry," there was a change in Doug's voice, "I'll settle for waiting until after Christmas, if you think it's wrong to walk out on your job before then, though I will grudge every single day. But when you talk about a column — what is it? Do you want to go on working or have you changed toward me and don't want to marry me? Is that the real problem?"

She looked at his worn face from which the confident happiness was fading into a kind of startled doubt. "Doug," she said gently, "it's been a long time."

"And I didn't let you know. But I couldn't!"

"I understand that. But in so many months — well, things change. Right now you seem almost like a stranger to me, a very nice, very attractive stranger, but I don't *know* you the way I did."

His hand tightened its hold on hers. "I think I understand. You want time for us to get acquainted again." There was a pause during which his mouth twisted wryly with disappointment; then he smiled at her. "All right, darling, we'll do it your way. We'll wait until you are quite sure I'm the same old guy, and I'll teach you to love me all over again. I'll find a place to stay near Waring where I can see you every day. All right?"

"Oh, Doug," she was half laughing, half crying, "you are so good."

"You're worth it. But don't try me too far, dearest. I'm only human and I'm in love and — we'll give it a try." He released her hand and got up. "Well, if I'm not to kiss you again for a while, I'd better leave you. Good night, Sherry. Dream of me."

ii

In her room, Sherry put out the light, tied the cord of her warm robe at her slim waist, and walked up and down, pausing to look at the fire crackling in the grate and to listen to the fury of the storm that raged outside the Folly.

Stanley loved her. That was the overwhelming thing that had happened. But Doug had come home, Doug who had been in danger, who had been wounded, who had aged from his experiences, and had found it all worth-while because she would be waiting for him, a compensation for all his trials, her loyalty unshaken, her love unchanged. At this moment Doug was under the same roof, deeply disappointed by her decision to postpone their marriage until they learned to know each other again but generously agreeing to it.

I will marry him, Sherry promised herself, and try to make it up to him for all he has suffered; I won't let myself think of Stanley again. But I need time, just a little time.

She got into bed. "Oh, Stanley," she whispered, and turned her face into the pillow.

iii

So that is Major Carleton, Stanley thought, staring into the fire in the library. A fine-looking man and very impressive in his uniform with that row of ribbons. More impressive, of course, because of the lines of pain and strain in his face, and crazy about Sherry. There's no question that he loves her. He'll take good care of her.

What rotten luck that Mrs. Fosdick knew they had been in the building with the lights out, a malicious woman like that! If she starts any gossip about Sherry I'll put a stop to it so fast she won't know what hit her. But suppose the Major hears it and believes it? No, he couldn't possibly suspect Sherry of anything dishonorable. Not possibly.

If only I hadn't taken her in my arms like that and kissed her. And she kissed me back! But I couldn't help it. I love her so terribly. What am I going to do without her? What am I going to do?

iv

Major Carleton climbed the great circular staircase to his room, walking slowly because of his lame leg. When he had removed his jacket and loosened his tie he stretched out his legs and leaned back, looking around him. A castle, no less! He shook his head in bewilderment. How on earth had Sherry met these people? He hadn't had a chance to find out much. Somehow there had been no opportunity to say all the things he had stored up to tell her during the long months since he had seen her. A lot had happened to him but, apparently, a lot had happened to her too. He had not figured on that. She felt that they were strangers. She wanted time before she married him.

He was sick with disappointment over the delay. He had hoped that they would be married in a matter of days, as soon as the local formalities of the license could be taken care of. But he must not rush her. And perhaps she would discover in a day or two that they weren't strangers at all, that they were as much in love as they had ever been.

She had seemed different in a way. More serious. Talking about her job as though it were a mission. Talking about writing a column of some sort. He grinned. His little Sherry setting herself up as a career woman! The thing was ridiculous. And so excited over a raise of thirty dollars, as though she would need it when they were married.

He would see that she had some real fun. He couldn't dance yet but the doctors had said the more exercise the better. It might hurt but it would restore flexibility. Perhaps they could get in some skiing in Vermont or fly to Bermuda for some swimming. It will be all right tomorrow, he decided optimistically. It's bound to be all right tomorrow

v

Eve tiptoed across the nursery with its dim night light to look at her sleeping baby. She pulled the light blanket over his shoulders and bent to kiss his cheek softly. Then she went back to her bedroom but not to sleep. She knew that she should rejoice in the happiness of Sherry and the Major, whose life was just opening up, but she could not help remembering that for her there was no such future. Something about Major Carleton's open-hearted manner had brought Bill vividly before her with his infectious gaiety. She had never felt so alone before.

How lovely Sherry had looked when she came in with Stanley, eyes glowing, a kind of radiance about her, almost as though she had known that her fiancé would be waiting. And his expression when he had gone to take her in his arms, so eager, so happy, so loving. How lucky Sherry was!

vi

Stanley had left for the *Courier* before Doug came down to the breakfast table where Ellen was still sitting. She looked him over, her impression of the night before confirmed. He was unusually good-looking with a gay and outgoing nature, a kind of exuberance that had been toned down temporarily by experiences that, she suspected, had been grim indeed, but he would recover his resilience in time, especially if he married Sherry. *If* he married Sherry. But of course he would marry Sherry. She would not jilt a man who had waited so many months for her. She could not.

"The butler said I'd probably find someone still at breakfast."

"We breakfast at all hours. Stanley and Sherry are first because they go to work, Eve comes down as soon as she can bring herself to stop admiring her baby for a moment, and Miss Holbrook has a tray in her room."

His face fell. "Then Sherry has already gone?"

"She caught a severe cold working in an unheated building yesterday and I sent her back to bed." Ellen added mendaciously, "She is awfully sorry not to see you but she doesn't want you to catch her cold and right now she's as much of a menace as Typhoid Mary."

"Can I send her a message?"

"Oh, of course. Good morning, Eve."

Eve, wearing a dark red sweater and skirt, her gold hair waved softly at the ends and brushing her shoulders, smiled at Doug who got to his feet. He had never seen such eyes, a true violet. How often, he wondered, does a man see beauty like this?

"Good morning, Major. Is your room comfortable?"

He laughed. "In a castle? After — uh — where I've been I still can't believe I am really here, that this can be a part of the same world."

"That reminds me," Ellen said, "Stanley wants me to tell you that you must stay here as long as you like."

"That's very kind of him." Doug smiled at Eve. "Both you and your husband have made me so welcome when I have no claim on you."

"My husband!" Eve was startled. "Oh, Stanley is my brother-in-law. I've just come here on a visit. I lost my husband a year ago." She turned to Ellen in order to forestall any word of sympathy. "Did Sherry go to work today?"

"She was in no shape to go out in the cold so I sent her back to bed."

"I'll go up to see her after breakfast."

"Don't do that, Eve. She is simply exuding germs. You'll pick up her cold and pass it on to Billy."

"Well — what are your plans, Major?"

"I don't quite know. I didn't have any plans beyond finding Sherry and getting married as soon as possible. She feels she ought to keep her job until after Christmas. She must find her job very interesting, working overtime and all that."

Seeing his expression, Ellen said, "An emergency came up."

Doug's lips tightened. The discovery that his host was not married to the beautiful Mrs. Holbrook had altered his attitude toward him. It was apparent to the two women that he was both jealous and disturbed. Before breakfast was over he had declined courteously to impose on Mr. Holbrook's hospitality for another night. There was bound to be a motel or a village inn nearby where he could establish residence so he could get a wedding license.

There was a charming inn about ten miles away in the

next village, Eve told him, and later that morning, with Doug at the wheel of the station wagon and Eve at his side, they negotiated the driveway and crept through Waring which, overnight, had been transformed into a wonderland by an ice storm.

"Oh, it's beautiful!" Eve breathed, lips parted in wonder while she looked around her.

"This is awfully kind of you," Doug told her.

"I wouldn't have missed this for anything. And you haven't interfered with my plans."

Doug stole a look at her exquisite profile, saw the melancholy droop of her lips. "Look at that! It's like a Grandma Moses primitive."

An artificial lake had been frozen and a colorful moving mob in red and green and blue and yellow was skating. Doug stopped the car and they watched for a few minutes, saw the hut against a background of dark pines and a blazing bonfire.

"Lord, I wish I had some skates!" he exclaimed.

"But, surely, with a bad leg —"

"The doctor said the more exercise I give it the better it will be in the long run. Prevent stiffening."

"Well, you can rent skates here. I read an article about this place in last week's *Courier*."

"Let's go."

"But I don't know how to skate."

"Nothing to it. I'll teach you." As she hesitated he said, "Oh, come on!"

No one had spoken to her in that tone of laughing cajolery in more than a year. "All right," she said impulsively, and found herself a quarter of an hour later, her hands linked in his, moving cautiously onto the ice, while small children staggered past, older ones raced, and an ambitious girl in orthodox skating costume practiced a dance step.

The cold brought color whipping into Eve's face, and Doug's instructions, somewhat marred when he fell flat, kept her laughing as she thought she had forgotten how to laugh. Instead of the usual fatigue that followed her plodding walks, she was exhilarated when at last they returned to the car. When they reached the Mayflower Inn it was lunchtime and it seemed natural for them to lunch together.

After Doug had arranged for a room he ordered lunch for two and they sat in a charming living room before a blazing fire while they waited to be called into the dining room. Bowls of steaming clam chowder were set before them and they ate heartily, talking with all the ease of old friends.

"This afternoon," Doug said, "if it isn't abusing your time and patience, I'll rent a car so I can get around. Tomorrow I'll go to New York to buy some civilian clothes."

Eve looked at the trim uniform with its array of ribbons. "It's rather a shame to abandon all that. Most imposing." There was a smile in her eyes.

"That's the past now. I like to live in the present. Don't you?"

"Well, I used to." She went on hastily, "About a car, there's a reliable dealer in Waring, according to Stanley, unless you have something special in mind."

He shook his head. "All I want is transportation so I

can go back and forth to see Sherry." The cheerfulness that had marked the morning faded. "What do you think of this job of hers?"

"I don't know much about it. I remember her saying she needed something to do while she waited for you to come back. This has been a difficult time for her, too, not knowing where you were or how you were."

"She said something about writing a column, beginning the first of the year."

"Did she? I never heard of that but she's so clever I don't doubt she could do it."

"When she marries me she won't need to work."

"Sherry is the kind of girl who likes to — oh, test herself, see what she is made of. I don't think she could be satisfied just to be a housewife like me. She's ambitious, you know."

"We used to have wonderful times together, laughing a lot, just enjoying ourselves." After a pause, Doug said, "I was surprised that a man like your brother-in-law would be running a village paper. He looks like the big time to me."

"For some reason it is important to him. There is a man who wants to buy the *Courier* in order to stop publication, which sounds absurd to me, but Stanley isn't going to permit it."

"A crusader, is he?" Doug was gloomier than ever. "Sherry always had a weakness for crusaders."

It was late in the afternoon when Eve drove the station wagon up to the Folly followed by Doug in a red Volkswagen. He had a long box of roses which he gave Wilson for Sherry before going to the room assigned to him the night before to collect his belongings.

"But you'll stay for dinner. Surely you'll stay for dinner," Eve protested and Ellen added her voice. She also reported that Sherry was greatly improved and her fever was gone.

"You are very kind to her. I can't tell you how grateful I am."

Ellen smiled and shook her head. "The gratitude is the other way. Sherry has been good for us all. She has been invaluable to Stanley and wonderful for Eve, shaken her out of the worst of her grief for her husband, helped her to find other interests, encouraged her to brighten up her rooms and her clothes." Ellen's eyes narrowed in thought. "But you did the most for Eve when you made her go skating with you this morning. What a wonderful idea! She loved it and she seemed more alive than she has ever been since I've known her. I wonder — while Sherry is busy at her job — perhaps it would be possible for you to take Eve skating again."

"I'd enjoy it very much," he said promptly. "Tomorrow I'm going to New York, but I'll be away only the one day."

Eve came down to say she had talked to Sherry from the safe vantage point of the doorway and that she loved her roses and was looking forward to seeing Doug as soon as he returned from New York.

She was followed by Miss Holbrook, her bracelets jingling as she walked. Tonight, and Ellen's heart sank as she recognized the symptoms, it was apparent that Miss

Holbrook was ripe for trouble. She inquired about Sherry in a perfunctory manner and hoped she didn't have anything contagious; if so she should not stay in the house at a risk of infecting other people. "So inconsiderate," she muttered.

"Sherry couldn't help catching cold," Eve retorted. "She got chilled working overtime, trying to help Stanley when the power went off at the *Courier* and there wasn't any heat."

"Oh?" There was amusement in Miss Holbrook's tone. "Sometimes, Eve, I think you are a little naïve. If you can really imagine that Sherry and Stanley were working in an unheated building where there were no lights, it is more than I can do. And the lights had been out a full hour before they left the *Courier*. Mrs. Fosdick telephoned this afternoon. She lives across from the *Courier*," she explained to Doug, "and she saw the lights go out and then, *a whole hour later,* Sherry and Stanley came out."

"And in that time," Stanley said from the doorway, his voice shaking with anger, "Sherry insisted that I get candles from downstairs and she finished typing the reports I took around this morning. The whole thing was her idea, her plan. I followed it out, saw my advertisers, and got back all but one of them, and, incidentally, saved the *Courier*. Mrs. Fosdick, and you might warn her, is asking for trouble if she makes any further comments or suggestions about Sherry Winthrop. I'll clap a suit for slander on her that will be epoch-making. And," he added, "that goes for anyone who repeats such comments."

"Stanley dear!" Miss Holbrook faltered, her color fading. "You'll have to admit that it is strange that the *Courier* was the only building to be affected by this so-called power failure."

Without reply Stanley turned to Doug. "Sherry is the finest human being I know, Carleton, and the most loyal."

"You don't need to tell me that."

"I just didn't want any misunderstanding."

"There isn't any misunderstanding," Doug said, thinking: He's in love with her too. I wonder if he dislikes me as much as I dislike him.

IX

NEXT morning Stanley informed his startled advertising man of the space that had been sold and sent him in a rush to get the advertisements. Neil Gordon irritated him by asking about Sherry and demanding to know whether it was true that she was going to be married. Perkins drove him to a frenzy by requiring decisions on everything. But for once that indeterminate man to whom a decision was agony had made one on his own without hesitation, and he told Stanley so.

"Mrs. Thomas Denton came in and wanted a big story in the *Courier* about that Christmas tree her husband is donating to the Green and the gifts to be distributed on Christmas Eve. She wanted the right side of the front page, no less. She," Perkins gulped and his Adam's apple bobbed up and down, "she offered me a hundred dollars to do it. A lady like that!"

Stanley grinned. "What did you tell her?"

"I said the *Courier* doesn't sell anything but advertising space."

Stanley clapped him on the shoulder, laughing. "Good man! May your shadow never lengthen. Did she want anything else?"

"She's got a story for the society editor who is to call in person." Perkins hovered irresolutely.

"What is it, Perkins?"

"It's that Mrs. Denton. I got the feeling she's the kind who won't give up, the kind who won't take no for an answer."

"She'll have to learn."

"Well, you might just give Sherry the wink. After all, she's only a kid."

"Sherry is as unlikely to sell out as you are."

"Sure, I know that, but she's not up to all the dodges and I'd guess that Mrs. Denton is. Something very shrewd behind that bright smile of hers."

"Stay in there pitching and don't worry about Sherry or about Mrs. Denton, and we'll have all the ads we can carry from now on."

Perkins beamed. "Mr. Saunders himself could not have done any better," he declared, offering the highest tribute he knew.

Stanley laughed, answered the telephone, talked to a couple of people who dropped in — everyone in Waring, he thought, regarded the *Courier* as his home away from home — and wrote letters, typing them laboriously in two-finger style, but all the time his longing for Sherry was like a physical ache. She had been so much a part of the *Courier* with her clear gay voice, her contagious excitement, her spontaneous friendliness, her quick step, that she was everywhere. If he felt like this without her for a day, what would it be like forever?

Aside from his longing for her physical presence he wanted to tell her about his talks with the advertisers, what he had said, what obstacles they had raised, how he had countered them and finally achieved his point. Without her eager response and her approval it was only half a triumph.

He did not see her during the two following days because he could not bear to see her with Carleton. He spent his evenings in the library and Sherry, he understood, dined out with the Major, carefully bundled up against the cold. A somewhat wan and silent Sherry, but a gentler girl than her fiancé had ever known, keeping the conversation firmly on him and his activities and the things he had seen and done that he was at liberty to discuss.

Sherry had been delighted to have Doug spend his mornings skating with Eve and she was grateful to Eve for helping him to occupy his time while she was regaining her strength. Still weakened and apathetic from her cold, she found it taxed her ingenuity to keep her relationship with Doug on the impersonal basis she had determined on until after Christmas. The situation could not last; it was clearly untenable and she was aware of the fact. For the time being he was content to give her her head, but with the New Year he would be more demanding, less manageable. Sherry refused to think beyond the New Year. She clung to this respite and kept the conversation moving feverishly, urging him to talk about the war and his plans for the future, his ambitions, his ideas and point of view, trying to get a deeper insight into the man she was going to marry.

But Doug, gay companion though he was, evaded her questions and laughed at her solemnity. "What big thoughts for such a little girl," he said indulgently and switched the talk to sports. When she was stronger they would get in a weekend of skiing in Vermont or New Hampshire, and take the beautiful Mrs. Holbrook along for the proprieties.

When she was stronger. Sherry was aware that she was deliberately sheltering herself behind the aftermath of the cold, using it as a protection against Doug and aware, in self-disgust, of the essential dishonesty of her attitude. But I can't let him kiss me; not yet; not until I get used to the idea. He is kind and generous and he is trying to do as I ask but this can't last forever.

It was not until Friday morning that Sherry appeared in the *Courier* office. Stanley was so glad to see her that it was all he could do not to welcome her with open arms. Instead he grumbled, "What on earth are you doing here? You go straight home."

A smile quivered on her mouth. "I won't go home."

"How did you get here? It is much too cold for you to be walking."

"Eve drove me down. There's a whole pile of items on my desk to verify and write up and Mrs. Denton wants me to call personally about some party she is giving."

"She is probably making another bid to get a big display for Denton's Christmas Eve party on the Green. We'll have to cover it, of course. As a matter of fact, we are announcing it in today's paper, and in the first issue after Christmas we will give it a real play with pictures. But that is as far as we go. Oh, by the way, take a look at these, will you?" There was boyish pride in his face when he saw hers light up.

"Stanley! You got all but one of them back. You did it. I knew you could. You did it."

"*We* did it."

At his expression Sherry flushed. "You forgot to return that box of candles. Here, I'll do it." She hurried away before he could stop her. He had a curious feeling that the sun was shining more brightly but when he looked at the window he saw only a gray cloudiness.

Sherry found Jones, the printer, setting type, and Dick, his face sullen, emptying wastebaskets and setting the place in some kind of order. He smiled at Sherry.

"Gee, I'm glad to see you back. We heard you were real sick. Trouble is that you've been working too hard, just being sweated. Someday, when we have a better system in this country and get rid of the Establishment —"

"What's got into you, Dick?" she exclaimed in astonishment. "I haven't been sweated. Neither have you. No one could be more considerate or more generous than Mr. Holbrook. As for the Establishment, what kind would you prefer? Or would you take anarchy with no establishment at all?"

Dick was full of grievances but he had only a mass of undigested and confused ideas about how they should be righted. "We should make a clean sweep," he declared.

Sherry grinned at the broom he was holding. "You'll have to do better than that," she teased him, and he flushed uncomfortably, too young to be able to accept ridicule with grace. "I don't know who's been talking to you, Dick, but whoever it is hasn't done you any good."

"You are wrong there," he said naïvely. "Didja get a look at that new motorcycle behind the building?"

"Yours?"

"Mine."

"I should think you'd freeze, riding a thing like that in this weather."

"Oh, I got a real warm fleece-lined jacket."

On the salary of a boy who earned only an office boy's pay? Sherry looked at Dick soberly, aware that someone must be providing him with funds if he could afford a motorcycle and a heavy jacket at the same time. And all that talk about making a clean sweep and exploitation and the Establishment. Often, she thought angrily, the people who incited the ignorant and the belligerent and the confused to resistance and violence were worse than the ones who actually performed the violent actions.

It was mid-afternoon before she was free to call on Mrs. Denton. The Dentons lived in a revolutionary farm-house with the original structure unchanged but, inside, disturbingly modern. Mrs. Denton in a crimson slack suit and dangling earrings, a potent perfume and an exotic wig, came to meet her, holding out a jeweled hand and smiling brightly.

"Miss Winthrop from the *Courier*. Oh, yes, do come in."

Sherry looked around her in stunned disbelief. One wall was a single huge mirror, reflecting the white baby grand piano. There were several paintings in strident colors and made up of designs that, to the untutored eye, looked like something that had failed to survive an earth-quake.

Sherry opened her notebook and turned to face Mrs. Denton, who was studying her closely.

"You are young to be a society editor, aren't you?"

"I am twenty."

"Well, I suppose you are just at an age to think small-town newspaper work is exciting." Mrs. Denton smiled brightly. "And working for a wealthy young bachelor like Mr. Holbrook must be exciting too." She saw the ring on Sherry's finger and said sharply, "His?"

"No."

Mrs. Denton laughed merrily. "Well, one would naturally expect an unattached man with all Holbrook's money to be attractive to women."

"I expect most women would find him so even without his money."

Mrs. Denton was checked in mid-flight, too experienced not to know when she had made a misstep. There was more to this girl than just a pretty face and it behooved her to feel her way more cautiously. She could be either a valuable ally or an antagonist to be reckoned with.

"Heavens, I wouldn't dream of criticizing Mr. Holbrook or minimizing his attractions. Both my husband and I are very fond of him. In fact, if he should ever be forced to give up the *Courier*, I'm sure Tom could find a place for him in one of his enterprises."

"I don't think Mr. Holbrook plans to give up the *Courier*."

"These days newspapers are so dependent on advertisers that one never knows what will happen. Practically overnight some drastic changes could occur."

"Oh, Mr. Holbrook has as much advertising as he can handle. His advertising manager has been run off his feet all week checking the ads that go to press today. Mr. Holbrook was just saying that he was considering making the

Courier a thirty-two-page paper, with more out-of-town news. He can get enough ads to carry it and people all over the state subscribe already. It has a lot of influence."

"So he is getting plenty of advertising. That's nice."

"Isn't it! This is a very — independent community, you know." Sherry smiled.

Mrs. Denton's lips compressed. So the *Courier* had all the advertising it could handle and was planning to extend its influence through the entire state. Somewhere along the line their man Ramsay had blundered badly. He had practically guaranteed that the advertisers would leave the *Courier*. Tom would make short work of him. Tom did not tolerate failure or people who promised more than they could perform.

What was equally obvious was that this girl knew what it was all about and she had got considerable satisfaction out of this temporary setback for the Dentons. She was definitely to be reckoned with. Mrs. Denton casually moved her foot and pressed a button concealed in the carpet. The door opened promptly and a young man with a long nose and hair that receded to the crown of his head on either side with a narrow patch of black in the center, like a dark path, walked into the room and paused as Mrs. Denton shook her head and glanced at Sherry.

"Oh, sorry," he said. "I didn't know you were busy." He looked Sherry over carefully, missing no detail of her appearance, and withdrew as silently as he had come.

Sherry looked at her watch and took the initiative. "You have a story for me, I understand, something about the Christmas Eve party for children on the Green."

"No, this is something else. I am giving a dinner party next week in honor of house guests from England, one of Tom's business associates and his wife, titled people, very distinguished. Sir Charles and Lady Remington. And some friends from New York, the Bruce Murgatroyds. And, of course, the Holbrooks from the Folly."

Sherry looked up, startled.

"Knowing how Lady Remington enjoys music, we are getting Henrico Belgali to play in the evening. He's one of the country's greatest pianists, as you know. Of course the price the man charges is outrageous but I didn't let that stop me."

"How generous," Sherry murmured.

"Oh, and among our guests will be Mr. and Mrs. Duffer, D-u-f-f-e-r, the presidential adviser, and Mr. and Mrs. William Fosdick of Waring. Mr. Fosdick is prominent in Connecticut politics, you know."

Mrs. Denton glanced at some notes scrawled on a piece of paper. "Oh, yes, of course, later on we will be extending our acquaintance and entertaining a number of Waring people, but they might feel out of place at this first party. However, there is the banker and several retired people from New York of fine position, and a couple of commercial artists and writers whom it is smart to entertain these days. And, in time, we'll see what we can do for the little people. Not entertain them, perhaps, but certainly try to improve their lot."

The little people. Sherry raged inwardly. It was like calling a sturdy midwest farmer a peasant. The little people, indeed. It would serve the Dentons right to let them ride headlong to their doom, addressing the citizens of Waring as The Little People!

None of this showed in Sherry's face.

"Winthrop!" Mrs. Denton exclaimed, with as phony and unconvincing a tone of surprise as Sherry had heard since she took part in high school dramatics. "Winthrop! But then you are going to be one of my guests. I remember now Miss Holbrook mentioned you as a — a kind of house guest — when I called her about the dinner party. Of course I said that you were to be included."

"You are very kind," Sherry murmured.

"Oh, not at all." As Sherry got up Mrs. Denton said, "My secretary refuses to come up here because she has a husband in New York. If at any time you would like to have a job, I would be happy to take you on and at a higher salary than a small-town paper could give you. You'd have an interesting life and be treated quite as one of the family. And any extra requirements, clothes and all that —" She left it for Sherry to fill in "all that" to suit herself.

X

I T was late when Sherry got back to the Folly. Major Carleton had been invited to dinner that night and everyone was in the small drawing room so she had a full house when she dropped her bomb.

Stanley had watched alertly when she entered the room, but she gave Doug the same smile she gave the others and went to sit beside Ellen.

"You look," Ellen accused her, "like the cat at the cream pitcher."

"I," Sherry informed her aloofly, "have been moving in the best circles."

"Have you indeed. Dear me, does it always have this appalling effect on you?"

"I," Sherry said haughtily, "am to be included, as a member of this household, when the rest of you dine with the Dentons next week."

"When we *what?*" Stanley exploded.

Miss Holbrook moved uneasily and her bracelets jingled.

"You are to meet the very best people," Sherry assured him. "Only the best. But later on the Dentons plan to extend their hospitality to humbler circles: the banker, some wealthy retired people, and a few commercial artists and writers whom it is now smart to entertain."

"Come off it, Sherry," Doug protested, laughing. "You've got to be kidding. People don't talk like that; they don't even think like that."

Sherry ignored this comment. "And then," she concluded triumphantly, "the Dentons are going to do something to improve the lot of The Little People, but not entertain them, of course."

Stanley was speechless.

"Well, I must say," Miss Holbrook declared, "I think it is very friendly of them."

"The Little People," Ellen said. "I wouldn't have believed it."

"And that is not all," Sherry said. "When the *Courier* fails, Mr. Denton will be happy to find some suitable spot for Stanley in one of his many enterprises. And," she went on before he could speak, "seeing at a glance my remarkable qualities, Mrs. Denton offered to pay me more than I am getting now to be her secretary, and I'm to be treated quite as one of the family and be allowed unspecified extras for clothes and what have you. I can't make up my mind whether to ask for double my present salary or to suggest that she give me the full amount of the bribe in one lump sum."

There was unbroken silence in the room for several minutes. Then Ellen said, "Sherry, how much of this story is true?"

"All of it; honestly, Aunt Ellen."

Doug looked up alertly as he heard Sherry call Mrs. Davis Aunt Ellen. She seemed completely at home in the

Folly, as though she had known these people all her life instead of a matter of weeks.

"Let's have the whole story," Stanley said.

Sherry repeated the conversation as accurately as she could. "And I can tell you one thing more. Mrs. Denton got the shock of her life when she found the *Courier* had all the advertising it needed. In fact, I told her you were getting so many ads you were thinking of building it up to thirty-two pages, using more news from around the state, and spreading the influence of the paper all over Connecticut."

Stanley began to laugh and then sobered. "You know, if I can get some guaranteed out-of-town advertising I might do that. You may have something there, Sherry. But what was that nonsense about me attending the Dentons' dinner party?"

"Everyone from the Folly is to attend the dinner party. Even me. It will help prepare me for bigger and better things in the future when I am practically a member of the Denton family."

"You can't be serious! With the campaign I am waging against Denton I can't afford to have people think I am hobnobbing with the guy on the side. When you write up that story be sure to leave out any reference to the people at the Folly."

"But, Stanley dear," Miss Holbrook protested, "you can't do that. I'm afraid it is too late to back down now."

"Back down?"

"You see, when Mrs. Denton called me and was so gracious, including everyone, even Sherry, I did not feel that I could refuse. And she is having some very distinguished guests and a famous pianist to entertain us. I know how you like music."

"You mean to say you actually accepted the invitation, Aunt Winifred, for all of us?" Stanley was incredulous.

She smiled toothily at him. "When you think it over, I am sure you will realize that we really can't afford to affront people as prominent as the Dentons."

"In the future I must ask you never to accept any invitation for me without consulting me first."

"What a fuss to make about nothing!" Miss Holbrook smiled with indulgent amusement as though arguing with an unreasonable small boy. "You've lived a solitary life too long, Stanley dear. You simply cannot be permitted to become a hermit." She managed a nervous laugh, startled by the anger in his face.

"We don't seem to understand each other, Aunt Winifred. I tried to express my wishes as a request; it seems I'll have to do so as an order."

For a moment Miss Holbrook was speechless with sheer surprise and indignation. Before she could gather her forces Ellen intervened hastily. "I have some Christmas shopping to do in New York. Would you care to go down with me tomorrow, Miss Holbrook? Eve? Sherry, I know there is no point in asking you."

Eve said hesitantly, "Well, I was going skating with Major Carleton in the morning."

Miss Holbrook laughed. "You had better look after your own property, Sherry."

Eve flushed. "Oh, Sherry, I never thought. Do you mind?"

"Of course I don't. I am glad Doug has someone to amuse him when I can't be with him."

"Sure?"

"Very sure."

Stanley, stealing a quick look at Sherry, saw that she was serious about it. She did not mind in the least how much time her fiancé spent with his beautiful sister-in-law.

ii

On Monday morning it seemed to Ellen that breakfast had lost all its gaiety and almost all its conversation. She was aware of the growing tension between Stanley and Sherry, of his brooding silence, of the unhappiness the girl was trying gallantly to conceal. This morning Ellen tried to fill the uneasy quiet with a lighthearted account of her shopping expedition in New York on Saturday.

"Taking Aunt Winifred was your Girl Scout's deed," Stanley commented.

"Actually, I enjoyed it."

Stanley grunted and broke toast into small pieces which he did not eat. He had lost weight during the past week, Ellen observed in concern, but she did not refer to it. Instead she said casually, "What has happened to your mysterious correspondent? I haven't seen one of those square blue envelopes lately."

"There won't be any more. I know what happened to her."

His tone discouraged further comment, but Sherry looked up to find his eyes on her face and she felt the color flooding into her own. "Come along, Sherry. I'll drive you down. You do enough walking in the course of the day."

It was not until they were in the car that he asked abruptly, "Why did you do it?"

"How did you know?"

"I saw you hand one of the envelopes to the New York bus driver, but I think I'd have guessed sooner or later. They were so like you. Why, Sherry?"

She told him about her reaction to his rejection of *The Shining Years.* "I guess I just wanted to — to show you I could write and hold your interest. And then I met you and . . ." her voice trailed off. "It was just a joke, really."

He turned on a side road beside the river, shut off the motor, and turned to face her. "What are you going to do, Sherry? I didn't intend to say anything after your Major came home but we've got to have it out, plain and clear, between us. I love you and you know it. There was one wonderful moment when I thought you loved me. If you are still in love with Carleton, you won't hear another word from me, but if you aren't — and you don't act happy — then break this thing off now. It will be kinder for all of us."

"I couldn't do that, Stanley." Sherry looked down at the hands clasped tightly on her lap. "All that time Doug was in danger, he was wounded, he went through awful things. . . . No, he hasn't told me about them and he won't. Even if he were free to tell me he wouldn't use anything like that as an argument in his favor. But he counted on me and he trusted me to be loyal to him. I can't walk out on him now. The most I can do is to postpone our marriage for a little while so we can get to know each other again. Maybe in that time he will find that he was as mistaken as I was. But if he doesn't —"

"Mistaken!" Stanley's face lighted up and he reached for her.

"No. Stanley." She did not move but her quiet voice stopped him.

"All right, let's admit that you are willing to sacrifice yourself, but do you feel you have any right to sacrifice me too?"

There was a long pause and then she said painfully, "That has to be Doug's decision."

After a moment Stanley turned the key in the switch. They did not exchange any further words until they reached the *Courier*.

Stanley went to his cubbyhole office where he began to write an editorial on the hidden ways in which unscrupulous politicians buy votes and goodwill:

Only the corrupt or the stupid person falls for the open bribe, but there are other methods, more insidious, harder to detect, by which the same results are achieved. The favor granted, the casual present bestowed on the unwary, the conferring of benefits that make a decent human being feel indebted. Of all the warnings the one to remain freshest in my memory is *Timeo Danaos et dona ferentes*.

Now bring on your Santa Claus, Stanley mentally challenged Denton, and shouted for Dick to come and get his copy.

A few minutes later Sherry, who had written an account of the forthcoming dinner party at the Dentons', took her copy down to the printer. Dick, who had been reading Stanley's editorial, looked up gloomily.

"Hi, Sherry, what you got this time? More dizzy activities of the idle rich?"

"Oh, for heaven's sake, Dick, what's got into you? You are always grousing about something."

"This stuff Holbrook is handing out sounds so noble it turns my stomach. A guy like that, stinking rich, so he can afford to refuse a little extra money on the side. He doesn't need it. I'd like to have him exposed, have people see him as he is, and stop the *Courier* from spreading his ideas. Yeah, sometimes I think they are right."

"Who are right?"

"The people who say papers like the *Courier* should be put out of business, and people like Holbrook too."

"I'm ashamed of you!" Sherry's face flushed. "There's no place in the world where a man can get ahead as he can in this country. Look at the men who come from no background at all and get to be president or the heads of great corporations. They didn't get there by feeling sorry for themselves or by resenting what other people have and trying to destroy them. Any idiot can destroy but it takes guts to build. You're only seventeen and you are strong and healthy and there is no reason why you can't make something of yourself. But you'll never do it by complaining. You'd be smarter to try to carry your own weight instead of carrying placards." She slammed her copy down beside him. "If it doesn't exhaust you, give this to the printer."

XI

WHEN Eve had removed her sable coat in the little hut near the skating rink, and sat down to put on her skating shoes, Doug gave a low whistle of admiration. Up to now she had skated in a sport skirt or wool slacks. But today she wore a skating costume of white, with a short full skirt that made her look like a powder puff. She was unbelievably beautiful. Under the frank admiration in his eyes, that had nothing of the bold appreciation expressed by Thomas Denton, she found herself flushing.

"I thought," she said, with the diffidence that always amazed him in this lovely woman, "that it would be more comfortable, but I feel rather conspicuous."

He suppressed his smile. Whatever she wore she would be conspicuous. People always turned for a second look at her as though they had not believed their eyes the first time.

"It's fine," he said casually, "and you'll be much more comfortable. Ready?" He took her hands and they started out slowly and then increased their speed; when they had swept around in a wide curve she laughed exultantly. "Now I want to try it by myself."

"Sure?"

She nodded and moved off with so much assurance that he ceased worrying about her. After watching her for a few minutes he was satisfied that she would be all right and he skated on by himself. Already he found the exercise less painful.

What fun it would be if Sherry could share these skating parties and have a little gaiety for a change instead of working all day. Well, that would be over by the first of the year. He would teach her to enjoy playing as she used to. Having to work so hard made her forget the joy of having a good time. After what he'd been through he never intended to spend an unnecessary minute being too serious over anything.

He was not so absorbed in his thoughts that he took his watchful eyes off Eve, skating easily through the crowd and unconscious of the looks of admiration she received. He was aware before she was that she was tiring and he joined her to suggest they call it a day.

They had almost accidentally drifted into the habit of lunching at the Mayflower Inn where a table by the window had come to be reserved for them, and where, after getting warm in front of the big fire in the attractive living room, they lunched at leisure and in a relaxed way. Eve was, he thought, the least demanding woman he had ever encountered, as well as the most beautiful. He was aware, as she was not, that the sympathetic and interested eyes of the waitress assumed she was watching the progress of a love affair. He wondered, in some amusement, what she would think if she overheard the long conversations that took place at the window table.

Just how it had happened Eve did not know, but she

had told Doug about Bill and their happy marriage and the vacuum that had followed his death when she had decided that her life had ended. They talked about Billy and discussed child psychology and child training, the proper balance between discipline and indulgence, and argued about the right schools. On one occasion they went so far as to discuss the best colleges. Doug had been the one to end that particular discussion by bursting into a laugh.

"Next thing we'll have married him off and start to worry about the grandchildren." And Eve had joined in the laughter.

Not that all the talk had been about her affairs. They had discussions about Doug's future career and made and rejected half a dozen preposterous schemes. Doug declared that his boyhood ambition had been to manage a circus and they weighed the idea solemnly.

"Or why not study wild game in Africa?"

"I've always wanted to be a deep-sea diver. I ought to get used to the climate down there as it may be man's last retreat."

"How about a shooting gallery at country fairs?"

"I'm a city boy myself. I was born in San Francisco and I feel more at home in the West than I do here."

"How about Sherry? Where does she want to live?"

Doug was taken aback. For the time being he had forgotten about Sherry. "I don't know," he confessed.

But that evening when he took Sherry out to dinner he remembered to ask her. Actually it was Sherry who brought up the subject. For the first half hour they talked fast and laughed a lot but somehow they did not seem as companionable as they had been in the past; they were both trying too hard. Doug found it more of a strain than it was to talk to Eve, who demanded nothing and whose soft laugh accompanied even his feeblest sallies.

In the whirlwind courtship he had not noticed that, for all her gaiety, Sherry was essentially a serious person. She had plunged into all the entertainment he offered as wholeheartedly as she did everything because she wanted to share his interests. He felt now that he was not quite measuring up to her standards and he wondered, fleetingly, whether Holbrook did. As far as he could see Holbrook was far too engrossed in his newspaper to provide serious competition. There had been only that one moment when the two men had looked at each other and mutely acknowledged their rivalry.

"How long," Sherry asked now, "can you afford to go without a job, Doug? You don't seem to be planning at all for the future."

He smiled lazily at her, arching his eyebrow. "I'm young yet and solvent. After all, I'm not exactly a pauper, you know. There's about a hundred thousand stuck away in the old sock for a rainy day."

Sherry was troubled. She studied the good-looking carefree face. "But don't you want to *do* something?"

"Such as?"

"Well, what did you do before you went into the army? I know so little about you, Doug, and you know so little about me."

He smiled at her confidently. She was a cute little trick. He'd never find a dearer girl anywhere and when she tilted her head on one side earnestly like that and looked inquiringly at him he wanted to reach across the table and kiss her, regardless of the waitress and the other diners, one of whom, a long-nosed fellow with receding hair, seemed to be taking a great deal of interest in Sherry.

"I enjoyed myself," he admitted. "My father has bought up a lot of land on the coast and turned it into a retirement resort. I can always run it if I feel like it."

"Is that what you'd like to do?"

He shrugged. This wasn't as amusing as making up absurd careers to entertain Eve, who was content to laugh at them and did not attempt to force him into choosing some boring occupation. Life was too short to waste that way. But Doug found himself somewhat on the defensive. In an attempt to switch her attention away from his future job he said, "By the way, do you know there's a lot of talk going around about the *Courier* and Holbrook? I hear it at the shops and in the garage and at the skating pond. People say that Holbrook is a Red and that the *Courier* is subversive and should be stopped.

"Ridiculous!" Sherry said hotly.

"Probably." He was indifferent. "Just gossip, I suppose. I thought I might pass it on but I am sure Holbrook knows what he is doing."

"He does."

Doug cocked an eyebrow. "You leap onto the barricades in his defense, don't you, the minute you hear his name? He's big enough to take care of himself, sweetie."

Sherry flushed but, with a healthy appetite, finished the last bite of her lemon pie while he watched her in amusement. Then she said, her face clouding, "Doug, you don't think — that is, there can't be anyone trying to damage the *Courier* or Stanley, can there?"

"Why would anyone bother? How important could a small-town weekly be to anyone?"

ii

"Well, what will it be?" Doug asked when they had finished dinner. "There's a good movie in the village." At least you didn't have to talk in a movie.

"Doug, would you mind awfully if we didn't go?"

"Why no, of course, darling. Whatever you like. Name your own program. After all, that is why I am here. Remember?"

"I keep thinking of the rumors you've been hearing about the *Courier*. I'm sure they are being circulated by Thomas Denton."

"Careful about using names in a small place like this where everyone knows everyone else," he cautioned her, aware that the attention of the long-nosed man had never wavered from their table.

"Sorry." She lowered her voice. "I'll bet that is where Dick's money is coming from and why he is all stirred up about the *Courier*. Doug, would you take me to see Mrs. Flint?"

"Who is she?"

"Her son is an office boy at the *Courier* who has been spending too much money. His mother works as a checker in the supermarket, which is open tonight."

"You are really worried about this, aren't you? Okay, let's go."

"You are so kind, Doug. I don't deserve it."

He grinned at her. "As long as you realize your luck, kid."

He helped her into the Volkswagen. As he backed out of the parking lot he saw the long-nosed man get into a white Ford. He drove slowly back to Waring, and behind him the Ford never tried to decrease the distance between them, never dropped far behind. He thought of mentioning it to Sherry but it did not seem important.

"I won't be long," Sherry said when they reached the shopping center. Mrs. Flint, a thin woman with hollow cheeks and sunken eyes, was busy at a checking counter, putting groceries into heavy paper bags, the weight of some of them clearly taxing her frail strength.

"Good evening, Mrs. Flint."

"You are Miss Winthrop, aren't you? Is it about Dick? Is he in trouble?"

"I don't know," Sherry admitted, "but I've been worried about him and I thought I'd like to talk to you. He's been different lately. Perhaps you have noticed it."

"He's a good boy." His mother was on the defensive. "Kids his age will be wild, you know, but it doesn't mean anything." She broke off to ring up a grocery order. "What have you noticed that is different?"

"Well, for one thing the wild way he talks about the *Courier* and the Establishment and saying they should both be destroyed. I began to worry for fear he would do something — silly." The word wasn't adequate but it was sufficient to alarm his mother.

"I've been bothered about him for quite a while. He has always been so good and so reliable and after his father died he was a real help to me. I don't have any training and when I had to go to work all I could find was this job and Dick helped all he could, shoveling snow in the winter and mowing lawns in summer. Of course he's not trained to hold a high-paid job."

Sherry laughed. "Well, after all, he's only seventeen."

"Dick isn't college material. He's slow in some ways. I don't know where he'd fit in. But he's not satisfied with the job he has."

"How much do you love your job?" Sherry asked bluntly.

"Oh, that's different, because I have to have it."

"I'm awfully afraid, Mrs. Flint, that he has got into bad company."

Mrs. Flint was encouraged by the warm sympathy in Sherry's manner. She said that she had been able to keep track of Dick until her illness when he had met some people whom he did not bring home. He was out at all hours, and when she questioned him he said he was old enough to live his own life and he didn't want his mother interfering.

The lights flickered and Mrs. Flint gave a sigh of relief. "We're closing now."

"My fiancé is waiting for me. We'll drive you home, Mrs. Flint."

The tired face lighted. "You're just as nice as Dick said."

Doug started the motor and then waited for a moment. The long-nosed guy from the Mayflower had followed Sherry into the market and now he was waiting for Doug to move. As he drove out of the parking lot the white Ford followed. Something was going on. As soon as he had left Sherry at the Folly he was going to find out what the guy was up to.

Mrs. Flint lived in a shabby rundown house next to a garage. She looked quickly at the windows and her face fell. "Dick's not home yet! I suppose he had to work over-time again."

Sherry's lips parted to say that Dick had never been asked to work overtime but she closed them again. Time enough for that later, if it became necessary.

"He gets tired, of course, but it brings in such a lot of extra money. We can certainly use it."

"What worries you most, Mrs. Flint? Is it the kind of friends Dick has?"

"Well, of course, his friends look like hippies, but then they all try to look that way now, don't they? I figure someone is trying to poison my boy's mind. But that's not the worst. A couple of weeks ago he offered to pay the rent because he said he'd got a raise. Then a few days later he bought a motorcycle and a heavy lined coat and a lot of little things. And he said that was from overtime. But when I sent his suit to the cleaner his empty pay envelope was in it with the amount written on it and his salary had not been raised. That's why I've been worry-ing about that overtime pay. Then I saw your face when I mentioned it and I knew he wasn't working overtime." She leaned forward, her face tense with anxiety. "So what is he doing and where is that money coming from?" Her hands twisted together, pulled at each other desperately. "What is he doing for it? Every time there is a knock at the door I wonder if he is in trouble."

"I keep wondering if he has been persuaded to spread some ugly rumors around town about Mr. Holbrook and the *Courier*."

"If he is taking money for something like that I know he wouldn't have done it if I hadn't been sick so long and used up all our savings."

"Why don't you ask him straight out, Mrs. Flint? And tell him if he is in trouble and I can help him I will. Honestly I will."

"I'll do that, Miss Winthrop. You've made me feel better just by giving me a chance to talk it out. I'll follow your advice and talk to Dick tonight, but if you'd talk to him yourself he'd really listen to you."

"I'll do it first thing in the morning," Sherry promised.

iii

Somewhat to Sherry's surprise but to her relief, Doug said good night abruptly, turned the Volkswagen and was down the driveway before Wilson had time to open the door for her.

Down on the road Doug saw a car turn off the Green. He followed, thinking that this time he was the pursuer. There was no point in speculating as to what this was all about; he'd find out sooner or later. Apparently Holbrook had been making powerful enemies and their interest extended to Sherry. Doug's lips compressed. He was not going to stand back and permit Sherry to walk into any danger or even any unpleasantness for the sake of the *Courier*. Then he remembered her talk with Mrs. Flint and her warmhearted offer of help for a boy who appeared to have gone pretty thoroughly off the rails. Doug smiled ruefully to himself. It would be no easy task to protect Sherry from her compassion and her championship.

The white Ford had turned the corner, had passed the garage, and had parked across the street from the Flint house. Doug, switching off his lights, pulled into the driveway of an empty house, made himself as comfortable as he could in the cramped space and prepared for a long wait. There was little doubt in his mind now that Long-nose was waiting for Dick. He had followed Sherry and knew that she had talked to Mrs. Flint.

Doug groped for a cigarette and then returned the package to his pocket. The glow of a cigarette would be like a beacon in the darkness of this quiet street.

His thoughts switched back to Sherry and her belief that he should be eager to plunge into some kind of work and build a career. She was ambitious not for money or for power but to have him use to the full all his energy and his intelligence. The trouble was, Doug admitted, that such a life of effort did not appeal to him. He wanted a pleasant and easygoing life. He could easily have one. He'd have to find a way to make Sherry see there was a lot of living she knew nothing of.

His thoughts drifted on to Eve. She had really knocked the breath out of him that morning in her skating costume. The loveliest thing on earth. And no vanity. Usually she was unaware of the eyes that followed her; when she did notice them she simply thought that people were rude to stare so and dismissed them from her mind. You could really relax with a girl like Eve. She spoke of herself, with humility, as being content to be just a housewife, as though Helen of Troy had so described herself, though Helen, as he recalled, represented few of the domestic virtues which Eve possessed in abundance. Like himself, he thought, she had no driving ambition.

The silence of the night was shattered by the sound of a motorcycle, which wheeled around the corner and came to a stop outside the Flint house.

"Dick," the man in the Ford called softly. The boy

wheeled around, startled, took one quick look at the second-floor windows, and went across the street.

The low-voiced colloquy went on for some time. Doug was too far away to hear a word but he could see, by Dick's gestures, that he was arguing violently, refusing to do something. A hand came out and fastened on the boy's arm, then the other hand slammed against the side of his head, hurling him off balance. The motor roared into life and the Ford pulled away.

It made a U-turn and passed Doug. As soon as it had turned the corner he started to follow. It was child's play as there wasn't another car in sight. It was equally easy, of course, for Long-nose to detect the lights of the following car. If it had not been for the brutality of the man's attitude in striking Dick's defenseless face, Doug would have abandoned the chase, but he could not let the man escape. In some way he obviously threatened Sherry.

The man ahead had begun some curious maneuvers, turning sharply to right or left at corners, obviously aware that he was being followed and determined to shake off his tail. Doug decided that it would be wisest to drop behind, which proved to be a mistake. When he reached the corner there were no lights. The street was deserted. Where could the man have gone in so few seconds?

He had moved on for two blocks when he saw car lights flash on, saw a car back, turn, and disappear around the corner. Long-nose had simply turned out his lights and waited for Doug to pass him. He had fallen for one of the oldest tricks in the book, Doug thought in disgust. He gave up and drove back to the Mayflower Inn.

XII

SHERRY found Ellen alone at the breakfast table next morning. Ellen explained that Stanley was still sleeping. It had been after four when she had heard him coming upstairs the night before. For a week he had been getting little sleep, he looked much too tired, and he was losing weight.

"He's in love with you, my dear."

Sherry made no reply. After a moment Ellen said, "I am not trying to pry, as I think you know, but I am very fond of you both and I'd like to see you happy together."

"There is Doug. I can't do that to Doug."

"To let him marry a woman who doesn't love him is hardly fair either, is it?"

Sherry made a despairing gesture. "Aunt Ellen, what would you do?"

"I can't help you there, my dear. No one could. But I can tell you what I would not do! Prolong an impossible and painful situation."

The weather did nothing to relieve Sherry's gloom when she left the Folly and started down the driveway to the Green. The sky was a dark, leaden gray and the air nipped her cheeks and nose and fingers. But her first sight of the Green stopped Sherry in her tracks and shocked her out of her depression. During the night a gigantic tree had been set up and decorated with lights, tinsel chains, monstrous plastic candy canes, gift-wrapped packages, and an outsize star at the top.

Sherry laughed until she was limp. Waring was running a close second to the tree in Rockefeller Center, but where the latter was dwarfed by its surroundings this one loomed over the village like the Eiffel Tower. When Thomas Denton made a gesture it was a big one. But the thought of Denton drove the laughter from her face and she began to walk swiftly.

Just what she had feared she did not know but she was relieved to find the *Courier* busy as usual. Dick's shining new motorcycle was parked behind the building. Before going upstairs she looked for him but he was not in sight. She waved to Jones, who was setting type. "Is Dick around?"

"Is he ever where he is needed?" the printer grunted. "I've about had it with Dick. He acts more screwy every day. From now on he toes the line and does what he's told when he's told or he will be out on his ear. I'd have fired him a long time ago if it hadn't been for his mother, but she's a real nice woman and she's had a hard time of it."

Seeing that Jones was thoroughly out of temper, Sherry did not ask him to send Dick up to see her. Time wasn't that important. She would look for him later.

Almost before she had time to strip off her wool gloves and get settled, the telephone began to ring with stories about holiday parties, an engagement, a European trip planned by one citizen, house guests being entertained by another. She was so busy that her personal preoccupations were driven to the back of her mind. Now and then in a quiet interval she remembered that she had promised Mrs. Flint to talk to Dick. Then something would distract her attention.

She was brought back to an awareness of him by hearing Perkins exploding with wrath. As he was generally a quiet, almost a retiring man, she was startled.

"What's wrong, Mr. Perkins?"

"If I've told Dick once I've told him a dozen times that he is expected to keep this wastepaper basket empty and to come up here every morning at ten to pick up the copy I have ready for the printer. Now I'll have to go down myself and I'm expecting an important call. When I get through with that boy —"

The telephone rang and Sherry reached for it. The voice that shouted in her ear was loud, unrecognizable.

"What?" she asked. "What? I can't understand you."

"Sherry!" That hoarse voice was Stanley's. "Get out at once. Do you hear? At once! Don't wait a minute, even for a coat. And shout that they are all to clear the building without delay. Danger. Hurry!"

The connection was broken. For a moment Sherry stared at the telephone as though expecting it to answer a question. Then she leaped to her feet and called, "Get out of the building at once. That was Mr. Holbrook on the phone. There's danger. Don't wait for anything."

She ran down the stairs, calling to the printer, "Get out of the building. Hurry. Tell Dick."

The printer looked up from his typesetting. "Are you trying to play Dick's game? Starting a bomb scare? When he started acting like a clown, and running around pretending he was looking for a bomb I'd had it. I knocked him out and I hope it will teach him a lesson."

"Bomb? BOMB! That's what Stanley meant. It's real. It's real."

The printer stared at her, open-mouthed, and then he lunged past her and out-of-doors. She could hear his feet pounding on the frozen ground.

"Dick! Dick!"

There was no reply. Sherry looked around frantically, saw the shoe beside the big press, saw the leg, saw Dick lying full length on his back, a reddish spot under one eye, breathing noisily.

She knelt beside him. "Dick!" She shook him, slapped his face. There was no response. She moved her fingers gently over his head, lifted it, felt the warm stickiness of blood.

Sobbing with panic she bent over, got her hands under his arms and tried to drag him across the floor. She had never thought of him as a big boy but now he seemed to weigh a ton, a heavy body that resisted all her efforts to move it.

"Dick!" she screamed and moved backward a few feet, dragging that heavy inert body after her.

She heard the clatter of feet on the stairs as the men raced for the out-of-doors and safety. Why didn't one of them offer to help her? But, she realized, except for Jones, no one knew that she was here. They assumed that she had been the first to reach safety.

Her heart was pounding and her breath came rasping in her throat. A dark fog seemed to cover her eyes and blur her vision. She sobbed to herself, "I can't do it! I can't," but she knew that she must. She couldn't leave a fellow creature to die if she could prevent it.

She tightened her grip and began that slow, agonizingly slow, backward shuffle toward the door and safety. One step. A second. A third. Then Dick's body stopped following her. One foot was caught on the leg of a chair. She let him down gently and ran to release his foot, grasped him under the arms again, took a long breath, and in the stillness she heard the ticking of an alarm clock. A time bomb!

If her progress had seemed intolerably slow before, it was infuriatingly more so with that inexorable ticking, measuring off the time that was left. Now she wondered that she had not heard it before. It seemed to be the only sound left in the world.

Tick — tick.

Bent over as she was her back seemed to be breaking. She kept stumbling over things so that she was afraid she would lose her balance and fall on Dick whose body, heavier every minute, moved so sluggishly, so reluctantly along, not a foot at a time but an inch.

Tick — tick.

One hand slipped and lost its hold and she saw that it was smeared with Dick's blood running down from the wound on the back of his head. Instinctively she wanted to wipe away that disgusting stickiness but she forced herself to take hold once more, to take another backward step and another.

Tick — tick.

She had believed that further exertion was impossible but terror seemed to give her new strength. It's adrenaline, she told herself crazily. They say it's adrenaline that saves you when you are scared. They say —

There was a strange sort of puff, a kind of giant gasp, and then she watched the side wall of the printing shop bulge outward. In that moment of shock Sherry did not hear the explosion of the bomb. She heard nothing at all. But she saw the wall blow out, saw dust and debris mushroom up and then begin to settle slowly, saw plaster drop from the ceiling and strike Dick on the chest, saw a great block of plaster drop away and fall. She watched, bemused. It did not occur to her to dodge.

ii

The call had come at eight o'clock and Wilson had taken it. It was after ten when Stanley came down to breakfast. After a week that was nearly sleepless he had slept as though he had been slugged. He paused in the lobby to greet Doug who had come to take Eve skating and heard him say to Wilson, "I suppose Miss Winthrop has left already."

"Oh, yes, she went at eight. Well, just a little before eight because the call came at eight sharp and she had already gone."

"What call was that?" Stanley asked in surprise. "People aren't trying to give her their social notes here, are they?"

"It was just someone acting smart," Wilson said. "A disguised voice said to tell her to be sure not to go to the *Courier* this morning, that it would be dangerous."

Ellen had come down with Eve and, mindful of what

Sherry had told her of the rumors going around, exclaimed, "Stanley, I don't like it! Suppose it was a
genuine warning."

"Cool it, Aunt Ellen. Who would want to harm the
Courier building?"

"Someone might," Doug put in. He repeated the rumors
he had been hearing and described Sherry's visit to Mrs.
Flint and the man who had followed her. "Look here,
I don't like this a bit. Excuse me, Mr. Holbrook. I'm
going down to the *Courier* myself."

Wilson said, "There's a telephone call for you, Mr.
Holbrook."

"Later. Take a message."

"She said it was desperately important and she sounded
that way. Just distracted."

"She!" Stanley went into the library and picked up the
extension. "Yes? This is Holbrook speaking."

"This is Mary Flint, Dick's mother."

"Dick?"

"He works for you in the printing shop."

"Oh, yes. Well?"

"I just tried to call him and I can't reach him. I'm
frightened. He told me he was going to try to dismantle
the bomb but it's been so long, over two hours —"

"Good God!" Stanley disconnected and telephoned
Sherry to issue his warning. He was running when he
reached the lobby, shrugging into his coat.

"Have Roberts bring the car around right away." He
was aware of the tense, anxious faces. "It's a bomb."

"I've got the Volkswagen at the door," Doug said.

"Let's go."

"How about the police?"

"I'll take care of that," Ellen said, her voice calm. "Don't wait."

"I'll come with you," Eve offered.

"No." Stanley brushed past her. "You'd only be in the way."

Doug gripped her hand. "Good girl," he said, smiled at her, and then he was gone, running for his car, the key in his hand.

Eve clasped her hands, "Oh, Aunt Ellen!"

"Keep your head," Ellen said tartly, ready to discourage hysteria. "We can't afford to get rattled." She went into the library and dialed the police. "It may be a false alarm, some perverted idea of a joke, but it may be genuine, and if so there may be real danger. I don't know — perhaps I should inform the fire department or call an ambulance —"

"Leave it to us, ma'am. That's what we are here for."

"And you'll hurry?" For the first time her voice shook a little.

"We informed a radio car while you were talking. They'll be there in a couple of minutes."

"Oh, thank God!" Ellen put down the telephone, her hands shaking. She turned to Eve who was white and trembling. "There's nothing we can do, but, oh, poor Sherry!"

Wilson came out. "Mrs. Davis, if I'd done something about that call at eight this morning — but Miss Winthrop had already left and I thought it was a joke."

"You aren't to blame, Wilson."

"I can't help blaming myself. She was always so pleasant and nice and gay around the house."

"Don't! You sound as though she were — as though

something had already happened." Ellen went upstairs to her own rooms in the tower where she gave herself up to a woman's most difficult task, waiting.

iii

The Volkswagen rattled over the little bridge, regardless of the "10 miles an hour" sign. Neither of the grim-faced men spoke. Stanley leaned forward as though by sheer will power he could force greater speed out of the little car. Doug, with the accelerator pressed to the floor, kept one hand on the horn to warn the unwary to make way for him.

For both of them the sight of the *Courier* building, intact and looking as usual, was an enormous relief. Then they heard the sound of a siren rising and falling behind them.

"It's the police," Doug said, glancing in the rear-view mirror.

Standing at some distance from the building, and shivering with cold, were the employees. Stanley looked from one to another. "Sherry!" he shouted. "Where is Sherry?"

It was Jones who said, startled, "Why she never came out. She and Dick —"

Before the car had rolled to a stop Stanley had the door open and he leaped out, running toward the building, ignoring the warnings shouted by Perkins. Then his ears were deafened by the explosion of the bomb, and the side of the building bulged out.

There were pounding feet and a policeman seized his

arm, trying to hold him back. "Stay here, Mr. Holbrook. It's not safe."

"Sherry's in there," he cried. "Sherry's in there." He broke away and ran with Doug beside him and the policeman close behind. The printing shop was a shambles, the equipment a mass of wreckage, the type scattered, the wall blown out and plaster falling from the ceiling. The air was so thick with dust that it was difficult to see.

Halfway between the wall and the door a boy was lying unconscious and, crumpled over him, a girl with bright hair, its brightness intensified by the sticky red of blood, lay motionless. As Stanley, with a cry of horror, lunged forward, the policeman shouted, "Careful! We don't want to bring down any more of the ceiling on them. Easy does it."

The two big grim men responded to the voice of authority and let the policeman take the lead, moving slowly, cautiously, testing every footstep. The policeman swallowed an oath as the cement shattered by the bomb broke under his foot and his leg plunged into a hole. He hauled himself up and after that they moved still more slowly.

At last they reached the two people who lay so quietly, so unconcerned with the danger all around them. As Stanley bent over Sherry he was shoved roughly aside and Doug, having assured himself no bones were broken, gathered her into his arms. "She's mine. Remember?" He carried her out to safety followed by the policeman and Stanley carrying Dick between them.

iv

It was mid-afternoon when Sherry opened her eyes in bewilderment. She was lying on a neat white bed in a neat small room. On the other bed a patient, propped on her elbow, was watching her with avid curiosity.

"So you're awake at last!" She rang the bell for the nurse. "They wanted to be informed as soon as you were conscious. Well, of all the excitement! And I thought it would be dull having to lie in bed for three days. Such goings-on! The *Courier* got bombed and you and some guy got knocked out and saved and you turn out to live at the castle. Talk about the movies! I wouldn't exchange this for my favorite TV program. In fact I haven't had the television set on since they brought you in, looking white as death and your face and hands and clothes smeared with blood. My! And people coming in to look at you every five minutes. And flowers! They must have bought out Burgess's shop. Just look at that display, will you?"

Cautiously Sherry turned her head, decided it would not fall off, and looked at the masses of roses, carnations, and plants on the table beside her bed.

"How's Dick?" Her voice was low; she felt if she spoke loudly she might awaken the pain that lurked behind her eyes.

"Who's he?"

"The boy who was hurt."

"I don't know, except that he is alive. Maybe that is

too bad. Someone was talking in the hall and said he was the one who set the bomb."

A nurse came in, smiling when she saw Sherry's eyes were open, but she gently moved the hand with which Sherry was groping at her head. She took her pulse and temperature and nodded with satisfaction.

"You're doing just fine." As she saw Sherry's indignant expression she smiled. "I know you don't feel like it, but the doctor says you'll be fit as a fiddle tomorrow and you can go home then. You just have a scalp wound but they had to take five stitches. It bled a lot, of course; scalp wounds always do." She laughed outright. "Your boy-friend is in a worse state than you are. Thought you were half killed. He's in the waiting room now, pacing up and down like an expectant father, and refusing to leave until he can see for himself how you are. I guess we'd better let him come in before he disrupts the hospital."

Sherry turned her face to the door. But it was Doug, of course, who came into the room, looked at her earnestly, took her hand and bent to kiss her. "Oh, darling, why didn't you run when Holbrook told you to?"

"Dick was still there and unconscious and couldn't help himself so I had to help him."

He covered her hand with his. "You're a little heroine."

"Oh, nonsense. Anyone would have done it, though I can't seem to remember how we got out. Is Dick going to be all right?"

"He'll live." Doug was not interested in Dick. "Though why you should care what happens to him I don't know Apparently he is the guy who set the bomb."

And again Sherry could hear that inexorable tick-tick as the seconds were eaten away and the margin of safety dwindled. She wondered whether she would ever again be able to listen to the ticking of a clock without fear. She managed to say, "Dick was just a tool."

"Tool or not, you aren't going to be soft on violence, are you?"

"It just seems so unfair that the real culprit won't be punished and there's no proof. We don't know who got in touch with Dick."

"I do," Doug told her unexpectedly.

"You do!" She tried to sit upright and then clutched her head with both hands. When the pain had decreased to bearable proportions she asked, "What happened to the *Courier?* Was there much damage?"

"You're a real girl Friday, aren't you? Why don't you think of yourself for a change? Well, this guy set the bomb and then he seems to have had a change of heart. He called just after you left this morning to warn you not to go to the *Courier*. Then later his mother telephoned. I didn't get that part clear except that she knew about the bomb and that she was scared. Well, the kid was acting so queer that the printer got fed up and hit him. Apparently Dick struck his head on something when he fell, but whether he has a fractured skull or a concussion I don't know. Frankly I don't care. I'm sorry for the boy's mother, who seems to be a nice woman who has had a lot of bad luck, but I'm tired to death of these kids who go off the rails for kicks and leave it to someone else to patch up all the damage they've done and give them another chance."

"But what about the *Courier?*" Sherry repeated, believing that she could understand what he said better if two demons with hammers would stop hitting her on the head.

"Oh, the place is a shambles, of course. But newsmen seem to rally to each other's support when they aren't competing for circulation. A weekly from upstate has offered its facilities until Holbrook can make other arrangements. He is up there now. The police are investigating and a special bomb squad came up and has roped off the building with a big sign UNSAFE, as the whole thing may collapse at any time. It was an old building, you know."

Doug turned to survey the array of flowers with a critical eye. "Best I could do."

"They are lovely. Really lovely, Doug."

A bell sounded in the hall and the nurse looked in to say, "Visiting hours are over. You'll have to leave now. She'll be home tomorrow."

Doug bent over and kissed Sherry. "I should never have listened to you. I should have married you out of hand if I had to beat you to do it. Then this would never have happened."

He had barely gone when the door opened stealthily and Neil Gordon looked in. He came in as cautiously as a thief in the night and approached Sherry's bed on tiptoe, acting so surreptitious that she had to smother a laugh.

He adjusted the shades and then proceeded to take three pictures of her.

"Neil, for heaven's sake, what do you think you are doing?"

"Hush! I'm not supposed to be here but I'm covering the story for the *Courier* and an upstate paper too, the biggest deal I've ever had. Give me your impressions real fast before they throw me out."

"Ask one of the others. They know as much as I do."

"But you caught Dick Flint in the act! There's never been anything like it."

"I did nothing of the kind." Regardless of the lancing pain in her head, Sherry sat bolt upright. "I didn't catch Dick at anything. He had been knocked unconscious and I was doing my best to drag him out. That's all I know and I'll never forgive you if you try to make people believe that Dick —"

The door opened and a middle-aged man with a stethoscope around his neck came into the room. He glared at Neil. "The rules apply to you. Out!" He opened the door and waited until the disgruntled young reporter went out. Then he came up to the bed and took Sherry's pulse, inspecting her. He put down her hand and nodded. "Well, you're out of the woods."

"How about Dick?"

"The boy who was with you at the *Courier?* He'd be a lot better off if you hadn't moved him." The doctor's manner was severe. "Haven't you ever been told that you should never move a head injury? Judging by the condition of his clothes you actually dragged him!"

Unexpectedly laughter bubbled up in Sherry. "Next time there is a bomb scare I'll let him stay there," she promised

XIII

I 'LL never forget this," Stanley said. "It's one debt I don't even know how to repay."

The upstate newspaperman grinned at him. "When my paper gets bombed out you can give me a hand. Actually we have more space here than we can use. Took over this building because it was cheaper than putting up a new one. Another thing, we don't keep our presses busy, which is wasteful. I'd been figuring on doing some job printing when our paper is out, so you can use the premises as long as you like. Matter of fact, what you have offered in the way of rent is more than it's worth but I'm not the guy to refuse a bargain. Anyhow it causes me no pain at all to be able to disappoint the people who tried to put the *Courier* out of business. I can tell you one thing. No one is going to plant any bombs in this building. I'm putting in a night watchman as of today. You'd better look out for yourself, Holbrook. A guy who would not hesitate to kill the people who were in the *Courier* building won't stop at much."

"I am aware of that."

A boy ran into the room bringing copies of the *Courier* just off the press. A banner headline read: COURIER BOMBED.

There were two pictures, one of the building with a gaping wall, the other of a girl in a hospital bed, her head bandaged, her eyes enormous in her small face.

Yesterday morning a bomb exploded in the *Courier* building, ripping out one wall, destroying the press, and causing considerable damage. The structure, according to a building inspector, is a total loss.

Six employees were in the building at the time. An anonymous warning to Stanley Holbrook, owner and publisher, at his home led him to call the paper and order everyone to leave.

Miss Sherry Winthrop, society editor, relayed the warning and on her way out discovered Richard Flint, office boy, unconscious. In a heroic effort to drag him to safety she nearly lost her own life.

A bomb squad found proof that the bomb was a homemade affair. All evidence is in the hands of our competent police force, who believe that the perpetrator of this cowardly crime will soon be under arrest.

Stanley Holbrook announced today that publication of the *Courier* will continue without interruption because of the generosity of the *Weekly Gazette*, which has offered the use of its facilities.

The week's paper had gone to bed, and Stanley drove slowly back to Waring. There had been a sudden rise in temperature, turning the white snow to a gray slush that sprayed up as he drove. He went over the past thirty-six hours from the time when he had taken Mrs. Flint's panic-stricken call. There had been his warning to Sherry and the wild ride to the *Courier,* the discovery that Sherry had not left the building, and the horror of the explosion.

Then came the nightmare of that cautious approach toward the two still bodies for fear the building would fall in on them, and Carleton brushing him aside to pick up Sherry, saying, "She's mine. Remember?" He wasn't likely to forget. He had had to stand aside while another man carried the woman he loved to safety.

At least, Stanley thought, I know now the lengths to which a man like Denton will go to get his way. He will not hesitate to destroy property. He will not hesitate to destroy human life. There might easily have been a dozen or more people in the building when the bomb went off. It's no longer a question merely of the *Courier;* this is one war I have enlisted in for the duration.

It was nearly dark when he drove up before the Folly. Roberts came around the side of the house. "I'll put the car up if you won't be needing it again."

"Not tonight. You aren't supposed to be on duty so late." Stanley noticed the grim expression on the outdoor man's face.

"I had to go pick up Mrs. Holbrook and get some new tires. Four new tires."

"Four!"

Roberts nodded. "That's right. She called me from the library in great excitement. She had left the station wagon while she went in to get some books for Miss Winthrop and when she came out all four tires had been slashed."

"She wasn't hurt?"

"Oh, no, and the car's all right. I've just been over it with a fine-tooth comb. But from now on I'm going to check both cars before they leave this place. It looks to me like someone is gunning for you bad, Mr. Holbrook; a bombing one day and this kind of sabotage the next day."

Stanley nodded, started to go into the house, turned back. "Look here, Roberts, someone took a chance on killing six people in the *Courier* and there might have been twice as many because people drop in all the time. That kind of violence may spread to my own household. I don't want to have any of you taking risks."

Roberts smiled sourly. "No one is going to scare us out of here, Mr. Holbrook. We're in this fight with you. Wilson and I have talked it over and the maids are fighting mad and ready to pour boiling oil out of the windows on anyone who tries to make trouble here, and you know Mrs. Davis. She don't scare."

Without attempting to speak Stanley held out his hand.

ii

Wilson was in the lobby, fastening a chain on the heavy door.

"Preparing for a siege?"

"For whatever comes," Wilson replied.

"No one will touch the Folly. The place is practically a fortress. That's how the old castles were built, to withstand a siege. Did they bring Miss Winthrop home from the hospital?"

"Yes, and she's fine. She had visitors all day, half the town, and flowers! As good as a funeral."

"Stanley, my dear," Ellen exclaimed as she came into the lobby, "you look tired to death."

"I'm all right," he said impatiently. "Sherry?"

"I've never seen anyone recuperate the way she does!" Ellen added quietly, "This has become a real vendetta, hasn't it? Did you hear about the tires on the station wagon?"

He nodded.

"Is Denton behind it?"

"Of course he's behind it; there's no doubt in my mind but I can't prove it."

"And the boy Sherry tried to save, is he the one who planted the bomb?"

"Apparently."

"What will happen to him, Stanley?"

He shrugged. "That's not up to me, Aunt Ellen."

"His mother called to see Sherry today."

"*His mother!* You didn't let her near Sherry, did you?"

"Of course I did. She's a pathetic creature and quite harmless. Oh, and that reminds me that Sherry wants to see you."

"She does?" Stanley ran his hand over his face. "I'd better shave and clean up first. I haven't been out of these clothes since yesterday morning. Anyone with Sherry now?"

"Eve and the baby. Sherry is crazy about Billy and she plays with him by the hour when she has the time. With her love of children she ought to have a brood of her own."

She's mine. Remember?

"I suppose Carleton is haunting the place."

"He came as soon as she was brought in from the hospital this morning but she insisted that he go skating with

Eve as usual. They both came back for lunch." Ellen laughed. "My dear, you wouldn't believe the number of friends Sherry has made in the few weeks she has been here. There has been a regular procession of people to see her or to make inquiries in person, and the phone never stops ringing. And flowers!"

A grin stretched Stanley's tired face. "Wilson told me it was as good as a funeral."

"But — and brace yourself, for this you won't believe — she received a box of orchids — three of them — from — guess who?"

"Not the Dentons? Well, I will be damned! You know, you almost have to admire nerve like that."

"And that's not all. Mrs. Denton came in person. Oh, no, I didn't let her see Sherry. But it seems she noticed Sherry's ring when she went to get the story of that horrible dinner party and she was curious about her engagement. Sort of hinted that it might be you. So I told her about Major Carleton and she called the Mayflower Inn and asked him to the dinner party too."

"Well, what a delightful evening that is going to be!" Stanley said savagely as he went up the stairs.

iii

Every time there was a tap on her door Sherry looked hopefully to see who was there. A steady procession of well-wishers had come and Eve kept bringing in boxes of flowers. The heavy turbanlike bandage had been replaced by a smaller one and, except for the shadows under her eyes and her pallor, Sherry was much her usual self. If she could only rid herself of the obsession of a clock tick-ing — but that would fade like all the rest.

Doug had come to look at her anxiously and she had sent him away, making him promise to take Eve skating as usual. After lunch he had come up for a little while. The exercise did not seem to have done him much good. He said his leg was beginning to hurt him again. Probably he had overdone the exercise. He would have to give up skating. He was unusually quiet. Just before he left he took her hand in a hard grip.

"Sherry, you've got to marry me at once. At once, do you hear? Things can't go on like this." There had been a curious look, almost like desperation, in his face.

A policeman had come to talk to her, a pleasant, quiet-spoken young man. Ugly comments about fuzz and pigs and unnecessary violence seemed preposterous in this man's company. He had smiled at her. "You must be tired of answering questions so I'll try to make this as painless as possible, but you do see that we have to know what happened."

"Yes, of course. I don't really know anything except what the others do. Mr. Holbrook called to warn us to get out of the building. You know about that?"

"Oh, yes. We've talked to Mr. Holbrook and to all the others. Go on, Miss Winthrop."

"I called for everyone to get out and then I ran down the stairs and told the printer. He thought it was all a silly joke but when I said it might be real he ran out. And then I saw Dick, and he'd been knocked out." She gave an unexpected giggle. "The doctor told me I shouldn't have moved a head injury. He was quite cross about it."

The young policeman joined in her laughter.

"Well, that really is all."

He looked at her in some amusement. "You'll never make it on a newspaper."

"Why not?"

"You don't know a story when you see one. You tried to save this guy at a risk of your own life and you don't think that is important?"

"I just happened to be there. You'd have done it."

"But that is part of my job."

"I guess it is part of everyone's job," she said soberly. "All I remember is the sound of a clock ticking —" She wiped her damp forehead. "Tick — tick. That was the worst part. I can't remember how we got out."

"You were struck by falling plaster and fell over this guy Flint. Mr. Holbrook and Major Carleton came in with my colleague. The Major carried you out to safety and Mr. Holbrook helped with the boy." His voice changed. "What do you know about Flint? The printer is making some pretty serious accusations. And the boy's mother told Mr. Holbrook her son came that morning to dismantle the bomb. Dismantle it!" He laughed. "Does that sound likely to you?"

"Yes, it does. It explains everything. It's just what Dick would think of. I believe he must have known about the bomb and he risked his life to find it and dismantle it."

"If he had nothing to do with it he wouldn't know how it worked."

"But he would try, just the same."

"Why not use his head and call us?"

"I think he was afraid to."

"Another of those kids who are taught to hate the police."

"Can't you counteract some of that feeling?"

"We do our best. We talk to the schools. We take kids who are interested around the station and tell them about some of our cases and how we handle them and try to make them see we are here for their protection. But when we find them engaged in malicious mischief or theft or driving recklessly or without a license, or roughing some-one up, we become the enemy."

It was after the policeman had gone that Ellen came in to say that Mrs. Flint was there and wanted to see her.

"I think she must be the woman who called Stanley to warn him about the bomb. She is awfully worked up but you don't have to see her if you don't feel up to it. The doctor did not want you to overtax yourself for a few days."

"Of course I'll see the poor woman."

She had been alarmed to see the ravages on Mrs. Flint's face. "Do sit down," she said warmly, "and tell me about Dick. Is he conscious yet?"

"They x-rayed his head and say he has a bad concussion. He has been conscious a couple of times, once just for a few seconds, and once for five minutes. He knew me but he didn't remember what had happened. The doctor says there appears to be no serious brain damage and he may remember the whole thing at any time or he may never remember it."

"But he's going to be all right, isn't he?"

"I don't know, Miss Winthrop. I don't know. There's

no denying my boy is in bad trouble. That is why I came to see you. The police say you tried to save him at the risk to your life. I hope you can help me. The police believe Dick planted that bomb. But it's not so. Well, I made him tell me the truth and I told him about your coming and saying you were worried about him and that you'd try to help if he was in trouble.

"And he cried, Miss Winthrop. I hadn't seen him cry since he was ten years old except when his father died. And he said he was in a mess. He had met this man who struck up an acquaintance with him and asked him all about the *Courier* and the people who worked there. He told Dick he was being exploited and that he should be earning three times as much money as he did.

"Well, facts are facts, and I know Dick isn't all that smart but I suppose a lot of kids that age think they are worth more than they earn. Anyhow, this man began to give Dick money. And he got Dick to go around dropping hints that the people who worked for the *Courier* were Reds and trying to undermine the country. Well, I ask you. Mr. Perkins has been a lay reader in the church for ten years and Evans votes Republican every time.

"Well, then, this man told Dick that he wanted him to order some material for a job he was going to give him. That's when he gave him the motorcycle and the money for the warm coat and all, and Dick put the stuff in his room.

"Then, that night, the man came to tell Dick not to go to the *Courier* next morning because a bomb was going to go off. Dick was nearly crazy. He said he'd tell the police and Mr. Holbrook. And the man said the bomb had been made in Dick's room and there was plenty of evidence to show it. And the material had all been sent in Dick's name. And the man had used a key to the *Courier* Dick had had made and the hardware store would remember him. Let alone the money Dick had been given. How was he going to account for it?

"We talked all night. I urged Dick to go straight to the police but this man had told him the police never play fair. So in the morning he called to warn you and then when it was too late he decided to see if he could find the bomb and get rid of it. And I — let him go. I had to, Miss Winthrop. He had to make up for what he'd done or he could never live with himself. But I couldn't go through another time like the hours I spent waiting to know what had happened."

She was surprised to find Sherry smiling. "There was a policeman here just now and I told him I was sure Dick had been trying to dismantle the bomb and not to plant it."

Mrs. Flint took Sherry's hand in hers, her eyes swimming in tears. "Thank you."

After Mrs. Flint had gone Sherry lay trying to piece the story together. One thing was clear. Dick himself was in danger, not from the police but from the man who had set him up for the bombing. They would have to silence the boy in some way. I'll tell Stanley, she decided. He'll know what to do.

Eve appeared, bringing books from the library. When she had come up after lunch she had been pale but now she looked ghastly.

"What on earth has happened to you?"

"Nothing."

"Don't be ridiculous. You look as though you had had a shock." Sherry's voice rose. "Not another bomb! Not Stanley."

"Not a bomb," Eve assured her.

"Then what?"

"Aunt Ellen thought I shouldn't tell you but you'd be better off with the truth." Eve described leaving the library to find that the tires of the station wagon had been slashed. "And none of us believes that it is a coincidence. Someone is really threatening Stanley. We called the police, of course."

"How awful."

Eve smiled. "There is one bright spot. Aunt Winifred has decided that it is too dangerous to stay on here, that we are all in danger. So she is going to leave the Folly the day after the Dentons' dinner party. It would take more than a bomb scare to keep her from that."

The two girls exchanged amused glances.

"Just think how peaceful it would be without those jingling bracelets," Sherry said.

"Oh, well, I don't suppose I'll be staying on after Christmas. I really must find a place of my own, perhaps in Florida or Arizona or somewhere out of the cold."

"But I thought you loved the winter."

"I thought so too." Eve got up, moving heavily and without her usual grace. "I'm going up to see Billy."

"Bring him down here," Sherry begged her.

But even the play with the baby that usually so delighted her had lost its magic today. Eve watched Sherry with brooding eyes. "It was Doug who saved you," she said suddenly. It was the first time she had called him anything but Major Carleton. "He — I don't think he is happy, Sherry. I think he is jealous of Stanley. I know you too well to think you would make a man unhappy deliberately. I think you ought to get married soon, Sherry, and end this situation."

She picked up Billy and went quickly away while Sherry stared after her in astonishment.

iv

She was having an early supper on a tray when the knock she had long expected came at last. In response to her call Stanley came in and stood beside her bed, looking down at her, a curiously intent look on his face. It was the first time she had seen or heard from him since the bombing. He was the only one who had not sent flowers or asked to see her.

"How are you feeling?"

"Fine, on the whole. I'll be up tomorrow and I can go back to work the next day."

"Don't overdo it." Nothing more. No concern. No sympathy. No anxiety.

"I won't overdo it." She raised her fork to her mouth and ate salad without tasting it.

"Good. Well, Aunt Ellen said you wanted to see me."

"Yes." Her voice and manner were as detached as his. "I wanted to talk to you about Dick." She told him of her talk with the policeman and with Mrs. Flint. "I believed her, Stanley. Whatever Dick may have been talked into I believe he was genuinely horrified to find out about the bomb and he did try to warn me and he took an awful chance trying to find and dismantle it."

"Why didn't he tell the police or me?"

"He was afraid to."

"Afraid of me?" Stanley was incredulous.

"Well, all the evidence was against him and this man told him he wouldn't have a chance. He's just a kid, Stanley, and not very bright. The kind who falls for anyone with a smooth-sounding line. He didn't understand what he was doing."

"Well," there was a touch of impatience in his manner, "what do you expect me to do about it?"

"I think he could be in danger," she said simply. "He can identify the man who actually did set the bomb. Can't you arrange to get him a guard?" As Stanley hesitated she said, "Can't you see how important it must be to someone to keep him from talking? He's the only one who can identify the man with the bomb. Oh, Stanley, there must be something you can do."

He took her hand, looked down at the face he so dearly loved. She had so nearly died. He had so nearly lost her. Lost her? He had never had her. He released her hand and stood back.

"Forget about it, Sherry. I'll take care of it at once. If the police can't spare a man to watch Dick I'll send Roberts over to the hospital. Ever since he had to change those four tires he has been spoiling for a fight. Good night." He went out and closed the door behind him.

XIV

NEXT morning, as she had done every day since her arrival at the Folly, Ellen looked quickly at the mail, but there was nothing for her. In all this time, though she wrote Bruce once a week assuring him that she was well and happy and having a most enjoyable time, she had had no response. Had Thelma persuaded him to cast her off? She remembered the old jingle:

> *A daughter's a daughter all of her life;*
> *A son is a son till he gets him a wife.*

Perhaps I should have been contented to stay quietly in that upstairs room in Bruce's house, she thought. But I wasn't more than half alive then. I wasn't part of anything and here at the Folly I am of some use. Stanley has told me so over and over.

She thought of Thelma's bitter denunciation and her saying that all her mother-in-law wanted was to bring shame and disgrace on her son, to make people believe that she had been thrown out of his house to starve and been treated like King Lear.

None of that was true, of course. She had simply rebelled against the emptiness and meaninglessness of her life. She hoped that when Bruce was her age he too would rebel if he found his life intolerable. She hoped he would want to do something about it; anything was better than to submit to your fate supinely.

The night before, Miss Holbrook had announced that she was going to return to San Francisco the day after the Denton dinner party; in fact, she had already made plane reservations. Stanley, with grave courtesy, had said that, much as he would like to have her remain, he felt he could not dissuade her from leaving while conditions were so unpredictable.

"I must say, Eve," Miss Holbrook announced, "I think you should take the baby away from the Folly without delay. I wouldn't put it past people who use bombs to kidnap Billy."

Stanley had intervened then. "The Folly is practically a fortress, Aunt Winifred. Billy is perfectly safe in this house. Of course, Eve, if you would feel safer somewhere else I'll try to arrange something, though I admit I hate the thought of Billy being driven out of his father's house."

"I've been thinking of going to Florida," Eve said in her soft voice, "to escape the cold weather, but I'm going to wait until this is all over. I was thinking after the tires were slashed that Bill wouldn't have run away."

"You're dead right about that," Stanley agreed. "Anyhow you won't be able to do much skating in Florida."

To his surprise Eve's face flamed with color. "I'm not going to do any more skating. I think I strained my back this morning."

Ellen looked up, looked down again. Major Carleton

had said he was going to give up skating because he had
strained his lame leg.

ii

At their last skating session, Eve and Doug had been
talking of the bombing and of Sherry's last-minute rescue.

"The policeman who talked to me at the Folly," Eve
said, "told me that you and Stanley went into that
bombed building and you were the first to reach Sherry.
It must have been an awful moment for you, loving her
the way you do."

There had been a startled expression on Doug's face
and he had ground his skates to a halt, while he stared at
her as though grappling with a new and totally unexpected thought.

"And you carried her out to safety."

"Yes," Doug said. "Yes." He saw in a blinding flash
that the impulse that had made him take Sherry away
from Holbrook had been jealousy. He had had to assert
his rights of possession, to prove to a male rival that she
was his. And yet from the night of his return there had
been a change in his attitude toward Sherry, though he
had refused to admit it to himself. In all those months
and through all the strain and pain and tension her face
had been before him; he had clung to the thought of her,
something good and lovely, sweet and clean, to return to
after all the frightfulness.

Sherry was a darling, as fine a person as you would
want to meet, only — only — something had happened.
He had met Eve, the most beautiful woman he had ever
seen, and whether skating or lunching together, relaxed

and at ease, he had fallen in love with her. How could any man see her and not fall in love with her? And the terrible thing was that Sherry was so devoid of jealousy that she trusted him, she had not dreamed that his feeling for her could change. He was bound to her. But his newly discovered realization of his love for Eve stunned him.

"Eve," he said abruptly, urgently. "Eve."

She raised her eyes to his. "Doug?" It was a startled question.

"Eve, what am I going to do? I love you. It's been you from the first minute I saw you and I never knew it until now."

"Doug, you mustn't. There's Sherry."

"I know that, but every day I've seen more clearly that it is only when I am with you that I am really happy. With Sherry — I don't know. She wants me to be a lot more of a person than I am."

"No one could want that," Eve protested hotly.

"Eve! You too!" It was a cry of jubilation.

She shook her head. "I can't do this to Sherry."

"You mean you've come to love me? Please answer me, Eve."

"I don't know how it happened," she admitted. "I thought everything had ended for me when Bill died. But then I met you and at first you reminded me of Bill; you are like him in so many ways, gay and such fun to be with, and not expecting me to be clever or anything, and I thought that was why I liked you so well. And then I discovered it was not on Bill's account but on your own. It was because you are you."

"I never dreamed this could happen," Doug said.

"It can't happen, Doug." Eve was unexpectedly firm.

"Sherry has loved you all this time, and she trusted us, even when Miss Holbrook warned her. She trusted us so much she just laughed at the idea you could ever change toward her. If you were to cheat her it would be between us always. It's no good, Doug."

"Then what are we going to do? To see you every day and to have no right at all —"

"I'll go away after Christmas and we won't meet alone until then."

"No, don't go."

"I'll have to go. To see you and Sherry together — I'm not generous enough for that. Darling, you'll have to marry her right away! Everything will be all right then."

"It will never be all right without you."

"It has to be. Let's go back to the house now. No, we won't lunch together alone again. There is no point in prolonging this. It makes us both suffer."

"I can't let you go," he groaned.

"You must. And we aren't going to speak of this ever again."

"Is that the way you want it, Eve?"

She made a despairing gesture. "That is the way it has got to be. And I think the sooner you and Sherry get married, the sooner you take her away from here, the better. She could be in danger if anything more happens."

"Let me kiss you just once, Eve. Just once. Give me that to remember."

She shook her head. "That wouldn't help much, would it?" She managed a wavery smile. "Let's go back now, but this is our real good-bye, Doug."

"Good-bye, my darling, but I'll love you all my life."

iii

Thomas Denton had come up to Waring for the week-end. He wanted, he said before the servants, to make sure the Christmas tree had been properly installed, and he had had his publicity man arrange for a picture of him looking up at the tree. "Might get it in *Time* or even in *Life,*" he said.

While the maid was serving them, the Dentons talked only of impersonal matters. As soon as she had left the room Denton said, "Well, anything new? So far as I could make out from Ramsay the big bang went off as scheduled. Saw something about it in the *New York Times.* Building a total wreck. That ought to take care of things. Mission accomplished."

"You haven't seen the *Courier,*" his wife said. "I have a copy on my desk." She explained that an upstate paper had offered Holbrook facilities for printing. "And there's a good deal of feeling in the village, Tom. Six people were in the building at the time and there could easily have been a dozen or more and they could all have been killed if Holbrook hadn't received a warning in time to call the building and have it cleared."

"A warning?" Denton looked at his wife with narrowed eyes. "Now whose idea was that?"

"Oh, it was the Flint boy, of course. The printer swears he came in acting frantic and talking about a bomb. Both the Flint boy and the Winthrop girl were nearly killed."

"She the one who came to see you and apparently was wise to the whole setup?"

Mrs. Denton nodded.

"Pity they weren't both rubbed out," he said viciously.

The maid came in with more coffee. "Of course," Mrs. Denton said, "I sent flowers to Miss Winthrop, orchids because I thought you'd like it. And I paid a call at the Folly to inquire about her."

When the maid had gone Denton asked, "Just what has happened to young Flint?"

"He is in the hospital, still unconscious. I called today. No change. No visitors. He can't talk yet."

"He mustn't talk — ever." Denton saw his wife's eyes widen with shock. "You see that, of course, Doris."

"He's only a kid."

"He's old enough to make plenty of trouble. Why Ramsay tipped him off I can't understand. The kid had served his purpose, he was set up as the patsy and the evidence was all planted. He was of no more use to us and a potential danger from now on. Ramsay should have seen that for himself. I seem to have to do everyone's thinking. And why a motorcycle? I told Ramsay to give him some money but I didn't mean that much."

"He reminded Ramsay of his own son, the one who died of polio and always wanted a motorcycle. I guess when it came down to it —"

Denton shrugged impatiently. "I don't often make mistakes about people."

His wife started to comment and then changed her mind. Her husband's most serious weakness was that he could not take criticism. He was a poor judge of people. He had overestimated Ramsay because Ramsay talked big. He had underrated Holbrook from the beginning because Holbrook was quiet-spoken, though any fool, Doris

Denton thought, should have known that the man meant what he said and said what he meant. Tom had thought Holbrook would scare. Instead he had become fighting mad. What had started as a matter of principle had now become a crusade. Her husband, Doris Denton admitted, had a tendency to underrate the human race in general. He did not see people as people but simply as forces to be manipulated.

"And how," he was saying, "Ramsay has made such a hash of things I can't understand. I would have said he was capable and thoroughly reliable, but he guaranteed to see the advertising was stopped and then he was proved wrong. The bombing succeeded but young Flint can identify Ramsay."

"Ramsay is doing his best. He figures a continued campaign of harassment will break Holbrook in the long run. The day after the bombing he slashed the tires on Holbrook's station wagon as a warning. And he telephoned the hysterical aunt to tell her the place was dangerous. And that Mrs. Davis — you know, Tom, I am positive I have met that woman before and, what's more, her name isn't Davis. Well, I'll remember one of these days; I always do."

"So Ramsay figures we can undermine Holbrook by scaring his women. It's not a bad idea but it won't work. Nothing will work as long as the Flint boy can talk. He has always been the weak link, too stupid and too young to be reliable."

"But he was the only one of the lot who was on the take for easy money. Ramsay checked on every one of them."

"Well, we've got to work fast before the boy is able to

talk." As the maid came in to clear the table he said jovially, "Looks like a white Christmas is coming up. I'm almost tempted to play Santa Claus myself. How are you doing on the presents for the kids? I can hardly wait to see their happy faces on Christmas Eve. Makes me feel like a kid myself."

iv

Roberts, looking very trim in a business suit, white collar and necktie, listened attentively to the police sergeant.

"Got all that clear?"

"Yes, sir. I'm to be the patient in the other bed. Have you cleared that with the hospital?"

"Oh, yes. The telephone operator is instructed to say that young Flint is still unconscious and can see no visitors. Your job is to watch. But don't make a move unless the boy is in danger."

"Is he really unconscious?"

"Last I heard, but the doctor said he could come out of it at any time. How much he'll remember is doubtful. If you can get him to talk so much the better, but don't force it or he might scare and clam up altogether. And do try to remember his exact words as far as possible."

"I can do better than that." Roberts indicated the case on the floor at his feet. "A tape recorder. Mr. Holbrook got it for me and showed me how it works."

"How did Holbrook land you for this job?"

"I've been working for him. Never knew a man to be such a square shooter. Everyone at the Folly is all set to be a one-man army, if necessary."

When Roberts had presented his credentials at the hospital, a nurse led him to a room with a No Visitors sign on the door. He went in, removed his shoes and jacket, slipped on the hospital gown over his clothes and got into bed after adjusting the tape recorder. He settled down for what might be a long wait, relieved to see that he had the bed nearer the door. Anyone approaching Dick would have to pass him.

The Flint boy slept soundly. He was younger in appearance than Roberts had expected; his face still had childish contours.

At the end of three hours Roberts found himself on the verge of dozing off, but he was instantly alert when the door was eased open and he lay with his eyes nearly closed. The nurse who had admitted him peered in, came quietly to look at Dick and take his pulse. She gave Roberts a conspiratorial wink.

"How's the boy?"

"Pulse all right. No change. He's to get no medication until he wakes up so you won't be disturbed again." She went out, her feet in rubber soles making no sound.

A half hour later Roberts was aware that he was dozing again and jerked himself awake. It would be a fine thing for Mr. Holbrook to trust him to look after a defenseless boy and then fall asleep on the job. He wondered what had awakened him and then saw that the door was ajar, that it was opening slowly, noiselessly.

Every sense alert, Roberts lay without stirring. Then he relaxed. A man in a white coat, a stethoscope hanging around his neck, appeared in the doorway. He started forward and then came to a stop when he realized that both beds were occupied. For a moment he was uncertain and Roberts tensed again but managed to keep his breathing heavy and even like a man in a deep sleep. Under cover of the bed he groped for the tape recorder and started it going. The man was moving toward the other bed now. He looked down at the sleeping boy.

Roberts studied his face. He would be easy to remember, easy to recognize again, and he looked fairly well-to-do. It wasn't starvation that drove him to an action like this. What then made him do it? The man was deathly white. He didn't like his job. That was obvious. You'll like it a lot less before we are through with you, Roberts thought grimly.

The man picked up the boy's limp arm, shoved up his sleeve, pulled out a hypodermic. The nurse had said that no medication was to be given until after the boy regained consciousness.

With a swift movement Roberts was on his feet. "How is he, Doctor?"

The man swung around, shocked at the unexpected interruption. Then he retreated. "Don't disturb him." He went out, closing the door behind him.

Roberts stared after him in frustration. Never in all his life had he minded anything like having to let a potential killer get away. He wished the police sergeant had not ordered him not to attack anyone who might approach Dick unless it was necessary to save the boy's life. Otherwise he was simply to make sure the boy was unharmed.

"The last thing we want is to create a disturbance in the hospital," the sergeant had said. "Just protect the boy; that's all you have to do."

Nevertheless Roberts was dissatisfied. It was maddening to let the fellow off, particularly as he might be the one who had planted the bomb, the one — and that was Roberts's special grievance — who had slashed the tires.

The boy stirred, turned his head, moved a hand. His eyes opened, looked in perplexity at Roberts, who grinned at him.

"How you doing, kid?"

"I — don't — know." The words came slowly. There was bewilderment in the boy's face. "Where is this and how did I get here?"

"This is the Waring hospital and you were brought here in an ambulance."

"What happened to me?"

"The *Courier* was bombed. But you knew about that, didn't you?"

"It really was?"

"The building was destroyed." Roberts came to sit on the foot of Dick's bed. The boy looked at the rugged face with its furrowed brow, friendly grin, and the big square hands that were accustomed to heavy work. He liked what he saw.

"I remember. This guy — this jerk — I thought he was my friend but he said he could prove I did it and I never —"

"Take it easy, kid," Roberts advised him, "but take it from the beginning."

In the best of circumstances Dick was not capable of marshaling his thoughts in any orderly way and now, suffering from concussion and shock and a human desire to put his own dubious actions in the best possible light, he was almost incoherent. But there was something about this stolid man with the kindly face he trusted. Patiently Roberts tied the pieces together, facts and explanations and excuses that tumbled out in confusion.

"And I thought all the time he was preparing me for a big job worthy of my talents," the indignant seventeen-year-old said, "and he was just making use of me like I was dumb or something. And then he said a bomb was set to go off in the *Courier* in the morning and if I didn't play along I'd be accused of it and I didn't know what to do. And then he hit me. Real hard."

"So what did you do?" Roberts's tone was casual.

"I called the Holbrook house to warn Sherry to stay away from the *Courier*."

"Why?"

"Because she's —" Dick searched for a word. "Well, like she said she'd help me if I was in trouble, you know. But she'd already gone. So then," he swallowed, "I knew I had to stop it somehow. That jerk — he couldn't have planted the bomb if I hadn't ordered the stuff and had a key made for the *Courier*. Well, I went down and I told Jones, he's the printer and another jerk, always trying to give me orders, about the bomb and I tried to find it and — that's all. Was I hit by the bomb?" In spite of his anxiety Dick was dazzled by the drama of this.

"No," Roberts said in a matter-of-fact way. "You were hit by the printer. Your mother called Holbrook and warned him and he got the *Courier* cleared of people, except for Miss Winthrop who stayed to try to get you out of the building. She was knocked down by falling plaster. You were both saved at the last minute."

"She tried to get me out?" Tears of fright and shame and weakness rolled down Dick's cheeks. He brushed them away with a pajama sleeve.

"What's the name of this — this jerk who sold you the bill of goods about the wicked *Courier* and the evil Mr. Holbrook and your cruel boss who thought he had a right to give you orders?"

Dick flushed at the casual amusement in Roberts's voice. "His name is Brown. John Brown."

"Oh, yes, from that well-known firm of Smith, Jones, and Brown."

"No," Dick said seriously, "I don't think he belongs to any firm."

"What does he look like?"

That baffled Dick. "Well, like anyone, I guess."

"Tall or short?"

"Medium."

"Young or old?"

"Medium."

"Coloring?"

"I never noticed anything in particular, one way or the other."

"Anything about his appearance?" Roberts asked without much hope. Dick might possibly have noticed if the man had two heads.

"No, just like anybody."

"Don't worry, kid. I think I've seen him for myself." Roberts did not say that the man had tried only a few minutes before to silence him permanently. If only they could catch him with the hypodermic in his possession! But that would be too good to be likely.

Roberts shut off the tape recorder. "I'm going out to

telephone but I'll be right back. If anyone comes in you yell bloody murder." He hovered near the desk, watchful eyes on Dick's door, until the nurse who knew him appeared.

"What would a doctor with a hypodermic be doing in young Flint's room?"

"He'd have no business to be there." She was startled. "Why for mercy's sake! There is only one doctor in the hospital at this hour and he's in the emergency room."

"No harm done," he assured her.

To his relief there was a telephone booth within sight of Dick's door and Roberts called the police to report.

"I don't think he'll dare come back today, knowing I'm in the room. But there could always be someone else with a different method."

"You stay there until we can relieve you. We'll arrange to have him transferred to the Danbury hospital and followed by an unmarked car to make sure no one is on his track. No one is to know except his mother. Okay, Roberts, you've done a good job. As soon as we move him bring in the tape recorder."

"All right but I can tell you one thing. I never hated anything as much in my whole life as letting that guy go without giving him a working over."

"Would he recognize you again?" the sergeant asked sharply.

"I doubt it. The shades were drawn and the room was quite dark and I had the sheet up over my face except when I spoke to him and he was too anxious to get out to notice much. But I could pick him out of a thousand."

"Well, next time you see him, hang on to him, but don't kill him, will you?"

$\mathcal{A}$ ND what do you think you're doing?" Stanley demanded as he pushed back his chair and got to his feet.

"I'm going back to work today," Sherry said. She was still rather pale but that was the only reminder of her accident, that and the small, inconspicuous bandage on her head. This morning she wore a nile green sweater and skirt which she had bought with her first salary from the *Courier*. "Good morning, Aunt Ellen."

"Aunt Ellen, tell this girl to go back to bed."

"Well, not, at least, until she has had breakfast. You are looking much better this morning."

"I'm all right now and I'm champing at the bit to get to work. I want to see how the *Courier* is making out in its new home."

"We'll settle down in another week or two," Stanley told her. "Of course getting out that first *Courier* was sheer chaos but I think we're beginning to get organized. All the staff is being taken back and forth in the station wagon. I don't intend to have anything happen to them. We have had extra telephones installed and some new equipment and supplies have been ordered. I'm keeping Roberts on the wagon full time so he can take Neil back and forth to get his stories and pictures, and to bring up anyone who must see us in person. It's all a nuisance, of course, but we're lucky to have a place to print the paper."

Sherry finished her grapefruit. "You think one of us could be in danger?"

"Let's put it this way: I don't think the campaign against the *Courier* has been stopped; I just think they will use different tactics."

"What are you going to do about a new building, Stanley?" Ellen asked.

"Nothing until after the first of the year. Then I'll call in an architect and get an estimate."

"All this is costing you a great deal more than you anticipated in the beginning, isn't it?"

"Well, yes, but I'm in this thing for the duration now." As Ellen was about to expostulate he grinned at her impudently. "After all, that's what Henry would do."

"So it is."

Sherry laughed and Stanley confessed, "The truth is out. I had to tell Sherry about Henry."

"Oh, dear," Ellen said in concern. "What will you think of us for all that nonsense?"

"I'm sorry about Henry. I began to feel he was the only man I could love."

"Better not let your Major hear that," Stanley said. "By the way, when are you two going to be married? I'll have to look around for a new society editor."

"I don't know. Right away, he says. But, Stanley, if Roberts is on the wagon who is looking after Dick? Roberts was going to see that no one tried to get at him."

"Someone did try." As both women exclaimed in horror Stanley told them what had happened at the hospital.

"And he let that man get away," Sherry wailed.

"The police warned him about the danger of creating a disturbance in the hospital, perhaps starting a panic among nervous patients. At least he got the man's voice on a tape recorder."

"Surely," Ellen said, "that would be sufficient evidence."

"No, but it is supporting evidence."

"But what will happen to Dick now?" Sherry demanded.

"He has been moved to the Danbury hospital where he is registered as Harry Williams. The Waring hospital is still reporting "no change and no visitors," and his mother has been instructed to pay her usual two visits a day. If anyone asks her about Dick she has been instructed to notice every detail of the person's appearance, clothing and all that."

"It's like a nightmare, isn't it?" Sherry quivered. "I had never realized there was so much evil in the world, or at least that people like the Dentons could have anything to do with crimes of violence."

Stanley looked down at her, his heart in his eyes, wishing that she was his to protect. He would never let evil near her. Then the look faded. "If you're ready we'd better get started. I heard the station wagon draw up a couple of minutes ago. Roberts collects the rest of the staff and then comes here to pick me up."

When she went out to the station wagon she found all the *Courier* staff waiting. When Stanley made no gesture she got in the middle seat beside Neil while Stanley got in front with Roberts.

There was an eager chorus of greetings and Sherry

found herself bombarded with questions. Only the printer waited until they had reached their destination and were alone for a moment to say, "I feel terrible, Sherry, for having knocked Dick out. I really thought he was screwy at first and then when I knew about the bomb I figured he was responsible. Now Mr. Holbrook says it is no such thing, but I'd already told a lot of people. But the worst is that when you gave me that warning I ran out and never noticed that you hadn't come along and here you were, trying to save Dick."

"Don't think about it anymore. I don't blame you a bit."

"You don't? Well, that's a weight off my mind!"

It was a strange day, working in strange surroundings, and Stanley, who had a private office here, was more remote, more inaccessible than he had ever been in the past. Even her own work seemed different because Roberts drove her back to Waring and waited while she made each call. And the calls required more time than usual because everyone wanted an eyewitness account of the bombing and her own experiences.

This so delayed her in preparing her own copy that she was still typing when Neil called, "Okay, Sherry, that wraps it up for the day. Our chariot awaits."

She looked up in dismay. "Oh, Neil, I can't leave now, not possibly. I have at least another hour's work."

"How are you going to get home?"

"I don't know. Maybe Roberts could come back."

He looked dubious but he did not argue. A few minutes later Stanley looked in. "What's this about not taking the station wagon?"

She indicated a sheaf of notes. "All that still to do. People kept me talking most of the time."

He went out without a word and Sherry's heart sank. Then she saw him coming back. "Okay," he told her cheerfully, "Roberts will deliver the staff to their homes and come back here for us."

"But, Stanley, you don't need to stay."

"Don't be a ninny," he said severely and she giggled. He pulled up a chair beside her desk and began to look over the material she had already prepared for the printer, commenting as he read:

"Mr. and Mrs. George Winslow are entertaining Mrs. Winslow's mother for the Christmas holidays. A number of social events are being planned, including a bridge luncheon and an Open House on Christmas Eve."

("Hey, they can't do that, taking the audience away from the party on the Green. But wouldn't it be wonderful if that happened and no one showed up to get Denton's presents?")

"Mr. and Mrs. Morris Hazelton announce the engagement of their daughter Maud to Mr. Foster Hare. Mr. Hare, a graduate of Harvard School of Business Administration, is now engaged in merchandising."

("Bargain basement at Macy's, but don't tell anyone. Ever see Maud? She has a face like a fallen soufflé.")

"Mr. and Mrs. Rupert Cox announce the birth of their son Harold. Mother and son are doing well."

("Good heavens, if that baby grows up to look like Rupert they'll be calling Waring a disaster area.")

"Stop it," Sherry said. "You are making me laugh so much I can't type."

Her laughter seemed to clear the air and by the time she had finished her work, left it for the printer, and gone down to the station wagon she and Stanley were on their old companionable terms, which lasted until Roberts pulled up at the Folly behind the red Volkswagen. Then the laughter died out of Sherry's face and Stanley's eyes were cold and bleak.

"Well, I see that your Major is here."

While Sherry went up to her room Stanley went in search of Doug. At first he barely recognized the man in a perfectly tailored suit, crisp white shirt, and figured necktie. Doug had been talking to Eve and something in his expression startled Stanley. *Just the kind of stinker I thought he was. Taking advantage of Sherry's being at work to flirt with Eve.* But certainly there was no indication of flirtation in either of the grave faces that were turned to him.

"Good evening, Major," Stanley said.

Doug smiled. "No longer, Holbrook." He indicated the civilian suit. "Plain Douglas Carleton from now on. Sherry all right?"

"Fine. She'll be down in a minute."

"As long as you are here to entertain Doug I'll go up to look at the offspring," Eve said.

"Wait, Eve," Doug said. "I think you had better tell Holbrook about the telephone call."

"What's this about, Eve?"

"Wilson called me to the telephone this afternoon. He had made a mistake. The call was intended for Miss Holbrook and not for me. The man said that, speaking as a friend, he would advise me to leave the Folly. It might be dangerous to stay. Then before I could say anything he hung up."

"Of course," Stanley said thoughtfully, "it could be a crackpot who heard about the bombing —"

"As who has not?" Doug put in.

"As you say. Someone trying to get in on the act."

"But someone did bomb the *Courier*. Good God, man, you can't deny it."

"Who is denying it?"

"And someone tried to get at Dick Flint in the hospital."

"How do you know?"

"Eve told me."

"I thought we had agreed to say nothing about that outside this house."

Her sensitive lips quivered. "I'm sorry, Stanley, but it was only Doug and, after all —"

"After all," Doug put in angrily, "Eve has a stake in this thing herself. She'd been riding in the station wagon when the tires were slashed. I can tell you that when I heard that I saw red."

She flung out a warning hand to silence him.

"If you can tell me," Stanley said rather tartly, "just how Eve could be injured in a stationary car with four flat tires I'll be glad to hear it." He wheeled and went out of the room.

"Oh, Doug, you shouldn't have spoken that way."

"When I heard what had happened to the station wagon while you were driving it —"

"But I wasn't hurt. I couldn't have been. Stanley was right about that."

"Oh, Eve darling, what are we going to do? I can't stand this. Seeing you in danger and unable to do a thing to protect you, having no right to protect you. I could see Holbrook didn't take that telephone warning seriously. If I could only take you back to San Francisco with me where you and Billy would be safe! I'd be good to the boy, Eve, not only on your account but because he's an irresistible child."

"Oh, do you really think so? Oh, no, no, no, no. You promised."

Whatever Doug intended to say was effectively checked when Miss Holbrook came in, her approach heralded by the rattling of bracelets and the jingle of sleigh bells. She came fluttering into the room, wearing the usual cluster of bracelets on her left arm and on her right arm a trinket with a dozen tiny bells hanging from it.

She laughed. "Isn't it the cutest thing! I couldn't resist it. So gay and so much Christmas feeling." She waved her arm to release a jangle of sound. "Dear Major Carleton, how very nice that suits looks! I do like a black suit on a man, though my father always said it was impractical, especially when you have animals." As Doug looked blank she explained, "House pets, you know, cats and dogs, all those hairs. They need so much brushing."

Without stopping for breath she rushed on. "Major, has Eve told you about that anonymous telephone call? That really sinister warning? It was meant for me, you know. And when Mrs. Fosdick called to ask what really happened about the bombing she told me she saw someone entering the *Courier* building late the night before."

"What's that?" Doug asked alertly.

Delighted to hold her audience enthralled, Miss Holbrook said, "It was a very dark night and there were no streetlights across the river. She saw the lights of a car stop outside the building and someone with a flashlight unlocked the door and then the man went in. She noticed he did not turn on the lights but the flashlight moved around and then, five or ten minutes later, he came out and turned his flashlight on the car and she saw it was white."

Doug gave a startled exclamation. "Then I've seen the man and I'd know him again. He must be the same one who trailed Sherry the night we went to Dick Flint's house!"

"I'll be afraid to sleep nights. Well, two more nights. Then I'll be flying back to the coast the morning after the Dentons' dinner party."

"Very wise of you," Doug agreed enthusiastically.

"I understand the Dentons have invited you too. So very kind of them. They even included Sherry, you know, when they found she was living here."

"I hope," he said gravely, "Sherry is properly grateful."

"Well, I don't pretend to understand young people. Stanley is just the same. He doesn't like the Dentons though they aren't at all pretentious. Just simple and pleasant and very gracious."

Sherry came into the room. "Hello, Doug! So you've become a civilian again." She looked from face to face. "You are all very serious."

"My dear," Miss Holbrook said in a tone that would have done credit to Lady Macbeth, "the Major has seen our criminal tracking you down. Actually tracking you!"

"Oh, come," Doug protested, "it's not as bad as all that, but I do think it's serious." He told Sherry about the man in the white Ford who had dined at the Mayflower and trailed them to the Folly where Doug had taken up the task of trailing him. He described following him to the Flint house and seeing his argument with Dick.

"That all bears out Dick's story, doesn't it?"

"Then," and Doug was rueful, "I fell for one of the oldest tricks in the book when he pulled in to a curb and turned out his lights. I sailed past and by the time he'd turned on his lights and cleared out, he had too much of a head start. I never found him again. But I wouldn't be surprised if he was Mrs. Fosdick's man at the *Courier* or the one who tried to get at Dick in the hospital. It isn't likely that two men are up to tricks around here."

"We'll have to tell Stanley," Sherry said and rang the bell for Wilson.

Ellen had come down by the time Stanley appeared so Doug was able to tell the story to all of them. Stanley listened to the story without comment. Ellen's fingers tightened over the arm of her chair but she did not speak. Miss Holbrook, though she had heard it before, punctuated it with little cries of horror.

"You didn't get the license number?"

"No, I never got that close except when we were both parked outside the Flint house and then I didn't want to risk scaring him off."

"Would you recognize him again?"

"I certainly would. Look here, why don't I make this my own pet project?"

"What's that?"

"Running down that white Ford. My days are free, you

know. I'll see if I can find out whether such a car is registered to Denton. I can try the filling stations. After all, the man must need gas."

"That's definitely an idea, Carleton. I'd be most grateful."

"No need to be. Sherry's safety is involved, you know." *She's mine. Remember?*

"I remember." Stanley turned to Miss Holbrook. "Aunt Winifred, I must warn you not to repeat anything we've been saying."

"How about Mrs. Fosdick?" Ellen asked. "Suppose she talks about seeing that Ford outside the *Courier?* The woman exaggerates and distorts things so and if the man should be warned it would make the Major's task impossible. Shouldn't she be asked not to talk to anyone about what she has seen?"

There were red spots of indignation on Miss Holbrook's cheekbones. "She knows quite well when to keep still. She told me herself she hadn't mentioned it to anyone except Mrs. Denton when she just happened to meet her in the drugstore. The poor woman is a martyr to headaches, Eve, and I told her about the terrible ones you have been having lately and she suggested the remedy she uses. She swears by it. I wrote it down for you and I have it in my room. Remind me when I go up to bed."

"Thank you, but really they aren't as bad as all that," Eve said uncomfortably.

Doug searched her face anxiously, started to speak and checked himself. "Ready, Sherry?" he asked abruptly. "The inn doesn't serve after eight-thirty."

"I'm coming but what a pity Mrs. Fosdick talked! Now you'll never find the white Ford."

"Maybe not, but I'll find that man if he is in Waring."

ii

"How long has Eve been having bad headaches?" Doug asked, breaking a long silence while they drove to the inn.

"I didn't know she'd been having them. She hasn't mentioned them to me."

"People can overdo this business of being unselfish. Eve certainly overdoes it. She makes a martyr of herself."

"I don't believe she thinks of herself at all, Doug. Her nature is as lovely as her face. She's just plain good. But I have noticed lately she isn't looking so well; maybe she needs exercise. Have you given up the skating?"

"My lame leg started acting up."

"Oh, I'm sorry, but can't you take her driving and at least get her out in the air? Take her along when you start hunting for the man in the white Ford."

"I didn't ask you out to dinner to talk about Eve," Doug said so harshly that Sherry was startled. "We've been waiting a long time. We've been engaged for months. What are we waiting for? Let's set a date now for the first possible day. I can't stand this business much longer."

Sherry was startled by the urgency of his tone. She felt cold at heart but she had no choice. Doug had depended on her loyalty and Stanley was making clear that his interest in her had been a sometime thing.

"All right, Doug, whenever you say."

"Good! Let's make it the day after New Year's. Start a new year and a new life. At least I can get you away from Waring and the guy who is gunning for Holbrook.

You'll be safe in San Francisco and you'll never have to hold a job again."

"But what about the column I was going to write? I might do it for a San Francisco paper, I suppose."

Doug shook his head. "One thing I couldn't stand would be a career woman for a wife. You'll like it out there, Sherry. A fresh start for us both. And there are lots of things to do. You'll see. We'll have a swell time and a lot of laughs when all this is behind us."

It sounded oddly as though Doug were trying to convince himself as well as her, Sherry thought.

When they had looked cautiously around the inn for anyone who might be trailing them and had ordered dinner Doug roused himself to ask her how the day had gone. Sherry answered him but again she was aware that both of them were trying too hard to appear gay, laughing immoderately at only mildly amusing jokes. When she was with Stanley the words could not spill out fast enough. She tried to ignore the pain that accompanied any thought of Stanley. She would forget him in a little while. But this was small consolation. She did not want to forget him.

"There's a good movie," Doug suggested when they had finished dinner.

"Not tonight, Doug. This was my first day back at work and it was confusing and I had to work overtime."

"Was that Holbrook's idea?"

"No, it was because people asked so many questions about the bombing it took more time to get my stories. And Stanley waited with me to see I wouldn't be left alone in the building."

"Least he could do," Doug grunted.

iii

When Sherry had said good night to Doug and submitted to his kiss, she went into the Folly feeling that she
was making an escape, though he had made no attempt to
detain her. It was not yet ten o'clock, too early to go to
bed, and in any case she did not want to be alone with
her thoughts.

Ellen was in the small drawing room, knitting needles
flashing, listening to a Haydn quartet on the hi-fi. She
said that Stanley was in the library, Miss Holbrook had
gone to bed, and Eve was in her own room. She searched
Sherry's downcast face but made no comment beyond
saying, "Don't overdo it, my dear."

"I won't. I'm going up now."

But it was to Eve's room and not to her own that
Sherry went. Eve was sitting before her fire in her transformed sitting room, a fashion magazine on her lap,
brooding over the fire. When Sherry came in, in answer to
her summons, she smiled brightly.

"Guess what I was doing!"

"What?"

"I'm planning your trousseau. You helped me change
my wardrobe and it's my turn now. My only talent is for
sewing and I want to make your wedding dress. I was
looking at this. It would be perfect for you."

"But," Sherry stammered, "but — Eve —"

"It would give me so much pleasure."

"Thank you but it will be a very simple wedding. Doug
wants us to be married on the second of January. Only

ten days off. I'll be married in the dress or suit I'll be
traveling in so there won't be a need for a wedding dress."

"The second of January," Eve echoed. "Ten days!"
She got up to kiss Sherry. "I'm so happy for you. So very
happy!"

XVI

Sherry looked around her and laughed. Stanley was looking as remote as an iceberg in his dinner clothes. Doug was grim. Eve, incredibly beautiful in white, was withdrawn and quiet. Ellen was worried.

"I must say I've never seen a more promising start for a party. With the exception of Miss Holbrook you couldn't look gloomier if you were going to a wake."

"I have never disliked anything more in my life," Stanley admitted, "than to be accepting hospitality from a guy who is doing his utmost to knife me in the back and whose ambition to be governor I am fighting tooth and nail."

"But I keep telling you, Stanley dear, you don't understand the Dentons. I had a feeling of rapport the moment I met Mrs. Denton. And the way she included all of us in her invitation, too!"

Over the head of Miss Holbrook the eyes of Stanley and Doug met and for once there was understanding and sympathy between them.

The Denton house was lighted from top to bottom and half a dozen outside lamps were burning, providing glimpses of hemlocks with their branches laden with snow. A small tree near the door had been decorated and spotlighted. There was a great wreath on the door and candles burned in the windows.

The door was opened by a servant who directed them to the room where they were to leave their wraps. They met again in the hall and were greeted at the door of the living room by Mrs. Denton, who held out both hands, glittering with diamonds, and beaming as though she were welcoming her oldest and dearest friends.

"Miss Holbrook! Mrs. Holbrook. How nice. Dear Mr. Holbrook. And you must be Major Carleton. And Mrs. — uh — Davis, isn't it? And little Miss Winthrop."

"Oh, dear! Are we the first?" Miss Holbrook exclaimed.

"You must meet my house guests, Sir Charles and Lady Remington."

A man and woman, both tall and gaunt and looking curiously alike as people so often do after years of a good marriage, had turned politely. Then the woman stepped forward eagerly, crying out, "Ellen!"

"Mary!"

The Englishwoman took Ellen in her arms and kissed her cheek. "Of all the wonderful surprises! Ever since Charles and I reached New York I've been trying to find you, but when I telephoned I was told that Bruce's wife had mislaid your address."

So it was not Bruce who had been at fault! In her relief Ellen could almost forgive Thelma's petty jealousy.

Denton, who had been in conversation with Sir Charles, came forward beaming and thrust his hand at Stanley. If he was amused at the predicament of his reluctant guest he was too wise to betray it. Anyhow Stanley saw at a glance that the English couple were equally reluctant guests, helpless, for business reasons, to extricate themselves.

While Ellen and her old friend talked vivaciously, Denton presented Sir Charles to Eve. "A real American beauty," he said, and the color heightened in Eve's face from annoyance.

The arrival of Mr. and Mrs. Duffer, the former a pompous-looking man with a round, expressionless face and an unexpectedly high, thin voice which did not so much speak as make pronouncements, was followed closely by that of the Fosdicks. Mrs. Fosdick was tall and thin while her husband was short and fat, with the jovial manners of a car salesman. When Denton introduced him to the great and powerful Duffer as "our local party chairman," it was easy to see why he had been included.

Then Mrs. Denton went to the door, exclaiming, "How nice of you to come! Did you find driving from New York difficult?"

"Not at all. The roads have been cleared, you know."

At the sound of that familiar voice Ellen wheeled around. "Bruce!"

He stood stock-still, a pleasant-looking man of thirty with an extremely pretty brunette wife. "Mother!" He sounded bewildered. "Mother! You here?"

"But I've written you every week, telling you I was living in Waring."

"I never got your letters. I thought —" Ellen looked at her daughter-in-law, who flushed. "What is this all about?"

"Later," Ellen said quietly. "Thelma, do let me introduce you to my dear friend, Lady Remington. Mary, this is Bruce's wife."

"I told you we had met before," Mrs. Denton exclaimed triumphantly to Ellen. "It was at the Murgatroyds' in New York. But why call yourself Mrs. Davis?"

"Davis is my maiden name. It's a long story and a dull one."

At first there was some danger that Duffer was going to monopolize the dinner party but gradually he became absorbed in the elaborate meal and was too busy doing it full justice to try to talk.

Mrs. Denton, with Duffer on one side of her and Sir Charles on the other, looked as though life could hold no more. Apparently she felt that she had done her duty by inviting Sherry and she paid no further attention to her, but Sherry was too interested in the crosscurrents at the table to be distressed by any personal neglect. There had been one unpleasant moment when Mrs. Fosdick had stared at her and said, "Oh, so you are the one!" but on the whole Sherry was engrossed in the human drama around her.

When she thought about it later it seemed to Sherry that it was Miss Holbrook, seated between Mr. Fosdick and Bruce Murgatroyd, who was responsible for stirring up all the trouble.

"But I had no idea," she exclaimed to Bruce, "that our faithful Ellen had a son."

"Your faithful Ellen?" There was an odd look on his face.

"Well, she really keeps the Folly on an even keel for

us all. Of course you know how close she has always been to dear Stanley because of her nephew Henry."

"Henry?" he repeated blankly.

"And I must say, for all she thinks the world of him, I suspect he is selfish and just out for what he can get. Why she told me herself her traveling days are over because he needed her money, and when I said frankly I thought that was wrong, she said it wasn't as bad as King Lear."

"King Lear?"

"The wicked daughters, you know," Miss Holbrook explained helpfully, "the ones who took all his belongings and then drove him out of his own house."

"Oh, my God!" Bruce looked for his mother and found her talking with the ease of old friendship to the good-looking young Carleton. Her expression was as serene as usual. In her black evening dress, unadorned, she was distinguished in an unstressed way. Could it be that she had given up all her financial independence to meet his needs? Had she taken a menial job, as this unpleasant woman suggested, because she needed the money? But that did not fit in with her presence at this dinner party.

Bruce's eyes traveled along the table in search of his wife, who was talking vivaciously to Mr. Duffer, but she felt his eyes and looked at him quickly, smiling. There was no answering smile. He turned back to Miss Holbrook but she was now engaged in conversation with the fat, dull little man who appeared to be active in local politics. A big frog in a little pond. Come to think of it, he looked rather like a frog.

"Say, what's this my wife has been telling me about

someone gunning for the Holbrooks, bombing the *Courier*, slashing tires, making threatening telephone calls?" Fosdick's voice rose above the general talk at the table, silencing it.

"Well," Miss Holbrook said helpfully, "I can't say anything because Stanley warned me not to talk but he'd feel different, I can tell you that, if he had been the one to get the warning."

"What is this, Stan, a local vendetta?" An adroit politician, Duffer had summed Holbrook up at first glance as one of the most important men in his community, and his use of the first name came from an awareness that most men were flattered to be recognized and addressed by their first names, particularly by men of more importance than themselves.

Stanley did not attempt to raise his voice. "A crude attempt to stop publication of the *Courier* that risked six lives and might have cost a dozen. But, of course, the joker who uses such tactics doesn't put a value on human life. People around here are worked up about it. If they could lay hands on the criminal they would make short work of him." Stanley leaned forward, smiling. "Don't you agree, Mr. Denton?"

Denton smiled back. "Nicest bunch of people around here you'd ever want to know. I'm sure if you wish to quote me on Waring you can't speak too highly."

Seeing Stanley's expression Sherry choked. Take it all in all, Denton knew how to parry the shots like a master. But there was something frightening in this open skirmishing, this frank declaration of war between two determined opponents.

Ellen, seated beside Douglas Carleton, saw his eyes rest on Eve, who was ravishingly lovely in a white dinner dress. On principle Ellen disliked interference but there were times, she assured herself mischievously, when Henry would approve of her taking a part. I feel like Puck straightening out the lovers in *A Midsummer Night's Dream,* she thought. She looked at her daughter-in-law and caught a pleading glance cast at her. Anyone would think I was a termagant, she thought, half amused, half indignant. Isn't Thelma sensible enough to know I won't betray her? But how ungenerous she was to hold back my letters to Bruce!

"You know," Mrs. Fosdick put in, "I think I saw the criminal when he was in the very act of setting the bomb." She described what she had seen.

"But you did not see his face?"

"No, only a white car."

"What are you going to do about this, Stan?" Duffer asked.

Stanley explained that a friendly newspaper colleague had offered the *Courier* facilities for printing until they could acquire a building of their own and that his employees were all being escorted to and from work. "And my driver is armed, with the consent and approval of the Waring police."

"Surely there would be no sense in attacking your employees."

"It looks like a campaign of harassment to make me lose heart. It won't succeed."

"I can understand how you feel," Denton said. "I enjoy a good clean fight myself."

"Well, I'm frightened," Miss Holbrook said. "As a matter of fact, I am flying back to San Francisco tomorrow, though why I should be the one marked out for a warning I can't imagine. After all, it is Major Carleton who saw the criminal clearly enough to identify him. I should think he would be the one to be endangered."

The conversation drifted away from the *Courier* and was grasped in Duffer's practiced hands. "As I was telling Dick Nixon just last week . . ." he began.

After dinner the pianist appeared to play Schubert, Chopin and Prokofiev — three thousand dollars for three little pieces, Mrs. Denton thought indignantly, but then it gave the party class and Lady Remington enjoyed it. Imagine her being a great friend of Mrs. Davis, who turned out to be Thelma's mother-in-law, living under an assumed name!

It was after the musician had left that there was a general shift in the party. Bruce Murgatroyd began a purposeful approach to his mother but she had been captured by Lady Remintgon, and the two women were so absorbed he could not intrude. He found himself beside Sherry. "I don't know any of these people except the Dentons who are friends of my wife. Tell me, do you know this man Holbrook?"

"Yes, of course. I not only work for him but I am living at his house temporarily. Have you ever seen the castle? It is really wonderful."

"Then you know my mother."

"Your mother?"

"She is using the name of Mrs. Davis for some reason."

"Aunt Ellen!" Sherry's eyes sparkled. "Of course I know her and of course I love her."

"Just what is she doing in Waring?" The young man's face was hard, resentful.

Sherry looked at him thoughtfully. "Just about everything. She is a substitute mother to Stanley as well as his hostess. She has been an aunt to me and to Stanley's sister-in-law, that beautiful one over there in white. She is, I think, the kindest and most understanding person I ever knew. If only I could grow old like that! I think she has more courage than any of us. She wrote to Stanley, you know, and described herself as a rebellious old woman, who was tired of being put on the shelf. At the Folly, I can tell you, Mr. Murgatroyd, she's the very heart and soul of the place."

"I — see."

"I wonder if you know how lucky you are to have a mother like that."

Thelma Murgatroyd, seeing her husband engrossed with a pretty redhead, came up to them in time to overhear Sherry's words. She met her husband's accusing eyes and blushed.

"Why didn't you tell me where Mother was?" he demanded. She had never heard such a tone in his voice before. She put her hand on his arm. "I — I thought she had taken a job as housekeeper somewhere just to humiliate you and I wanted to spare you, dearest."

Sherry left the couple alone to settle their domestic crisis in privacy.

After a few patronizing comments to Fosdick, which the latter would be able to quote, Duffer turned to Sir Charles, determined to find out what he did, why he was here, and what useful contacts he might have, but in the Englishman he found a man perfectly capable not only of fending off impertinent questions but making clear their impertinence.

After a glance at her husband for instructions, Mrs. Denton took Doug away from Sherry and began to question him about the man whom he could identify. She found him extremely vague in his impressions.

Ellen turned to find her son beside her, white and grim. "Mother," he said urgently.

"Yes, dear."

"Why did you run away like that?"

She smiled at him lovingly. "Just an old lady's last fling."

"But why didn't you tell me?"

Her lips parted and then she was silent. Thelma had kept her letters from Bruce. She could not tell him that without causing trouble between man and wife.

"Well, I —"

"I understand. I should have realized in the beginning that you wouldn't do that to me. But Thelma is young and she has no family of her own, and she is uncertain socially. She was afraid you had done something to embarrass me, as if I could ever be anything but proud of you, whatever you do."

Ellen's eyes were bright with tears.

"You see," Bruce went on with difficulty, "Thelma is such a dear girl but she — well, she was a salesgirl when I married her, as you know. That was fine with me and I know it was with you as long as I loved her. But she never had a chance to meet — oh, society people. She thinks they are glamorous and important. She thinks her friend Doris Denton is more to be envied than anyone she knows because she went from being a salesgirl to marrying a rich and prominent man like Denton. But Thelma will learn real values. I'm sure of that."

"Of course she will," Ellen said warmly.

"Then you'll come home with us? Come home tonight?"

"But, Bruce —"

"Hey, what is this?" Stanley exclaimed. "I'm being undermined on all sides. Aunt Ellen belongs to the Folly. You get her over my dead body!"

Ellen laughed. "I'll come down on a visit after Christmas. But Mary is leaving Waring tomorrow and we have so much still to say to each other!"

"Why," Stanley suggested, "don't you ask the Remingtons to come to the Folly and stay until after Christmas so you can have a chance to catch up on old times?"

"I would love to."

Something in Stanley's tone completely reassured Bruce about his mother's standing in the Holbrook household.

The Dentons heard Ellen, seconded by Stanley, ask the Remingtons to the Folly on the following day.

"And," Stanley said, "why don't you have your son and his wife spend Christmas with you? That is," and he grinned at Bruce, "if you promise not to break up my happy home."

Bruce gave his wife a look of inquiry and she turned timidly to Ellen for guidance.

"Do come," Ellen told her. "You'll love the castle."

Mrs. Denton laughed shortly. "Well, it looks to me as though the Holbrooks are taking over the Denton guests. At least you'll all be here for our Christmas Eve party on the Green. Tom himself is going to play Santa Claus."

"A very good move," Duffer declared. "Very sound.

Builds nice relations and a fine image. By the time you announce your candidacy you'll have the ground laid."

While the good-byes were being said Mrs. Denton drew Miss Holbrook aside. "This is really good-bye then. I am so sorry. I'd have liked to know you better."

"I, too, dear Mrs. Denton! What a delightful party. But what with that warning and Sherry nearly killed and that poor boy still unconscious —"

"Have you heard how he is? I suppose you people would be the first to know."

"Well, all I know is —"

Stanley, who had come up beside her, intervened swiftly, "All we know so far is that he hasn't talked — yet." He smiled at his hostess and wished her a good night.

ii

"I think," Mrs. Duffer said as their car sped through the night to New York, "Mrs. Denton will make an excellent political hostess. She has the right manner."

"Yeah?"

"And he is certainly willing and able to put up enough money to buy all the TV time he needs."

"Yeah."

"People like the Remingtons — he's shipbuilding in England — are always useful to know and they look well on an invitation list."

"You run the house and keep out of politics, honey. Remington doesn't have a vote in America, and votes are what count. Also he and his wife were furious at being roped in as guests to be exploited by the Dentons. Not their kind. Snobs. And that applies to Holbrook too. I've been checking on Connecticut and especially on Waring, which is where Denton would have to make his start. Holbrook carries weight. The *Courier* carries weight. And they both hate Denton's guts."

"But Mr. Holbrook seemed so pleasant!"

"What did you think he would do? Spit in Denton's eye? He's a gent, after all. But if he wasn't maneuvered into going there tonight I'll eat my hat. Nope, right up to the last minute I was wavering, but when I said something about Denton's public image I got a load of Holbrook's face. If he could destroy Denton's public image he'd do it like a shot."

"What makes you so sure?"

"I don't know. There were some undercurrents that baffled me. For instance, when he said his driver was armed he was sounding a warning."

"So?"

"So I look around for someone else to groom for the presidency, honey. There's a senator from Pennsylvania I've got my eye on. Promising. Good record. Can't tell where he stands by the way he votes. Enough money to carry him until we get backing."

"You're giving up Tom Denton just because one guy looks cross-eyed at him?" his wife protested.

"Because of the kind of guy he is. Don't argue, precious. You just stick to the things you know about and leave politics to papa. As I was saying to Barry —"

"Save it for the next meeting," his wife said wearily She yawned.

iii

"Thelma."

She interrupted nervously. "I never was so surprised. I had no idea your mother knew people like Lady Remington."

"Would it have made any difference?"

"Well, of course it would make a difference! I thought she hadn't been around much and that she wouldn't be at home in our kind of life."

"Or in our home?" When Thelma was silent he said, "No, she wasn't. She was so unhappy she had to leave our house, the house, incidentally, she paid for. I can hardly grasp it. What on earth did you do? What did you say to her, Thelma?"

"Nothing. I tried. Honestly I tried to make her comfortable. I thought she'd make some friends her own age and be out of the way. I didn't think she would fit in with us." When Bruce made no comment she stole a look at his profile. He was staring ahead at the road, his expression stern. "I did it for your sake, Bruce. With all the people we are beginning to meet —"

"Like the Dentons?"

"Doris and I are best friends." She was sulky now. "And Tom is one of the big men, the coming men."

"It's because of people like the Dentons you wanted Mother to go away?"

"I didn't want her to go away. I found her packing that last day and demanded an explanation."

"Demanded?" Bruce's tone was smooth.

"She owed us that. And she said she had applied for a

job as a housekeeper where she'd have something useful to do. I told her she just wanted people to think you'd driven her out of your house to starve."

"God! And when she wrote to me you took her letters."

Thelma was silent for a long time. When she saw that her husband was not going to break the silence she said, "It was such a nice party and nice people and I looked forward to it and now you've spoiled it all!" After a while she played her last card. She began to cry.

iv

"I had no idea," Miss Holbrook exclaimed, "that you knew Lady Remington. You've never mentioned her." When Ellen made no comment Miss Holbrook went on, "So your name is really Murgatroyd."

"Yes."

"What a charming son you have, a friend of the Dentons too."

"My daughter-in-law and Mrs. Denton are old friends, I believe."

"And you never told me that!"

Stanley intervened. "You had better get some rest, Aunt Winifred. And we'll say good-bye now. Roberts will be ready to take you to your plane at seven."

"Well, I — with so many interesting guests coming to the Folly I'm almost tempted to cancel my reservation."

There was a moment of general consternation and then Doug leaped into the breach. "Do you think that is wise? Particularly after the warning you got?"

"Well, perhaps not. When I think of that telephone call — and the tires — and the poor boy still in the hospital. Did you notice how concerned and interested Mrs. Denton was?"

"I noticed." Stanley recalled that he had intervened just in time to prevent his aunt from confiding that Dick had been moved to another hospital. "I'm afraid if you cancel your flight you won't get another until after the holidays. There's always such a rush, you know. College kids going home. All that."

"Well." Miss Holbrook wavered. "But the Dentons' Christmas Eve party on the Green —"

"It will be out-of-doors, you know," Eve reminded her. "And you feel the cold so much — and especially with this flu epidemic —"

With everyone so interested in her welfare and determined to look out for her, Miss Holbrook yielded. "Then I'll say good night and good-bye and a Merry Christmas to you all. And remember, Stanley dear, when your guests go and all is well again you have only to say a word and I'll be quite at your disposal."

"I'm sure of that. A safe trip and a happy holiday to you, Aunt Winifred."

XVII

S TANLEY went in search of Ellen. It had become a habit to go to her for advice and he wondered what the Folly would be like when she left it to return to her son's house, as he supposed she would eventually. He found her in the rooms that had been Miss Holbrook's, making sure that they were ready to receive the Remingtons.

"So nice of you to ask them, Stanley. Mary is my dearest friend and we haven't seen each other in nearly three years, when I was last in England. And asking Bruce and his wife to come so we can spend Christmas together —"

"I wish you would consider the Folly your home, Aunt Ellen."

She smiled mistily at him. "No, my dear. I have learned a lesson. From now on I must have my own rooftree. I made a bad mistake when I agreed to move in with my son and his wife. The house was, and quite rightly too, hers. This house is yours and your future wife's."

"I don't expect to marry. The only girl —"

"I know. I think I guessed how you felt about Sherry even before you did."

"Then you know it is impossible. She is engaged to Carleton and they're to be married in a week."

"Be patient a while longer, Stanley. As my nephew Henry would say, 'Don't give up the ship.'"

"What could happen in a week to change things?"

"As a last resort there is always Aunt Ellen."

He gave her a hug. "You're a darling but even you can't perform miracles."

"Don't be so sure of that! Why were you looking for me?"

"The Danbury hospital called. They desperately need beds and Dick Flint is in a two-bed room. I figured we had better have him brought here where we can look after him until we round up this joker and take him out of circulation. And there is enough room for his mother. Might be better to get her up here in case of any attempt at retaliation."

"Of course. I'll talk to Wilson about it. You know, Stanley, this house really needs a housekeeper, one who is willing to subordinate herself to Wilson but can handle a lot of problems he's poor at. The house linen, for instance, needs overhauling, and there is too much waste in buying. Well, we'll work out something. Is the Flint boy coming by ambulance?"

"He doesn't need one and it would just advertise his presence here. Carleton is downstairs discussing plans for tracking down his friend with the white Ford. He's offered to collect the boy and his mother and get them here if you'll make the necessary arrangements with Mrs. Flint."

Mrs. Flint interrupted Ellen's invitation by breaking into tears. "It's like the answer to a prayer! I didn't know where to turn. I got laid off yesterday because I've been sick so long and only on part-time and with the holiday rush they needed a full-time checker."

Doug delivered a wide-eyed Dick and his silent mother to the Folly and left them in Ellen's capable and welcoming hands. Then he considered his own course of action. The chances that the white Ford was still on the streets of Waring were remote. The car might, of course, have been taken out of town, but the Dentons had not had much time in which to make plans.

Now where, he wondered, would I put a car I didn't want found in my possession? Too risky to sell it or to give it away. No time to have it repainted. I'd leave it with a lot of other cars; that is, if I could afford to scrap it. And Denton could scrap a fleet without feeling any pain.

Somewhere in the past few days he had seen an old-car graveyard. He had been driving with Eve at the time. Eve! Doug tried to thrust away the thought of her. Eve smiling at him across a table, her soft laugh greeting his sallies. He always felt witty when he was with her. Eve with her son in her arms. I've never even kissed her, he thought bitterly. Hey, man, get back on the job.

He remembered now where he had seen the old-car graveyard and drove there. When he had parked he got out and began to make his way over the frozen snow. There were so many wrecks that he nearly gave up but he went back and forth painstakingly until he had checked every one. Well, it had been a good idea but you can't win them all.

He started back to the Volkswagen but he was nagged by the feeling that he had missed something. There was some clue whose meaning he had missed. And for the past few minutes he had been increasingly aware that someone was following him. He could hear the crunch of foot-steps over the frozen snow. He found himself turning swiftly but he saw no one.

He was retracing his steps toward the Volkswagen when he noticed the moving van. Apparently a portion of the roof had been sheered off and the front had splintered. Now Doug recalled what had attracted his attention in the first place. There had been scuffed snow behind the truck. He stood looking at it, biting his lip. Someone had tried to remove the traces of tires leading up to the van. Doug tilted back his head. It could be done. The back of the truck unhinged. A car could be driven up as though on a ramp and be hidden inside.

He reached up to unhinge the back of the truck. . . .

ii

Ramsay bent over the unconscious man. Automatically he looked around but there was no one in sight. This road was always sparsely traveled and always the last to be cleared.

He tried to hoist Doug over his shoulder but he was too heavy and he had to drag him. Behind the Volks-wagen there was a pickup truck with the sign MORRIS'S BOTTLED MOUNTAIN WATER.

With a great deal of difficulty he hoisted Doug over the side of the truck and let him drop. Ramsay enjoyed letting this big fellow fall hard.

"Get rid of him," Denton had said late the night before when the dinner party was over.

"How?"

"That's up to you. Just remember that he can identify

you. When you shadow a girl you must wear a placard."

Ramsay found the Volkswagen keys in Doug's pocket and drove it inside the graveyard. Then he returned to toss a gunnysack over Doug's body, inert in the back of the truck among the big bottles of water.

"It's got to be an accident," Denton had warned him.

Ramsay knew there must be no more slipups. He had failed with the advertisers. He should not have warned Dick that the bomb had been planted. He should not have been frightened away from killing Dick by the unexpected presence of a patient in the next bed. The man Carleton must be eliminated and there could be no mistakes.

Where, Ramsay, wondered, could he leave the guy so it would be a long time before he was found, so long that no one could tell for sure what had happened to him? The answer leaped to his mind: the bombed-out *Courier* building. It might be months before anyone ventured inside, perhaps not until the building was demolished in the spring. And when the body was found it would be anyone's guess as to why he had gone there. Probably just curiosity to see the damage. And he had fallen and knocked himself out and died of — of — why, of exposure, of course.

Ramsay drove the truck as close to the building as he dared, climbed inside, hoisted Doug over the side and let him drop heavily on the frozen ground. Cautiously he crept inside the building, feeling a kind of pride when he saw the extent of the devastation he had caused, the bulging gap in the wall, the fallen ceiling, the ripped staircase with a dangling railing.

He went back and got hold of Doug and brought him

in, moving carefully, feeling the weakened building vibrate with his steps. There was a trickle of blood on Doug's cheek from a piece of plaster he had struck when he was dropped. For a few minutes Ramsay looked down at him, his lips pulling in and blowing out. There was a heavy piece of metal beside him, torn from the presses during the explosion, and he picked it up, weighed it in his hand, put it down again.

Then his eyes fell on the truck and he began to smile. He went to hoist out one of the big bottles of water, rolled it toward Doug's body and then let the water pour over him. When the bottle was empty he tossed it back into the truck. What a piece of luck it had been to find this truck with the key left in the lock and the means of death at hand.

iii

"Are you sure, Eve, Major Carleton planned to lunch here?"

Eve nodded. "He is going to tell us about his search for the man he calls Long-nose."

"Well, I think we won't wait for him any longer. The cook has made a soufflé." Ellen turned to the Remingtons. "All this must sound very cryptic but the truth is that we've been involved in a great deal of excitement." Without identifying the Dentons she described the struggle for control of the *Courier*.

"What an extraordinary tale," Sir Charles exclaimed.

"I thought things like that happened only in thrillers," his wife said.

"I wish that were true but there is no doubt that something very bad is going on and Stanley is in the center of it."

"Right now," Eve said, with sharpness in her soft voice, "Douglas Carleton may be in the center of it."

"He may have been delayed by a flat tire."

"Maybe." Eve helped herself to soufflé and let it get cold on her plate.

"You are really worried, aren't you, Eve?"

She nodded mutely, folding her napkin into pleats, straightening it out again. With an effort of will she forced herself to talk to the Remingtons while her mind was crying, "Doug! Doug! Where are you? What's happened to you?"

When the endless luncheon was over she said, driven by a compulsion too strong to control, "Can't we do anything?"

"But, Eve, the man is only an hour late."

"He'd have called. He would know I — we would all be concerned."

Ellen went into the library and called Stanley to ask him what to do. "Major Carleton should have been here an hour ago for lunch and he hasn't called. He may have had a minor accident. I didn't want to alert the police for fear they will think we are all becoming hysterical."

"Not after what has happened. You call them now. Say he was looking for that white car and someone may have been looking for him. Last night my dear Aunt Winifred told everyone he could identify the car, which was just asking for it! I'm on my way home."

Ellen called the police and reported that Doug was missing. "This is the second time I have called you. This may be a false alarm."

"Do you know the license number of that Volks the Major was driving?"

"No, I don't, but wait —" Ellen called, "Eve!" Eve came running. "Did you ever happen to notice the license number of the Major's car?"

"Yes. It's AV 4488."

A few minutes later Wilson appeared in the small drawing room. "Mrs. Fosdick is on the telephone and insists on speaking to someone. She says it is terribly important."

"Oh, not now. I want to keep the wire open in case the police or the Major should call."

"She sounded quite distraught."

"She always does." Ellen made an impatient gesture and went into the library. "Mrs. Fosdick," she said crisply, "an emergency has arisen and we must keep our telephone line open. Will you please call later?"

"Mrs. Murgatroyd — Mrs. Davis, this is important. I just saw someone in a pickup truck outside the *Courier* building."

"But —"

Mrs. Fosdick's voice rose. "Wait! The man went inside and he was dragging a body."

"A body!"

"I thought you ought to know before I call the police."

"Do so at once and tell them what you saw. Tell them — if he is still alive — to bring him here." Ellen turned as she heard a crash. Eve had fallen on the floor in a faint.

There was a scream of tires, a motor raced and cold air swept through the lobby as the front door was flung open and Stanley came in with Sherry.

He bent over Eve. "What happened to her?"

"Shock. She'll be all right. Ring for Wilson, will you, Sherry? And, Stanley, I think you had better go to the *Courier* at once. The police have been alerted. Mrs. Fosdick just saw someone drag in a body."

The door slammed and Stanley was gone.

iv

A thin layer of ice was forming over the still figure when the police crawled cautiously into the *Courier* and dragged it out.

Stanley's car had come to a screaming halt behind it. He looked down in horror. "How diabolical! What a way to die."

The sergeant got up from his knees. "He's not dead. There's a pulse and fairly strong. But what chance he has —"

"Take him to the Folly. Get a doctor over your radio. Nurses. Whatever may be necessary. You haven't the manpower to protect him, and his life is a threat to the people behind this."

"All right, Mr. Holbrook."

"I'm going to see Mrs. Fosdick and try to keep her still if it isn't already too late."

The sergeant grinned. "You can't do it. No one ever has."

He and his companion lifted the stiff body and Stanley shot away, crossed the bridge, and lifted the heavy knocker at Mrs. Fosdick's door.

She opened it at once. "Well, Mr. Holbrook! I've been watching the *Courier* ever since I talked to Mrs. Davis."

"Have you talked to anyone else?"

"No, I haven't been able to tear myself away from the window."

"Good. Now, Mrs. Fosdick, a man's life is quite literally in your hands. A single word, a vague hint to any human being, and that includes your husband, and you could do more harm than you can even imagine."

"I know when to keep still."

"I hope so. I very much hope so. But if, through any indiscretion of yours, anything you saw today becomes known to anyone you will be responsible for the result and that fact will appear in the *Courier*." Without waiting for a reply, Stanley ran for his car and headed for the Folly.

Ellen, Sherry, and a white-faced Eve were waiting for him. "It was Carleton," he told them, "and he is alive. They are bringing him here." He explained what had happened. "He was supposed to die of exposure, of course, but I hope we got him in time. Aunt Ellen, will you see that a room is prepared for him?"

"That's already been done."

"Bless you." He put a hand on Sherry's shoulder. "I am sorrier than I can say. I should never have involved him in my problems."

"It's not your fault. It was his own choice."

Eve was the only one in the lobby when the little procession came in. She bent over and touched his cold cheek gently with her fingertips and then waited, dry-eyed, while they passed her and went up the stairs.

There was a half hour of confusion while Sherry ran back and forth with hot-water bottles and Billy's nurse took charge. Because of the desperate shortage of nurses none could be found in Waring.

"I studied first aid and I'll take over at night," Eve promised.

"The chief thing right now," the doctor said, "is to get him warm. I've shot him full of antibiotics. There's danger of pneumonia but the man is in superb physical condition, aside from that bad leg. He's the kind who could come out of this with nothing but a cold. I'll be back again this evening. The nurse is watching his temperature closely. She seems to be a sensible girl and you are lucky to have had her on hand." He looked at Eve. "If you are going to take over tonight you must have some rest now."

"I don't need any rest."

"You'll obey orders, young lady."

Eve made herself lie down on her bed, with the door open to the nursery where she could watch Billy napping peacefully. She lay staring at the ceiling. At this very minute Doug was fighting for his life and there was nothing she could do but wait. But, she reminded herself, Sherry was waiting too, and waiting in the same anguish.

Sherry, having delivered an electric blanket to the nurse, went down to find Stanley pacing the library floor. "The nurse says he is much warmer and his breathing is better and she thinks he is going to make it without any complications. Isn't that wonderful?" She laughed. "Oh, and Aunt Ellen said to tell you that Dick and his mother are here."

"I seem to be running a bureau of missing men."

The doctor returned later to report. "The man seems to be made of iron. He is conscious and throwing off the infection and he has only a slight fever."

That evening, before settling down to bridge with Ellen and the Remingtons, Stanley had a talk with Dick and his mother. Dick had flinched like a nervous horse when Stanley pulled up a chair beside the bed.

"I'm going to give back the motorcycle and the coat and everything to the man who gave them to me, and I'll go around telling everyone I was mistaken about the *Courier* and it wasn't true. And I'll repay the rest of the money I spent as soon as I get another job."

"What's wrong with the one you have?" Stanley asked him.

"You'll let me stay?" Dick was incredulous.

"Well, you tried to make up for what you had done when you went in to find the bomb. Do you think you can learn to take orders from Mr. Jones?"

"Yes, sir! And I'll try real hard."

"Good! That's settled then." Stanley turned to Mrs. Flint. "Mrs. Davis tells me you were a big help to Wilson this afternoon. Would you care to stay on at the Folly as housekeeper?" The answer was in her face and he nodded and went out quickly to avoid her thanks.

While the bridge game went on in the library, Sherry crouched over a fire in the small drawing room, thinking of Doug who had risked his life because she was involved. And Eve sat beside Doug, her eyes on his face. She wanted him to continue his deep sleep but part of her mind hoped he would wake up and see her there.

Doug was the only one who slept soundly that night at the Folly.

XVIII

E LLEN looked down at Doug who groped for the lump behind his ear and winced. "So I was supposed to freeze to death! You've got to hand it to that guy; he never runs out of ideas. You know, there's nothing I'd like as much as to meet this joker face to face. He won the first two bouts but the third one is going to be mine."

"Men!" Ellen laughed and shook her head. "Fighting animals, all of you. Haven't you had enough of violence?"

"I have a few tricks of my own," he admitted. "Which reminds me, you might call the police and say I think they will find that missing white Ford inside a huge van in the old-car graveyard north of the village."

Ellen went to the nearest extension phone and relayed Doug's message.

"We'll check it out at once," the police promised.

"Now," Doug said, when she had returned, "please tell me how I got to the Folly."

"The police brought you at Stanley's suggestion. Billy's nurse looked after you all day and Eve took over at night."

"She did!"

Ellen looked at his revealing face, looked down at the knitting needles flashing in her fingers. "I was afraid she wouldn't be quite up to it because I stupidly repeated a comment of Mrs. Fosdick's about a body being dragged into the bombed-out building and Eve thought you were dead and she fainted." Doug's hand tightened convulsively on the blanket but he did not speak. "Actually it was Eve who stirred us all up about you. She — forgive me if you think me impertinent, Douglas, but are you being quite fair to Eve?"

"*Fair* to her?" He waited until he could control his voice. "I think you forget I am engaged to Sherry."

"Well," and she smiled, "perhaps I should ask if you are being fair to Sherry. As an outsider I see a great deal. You are four extremely fine young people and what frightens me is that you are going to ruin your lives for misguided reasons. You are determined to marry Sherry because you were once in love with her and she was once in love with you. But you have fallen in love with Eve, and Eve quite obviously is in love with you. If you persist in being so noble and so — so stupid instead of having a little plain speaking, you'll all be unhappy. Can't you see that you and Eve belong together? You are the same kind of people."

"And Sherry?"

"Sherry is head over heels in love with Stanley Holbrook and he with her, but they are both determined to be fair to the returning soldier."

Doug sat high on his pillows. "Is this true?"

"Why don't you talk to Sherry and find out for yourself? Shall I send her in to you? She is here, you know, because Stanley insisted that she stay home today to be with you."

"Are you sure about all this?"

She nodded, smiling. "Shall I get Sherry?"

When Sherry came in Doug found himself oddly tongue-tied. "Aunt Ellen says the doctor is dumfounded at the way you are recovering. You've made some kind of medical history."

"I'm an unusual guy." He grinned at her. "What an odd light!"

"There was a heavy snowfall in the night. This is going to be a white Christmas. And tonight is Mrs. Denton's Christmas Eve party on the Green."

"That is one function I am not going to miss."

"You were never more mistaken in your life. You are supposed to have disappeared. Roberts is hiding out at Mrs. Fosdick's house watching the *Courier* in case anyone comes to check on you. And I've called the Mayflower several times to ask about you and leave urgent messages." She laughed. "They said some other woman was making calls too and they wondered if it was the girl you usually lunch with."

"Did you mind? About my lunching with Eve?"

"Of course not."

"Why didn't you mind, Sherry?" Seeing that she was at a loss for a reply, he said, "When I came home you said — I don't remember the exact words — that people change, that we had to learn to know each other again. And I, like a blind fool, have been trying to force you to love me. And I failed. Didn't I, Sherry? Didn't I?"

Her eyes widened in a startled question and then they were brimming with laughter. "Oh, Doug! You too! Who — oh, Eve, of course. Oh, Doug, I'm so glad. I'm so

glad!" She bent over and kissed him, the only spontaneous kiss she had given him since his return. Then she
removed her ring and laid it on the bedside table.

He laughed happily. "A girl couldn't jilt a man in a
nicer way. But —"

She sobered. "But, Doug, you missed the point about
the woman who called the Mayflower, asking for you.
What woman do you know here aside from those at the
Folly and those you met at the Dentons' dinner party?"

"So it was Mrs. Denton, checking up to see how their
side is doing. That means she knew about the attempt to
kill me. A fairly cold-blooded female, wouldn't you say?"

There was a tap at the door and Ellen came in. She
looked from one glowing face to the other, noticed
Sherry's ringless hand. "The police called, and are feeling
triumphant. They found the Ford where Douglas said.
Registered to Mrs. Thomas Denton. They went over it
for fingerprints and found some inside the glove compart-
ment, which match prints on the wall in Dick Flint's
room, the only ones the man had overlooked. They said
he was a very cool customer. And, slipped down under the
driver's seat, they found a big key."

"Not the key to the *Courier!*" Sherry exclaimed.

"Yes. The police called Mrs. Denton to say they had
found her car. She didn't like that at all. When they
asked why she had not reported it missing she said she
had assumed her husband had it in New York. He often
lent cars to his friends. She couldn't get over her surprise
at where it had been hidden and wanted to know what the
police made of it. They told her they were baffled."

Sherry laughed, and Ellen did not repeat the rest of

her conversation with the policeman, who had said, "Well, we'll see you at the festivities tonight and keep an eye on you."

"Why?" Ellen had been startled.

"Oh," the sergeant said vaguely, "a big crowd milling around, everyone watching the Santa Claus to see what their kids are getting and whether they remember to say thank you. Might be a good time to make trouble."

Ellen decided not to mention the sergeant's ideas about possible trouble. If Doug heard about that nothing would prevent him from attending the Christmas Eve party as a bodyguard. I'll tell Stanley when he comes home, she decided. He'll know what we ought to do.

ii

Ellen's son and daughter-in-law arrived in time for lunch. Wilson had shown them to their room and then conducted them to the big beautiful drawing room, where Ellen was talking to the Remingtons, a glowing Sherry, and a quiet Eve. Thelma, overwhelmed by the castle and terrified of a mother-in-law to whom she had been so disagreeable, clutched at the arm of her tall husband, feeling frightened and uncertain. Then Ellen came forward to welcome her, bending to kiss her cheek. She smiled at her son.

"How wonderful that you could both spend Christmas here! It's all I needed to make it perfect." She looked around. "You know my son and daughter. You met them at the Dentons' party."

While Lady Remington made a place beside her on a

couch for Thelma, Bruce looked around. "Where is Holbrook? I'd like to thank him for being so kind to you, Mother."

"You'd better not let him hear you say that, Mr. Murgatroyd," Sherry warned him. "Stanley doesn't believe the Folly would survive for one day without Aunt Ellen. What we all owe her," and she caught Ellen's eyes and smiled, "is beyond calculation."

Eve heard the jubilant sound in Sherry's voice, saw her radiance, noticed the ringless finger. "What's happened?" she whispered.

Sherry smiled. "Ask Doug. He can hardly wait to tell you. Oh, Eve, don't hesitate! Be happy."

"You mean it?"

"With all my heart."

"We're having just a light lunch," Ellen explained, "because we must have an early dinner on account of the Christmas Eve party."

"Are you giving a party?" Thelma's eyes shone. "What fun! I bought a lovely evening dress, just in case."

"Another one?" Bruce protested.

She turned to him cajolingly. "Well, Doris Denton told me this was a regular castle and I knew, if there was a party, Doris would be in evening dress so —"

"This isn't our party and it isn't a dress affair. A community tree on the Green, sponsored by the Dentons."

"Mother," Bruce said when lunch was over, "we've got to have a talk."

"Of course, dear. Now if you like. Come up to my little sitting room where we won't be disturbed. Mary is taking a nap; the girls have their own concerns," and she smiled a little, "and Charles has gone for a walk."

"I want to come too, please," Thelma said. "This is a — a family matter."

A few minutes later, in Ellen's pretty sitting room, Thelma was using the same words again. "A family matter. I suppose that is part of what went wrong. You see, I never had a family. I didn't understand that families count. And I didn't understand you. I've been stupid and selfish and unkind and extravagant. But we're going to start all over. Because I love Bruce, Mrs. Murgatroyd. I truly do. All I want is to make him happy and if you'll just come back and help me —"

"Oh, no, no!" Ellen exclaimed. "You don't need me. Just trust your love for Bruce, my dear, and you can't go far wrong."

"But the house and the money — I truly didn't understand until Bruce explained last night — and we're going to sell the house and get a small apartment and live on what Bruce makes and — and sort of get squared away. That's what Bruce wants. He never wanted to start with more than he earned."

Ellen put her arms around the girl. "You're going to work things out beautifully. Now, Bruce, take this girl away so your mother can rest before the night's festivities. Even rebellious old ladies need to rest."

He hugged her. "Okay. We'll let you prepare for all the wild excitement."

"Well," she said thoughtfully, "at least I'm prepared for fireworks."

iii

"I thought you'd never come," Doug said when Eve tapped on his door. He was fully dressed and lying on a chaise longue, holding a book which he had not attempted to read.

"But you shouldn't be up!" she exclaimed in concern.

"Of course I should. Got to get up strength for to-night."

"Douglas Carleton, you're crazy if you think you are going out tonight. That man is probably still in town. In a crowd he could — no, Doug!"

"The words," he instructed her, "should be, 'Yes, Doug.' I am a free man, my darling. Are you coming here to me or am I going to come to you?"

They met in the middle of the room and stood holding each other, wordlessly. At length he bent his head and kissed her mouth. "Oh, Eve, I do love you so. Let's get married at once and go back to San Francisco, you and Billy and me. I'll make you happy."

"I'm happy now, so happy I can't bear it."

"You'd better start getting used to it."

She pressed her head harder against his shoulder. "How did it all happen?"

"Aunt Ellen, of course."

"Oh, of course."

XIX

THE snow had stopped and the air was crystal clear. Streetlights shone on snow that sparkled like jewels, on snow-laden hemlock and oak, maple and elm. Around the Green, windows with their curtains wide open on this night showed candles and lighted Christmas trees. At one end of the Green, near the big tree, a group of children had gathered to sing Christmas carols at the appropriate time.

Mr. and Mrs. Denton made an impressive arrival, escorted by a police car with siren screaming and followed by a truck filled with baskets of presents which two men unloaded near the big white-covered throne beneath the tree. The Dentons were accompanied by a Santa Claus in full regalia of red suit and stocking cap and flowing white beard.

Stanley, who had been watching through binoculars from a vantage point in the library window, gave an exclamation of surprise. "I understood that Denton himself was to be Santa Claus."

Sherry clutched his arm in excitement. "Stanley! They've got to conceal that man somewhere. What could be better than a Santa Claus beard? A man doesn't really have a face when he is wearing one of those."

"They wouldn't dare!" Eve exclaimed.

"Oh, wouldn't they?" Doug said. "Well, that settles it. I'm going down there." He ignored a chorus of protests. "I have a score to settle with that guy. Quite a score."

"But it's just asking for trouble," Eve wailed. "And as long as they think you are dead, you'll be safe from any more attempts."

"I'll cover up as much as I can and I'll be with you, Eve. That ought to throw them off the track. They'd expect to find me with Sherry, provided I was in any shape to go anywhere. But I've got to go. I'm the one who knows the man by sight."

Seeing that he was not to be diverted from his purpose, Stanley gave in. "All right, but in that case Roberts is coming with us and Roberts is armed."

Ellen turned to the Remingtons. "You didn't bargain for anything like this. Of course it may be nothing but a community party for children. On the other hand there may be trouble. Perhaps you had better stay here. From these windows you'll have a box seat — in case anything does happen."

The Remingtons exchanged glances and smiled. "We wouldn't miss this," Sir Charles declared.

From below there came cries of excitement.

Thomas Denton, with cameras focused on him, had stepped forward to turn a switch and the lights on the great tree came on. It was a most impressive scene. Children began to surge closer to the tree, and Santa Claus, his great white beard covering him from beneath his nose to halfway down his chest, settled himself on the big white-covered throne with baskets of gifts beside him. Neil Gordon, hovering near, was taking pictures of the tree, the crowd, the Santa Claus, the gifts, and, of course, the beaming Thomas Dentons.

That was when the party from the Folly made an unobtrusive appearance. Stanley led the way with Sherry and Ellen, followed by the Remingtons with the Murgatroyds, and behind them Doug flanked by Eve and a grim-faced Roberts. Doug wore dark glasses and he had a muffler pulled up over his chin. Stanley saw a man in plain clothes drift casually away from the crowd to stand near them. He also saw that the man, instead of watching his party, turned his back on them, like Secret Service men guarding a president, to watch the crowd. Apparently the Waring police force had drawn on other communities for extra men. It was a comforting thought though, as Sherry whispered, it seemed odd to invite the police to a Christmas party.

The Dentons stepped forward to greet them, giving Stanley the curious illusion that he was being welcomed to his own village. Then there was a cry of "Hi, Sherry," and she went to join the young choristers. Doug in the background, shielded from observation by Roberts and Bruce Murgatroyd, never took his eyes off the Santa Claus. If this was Long-nose, it was as daring an action as he had ever seen, a mocking defiance in the face of law and order.

And now Santa Claus, his voice amplified by a loudspeaker, was going into action. "Ho, ho, ho," he began. "Step forward, boys and girls. From the North Pole —"

Roberts could not recognize the tones of the voice he had heard in the hospital. He looked at Doug who shook his head. "I can't tell," he whispered.

While he kept up a line of patter the Santa Claus was distributing gifts to the children who filed past.

Slowly Doug and Roberts were converging on the throne while Bruce and Stanley provided what cover they could and the plainclothesman accompanied them step by step, never quite in the group, never taking his watchful eyes off the crowd and the Santa Claus.

Then Roberts gripped Doug's arm. "Look at that, will you?"

An enterprising small boy of three had clambered onto the lap of the Santa Claus and tugged at his coat for attention.

"Santa Claus, I've been a good boy. I want a train and —"

"And this is for you, little girl. Merry Christmas!" Santa Claus handed a doll to a passing girl and tried to push the tenacious youngster off his lap.

"Santa Claus, I've been a good boy." The child's voice rose in indignation. "Listen to me! I want a gun and —"

"Quiet!" Santa Claus muttered. "And for the boy in the big cowboy hat here is a sheriff's belt."

"Santa Claus!" The small boy was not accustomed to being ignored. He released his hold on the red jacket, caught at the long white beard and tugged. The beard came away in his hands and the startled child tumbled off his lap, howling.

"That's the man!" Doug plunged forward, unaware that Eve was clinging to his arm. Roberts had his gun in his hand.

The crowd, which had laughed when the beard was torn away, was intent now as Doug lunged toward the man on the throne, Eve still trying to restrain him. The Santa Claus recognized Doug in horror and disbelief. The man was supposed to be dead. He couldn't be here. But he was at hand and there was purpose in his face. This time Ramsay was caught. Nothing could get him out of this. He snatched at Eve, dragged her in front of him, holding her like a shield with his left arm.

"I have a gun. One move and she gets it. That clear? I'm leaving here. When I get away I'll let her go. Otherwise —"

There were two quick shots. Both Roberts and the plainclothesman had aimed for the man's legs and both bullets had found their target. As Ramsay fell, Doug caught Eve in his arms and the plainclothesman bent over to snap handcuffs on the man's wrists and search for his gun which he slipped into his pocket. He blew a whistle and a deputy ran forward to take the Santa Claus away.

Ramsay looked from side to side for help. Like most killers and bullies he was a personal coward. What a fool he had been to give himself away in a moment's panic by grabbing the girl. He could have denied everything if it hadn't been for that. At least Denton would get him off. Denton would have to get him off. He had too much on him. But Denton and his wife, with exclamations of horror, were turning their backs on him. If he was going to jail he wasn't going alone. He pointed to Denton. "He made me do it! He made me do it!"

"That's a lie!" Mrs. Denton cried shrilly. "We never saw the man before."

"Then how come you hired him to be Santa Claus?" the sergeant demanded.

"I saw him in your house," Sherry said.

"I saw him try to kill Dick Flint with a hypodermic," Roberts said.

"He's the guy who followed Sherry Winthrop and left me to freeze to death," Doug said.

"He's been driving your car," the sergeant said. "You won't be running for governor in this state, Mr. Denton. We can get along just fine without people like you."

So the Dentons returned home, as they had arrived, with a police escort. Thomas Denton had only one comment to make. "I am calling my lawyer before I make any statement. I have only this to say: I am being framed by Stanley Holbrook because I refused to buy the *Courier* at an exorbitant price."

"Doug," Eve cried, "you might have been killed."

He took her in his arms and kissed her. "I'm all right, darling."

Stanley started forward. "Why you —"

Ellen restrained him. "It's all right. I told you to leave it to Aunt Ellen."

"But Sherry —"

"She hasn't been wearing her ring all evening, my dear. But you had your mind on something else."

"Where is she?"

A child wailed, "What happened to Santa Claus?"

Then Sherry's voice rose, clear and sweet, "O little town of Bethlehem," and the choristers joined her, filling the night with their young voices. The lights of the tree continued to shine on the frozen snow and the joy and peace of the season fell on the village of Waring.

Neil Gordon accompanied the party back to the Folly

and demanded the full story. Stanley grinned at him. "Call Hartford. Maybe they could use an eyewitness account."

"May I, Mr. Holbrook?"

"Go ahead, Jack London, and more power to you."

"This," Lady Remington declared, "has been the most surprising evening of my life."

"When you said fireworks," Bruce accused his mother, "you really meant it. Why didn't you warn me?"

Her eyes twinkled. "I didn't want to alarm you. It takes an old lady to face these things."

"A rebellious old lady," he teased her. "You're just plain adventurous. When you get your money back in a few months what do you plan to do next?"

"I think I'd like to drive through Spain and the Pyrenees into France, or perhaps take that trip through the canals of Sweden, or — I've never seen the wild game in Tanzania."

Bruce laughed. "There's time for it all."

At last Stanley went to kiss Eve. "I'm awfully glad about it. Now that I am not jealous of him I like this guy you are going to marry." He smiled into the big violet eyes. "Bill would have liked him too, Eve. He would have wanted this for you. But remember the Folly is Billy's home whenever he wants to come here."

When he had shaken hands warmly with Doug he went in search of Sherry. He found her alone in the darkened library looking down at the Green, her slender body silhouetted against the dim lights from the great tree and the faint glow of the village. He joined her and they watched while the lights on the Denton tree were switched off and those in the houses around the Green went out, one by one.

"Sherry —"

She drew a deep breath. "So that's the end of the Dentons' Christmas Eve party."

"And the end of Denton's political ambitions. Sherry —"

"I like Aunt Ellen's son, don't you?" She sounded oddly breathless.

"Very nice guy. Sh —"

"I suppose she will be leaving the Folly."

"They will all be leaving the Folly. It looks as though I am going to be a very lonely guy around here." When she made no comment he said, "Of course I could ask Aunt Winifred to come back, now all is safe."

She gave a tiny chuckle.

"Eve is going to marry Carleton, you know."

"Yes, I know."

"Well," he demanded indignantly, "why didn't you tell me?"

"It happened only this afternoon — and you were worrying about trouble tonight — and you didn't even notice I wasn't wearing Doug's ring — and — and —"

He took the ringless hand. "Something ought to be done about that. Any suggestions?" No reply. He took her in his arms. "Unless you have some objection I am going to kiss you." There was no objection.

After a long time they turned to look down on the darkened village. "It's going to be a good life," he told her. "I may not go out and slay any dragons —"

"In a way, though, that's just what you have done,

Stanley. A very big, very dangerous dragon. All it took was one brave voice."

"I was thinking of your novel," he said unexpectedly.

She laughed. "Oh, that! I had almost forgotten it."

"You called it *The Shining Years*. That's what we have ahead of us."

She stood on tiptoe to kiss his cheek. "They won't always shine. There will be trouble and sickness, perhaps, and disappointments and failure, but as our Puritan ancestors said, 'With courage enough.' Like Aunt Ellen."

A clock struck midnight with a silvery sound from behind them and then from the church tower on the Green the carillon began to sound the notes: "Joy to the World."

"Merry Christmas, Sherry!"

9

PART I

Road